THE
SAMURAI'S
GARDEN

THE
SAMURAI'S
GARDEN

GAIL
TSUKIYAMA

ST. MARTIN'S PRESS
NEW YORK

THE SAMURAI'S GARDEN. Copyright © 1994 by Gail Tsukiyama.
All rights reserved. Printed in the United States of America.
No part of this book may be used or reproduced in any manner
whatsoever without written permission except in the case of
brief quotations embodied in critical articles or reviews. For
information, address St. Martin's Press, 175 Fifth Avenue,
New York, N.Y. 10010.

LIBRARY OF CONGRESS CATALOGING IN PUBLICATION DATA

Tsukiyama. Gail.
    The Samurai's garden/Gail Tsukiyama.
        p.   cm.
    ISBN 0-312-11813-9
    1. Japan—History—1926-1945—Fiction.   I. Title.
    PS3570.S84S26   1995   94-44996
813'.54—dc20   CIP

First Edition: March 1995

10   9   8   7   6   5   4   3   2   1

Book design by Ellen R. Sasahara

No one spoke,
The host, the guest,
The white chrysanthemums.

—Ryōta

ᴀCKNOWLEDGMENTS

I wish to thank Catherine de Cuir, Cynthia Dorfman, Blair Moser, Norma Peterson, and Abby Pollak for their continual grace and support. And as always, many thanks to my mother and brother for their ongoing strength and encouragement.

AUTUMN

TARUMI, JAPAN
SEPTEMBER 15, 1937

I wanted to find my own way, so this morning I persuaded my father to let me travel alone from his apartment in Kobe to my grandfather's beach house in Tarumi. It had taken me nearly two weeks to convince him—you would think I was a child, not a young man of twenty. It seems a small victory, but I've won so few in the past months that it means everything to me—perhaps even the beginning of my recovery. Just before leaving, I bought this book of Japanese parchment paper to record any other prizes I might be lucky enough to capture. It opens before me now, thin sheets of sand-colored paper, empty and quiet as the beach below the village.

Since I became ill last spring in Canton, I've had no time to myself. When I was too weak to continue studying, my instructors at Lingnan University ordered me home. My friend King accompanied me on the train, and hovered over me all the way home to Hong Kong. I'll never forget the frightened look in my mother's eyes the day I returned. It was like an animal's fear for her young. I couldn't stop coughing long enough to catch my breath. When King and a manservant carried me up the concrete steps of our house, my mother stood in her green silk *cheungsam,* lips pressed tightly together in a straight line as if she were holding back a scream. Once home I was constantly under her cautious eyes, and those of our old servant Ching. The two women monitored my every move, as if I might wilt away right before their eyes. That's how they looked at me sometimes, as though I were already a memory.

I can understand their concern. My days were still punctuated by fevers in the late afternoon and a persistent dry cough. All through the thick, sticky summer, the heat made things worse. When my illness was diagnosed as tuberculosis by an English doctor, my mother sent a telegram to my father in Kobe. Her concern

3

turned to dread and she forbade my younger sister Penelope, whom I've called Pie ever since she was born, to enter my room.

Every morning Pie balanced on the threshold and smiled at me, looking smaller than her twelve years. There are four of us children in all. My older sister Anne and my younger brother Henry are now back at school in Macao. My parents gave us all Christian names at birth, since my father believes it an asset in the business world to be addressed with ease by Westerners. His import-export business thrives on such progressive ideas. It seems the apartment he keeps in Japan is more his home than our family house in Hong Kong. He makes his life in both places and the way he bows low with eyes averted seems at times more Japanese than Chinese to me.

By late July, the heat had settled in on Hong Kong, while my fevers advanced and retreated. A heavy stillness had descended on our house, as if everyone was moving in slow motion. My mother was even more nervous than usual. Two days later, the news came over the radio that the Japanese had captured Tientsin and surrounded Peking.

Hong Kong was stifling in August. Some afternoons I could barely breathe. My father wrote: "Send Stephen to me in Kobe, I will take him to Tarumi. The climate is drier there, and the air is much fresher than in Hong Kong." My mother ordered Ching to prepare for my journey to Japan, while the Japanese occupied Peking and sent their warships to Shanghai. I hated to leave my family and friends, even though I hadn't been allowed to see them. I felt lonelier than ever.

In some ways I can't help thinking my time in Tarumi will be a quiet resembling death. At least the sea breezes are much more soothing than the hot, humid heat of Hong Kong.

Late in August, the Japanese invaded Shanghai where a bloody standoff continues. Thousands of refugees have fled China and have built their makeshift homes in the crowded streets of Hong Kong. On the way to the harbor, we smelled their greasy street cooking and saw their gaunt, desolate faces begging for money and understanding. Then, at the pier in Kowloon, my mother and Pie looked bereft, too, as they waved good-bye to Ching and me.

Only after she thought I had disappeared into the crowds did my mother lift her white lace handkerchief to her eyes.

All the way to Japan on board the *President Wilson*, Ching refused to let me sit on the sun-drenched deck without wearing at least three sweaters. When we finally arrived in Kobe, she clung to me whispering and hissing, "These are the Japanese devils who have driven our Chinese out of their homes." I looked out through the taxi window at the bustling crowds, but except for small groups of soldiers loitering in public places, rifles slung on their shoulders, these Japanese appeared harmless to me. I was relieved when Ching left me with my father and hurried home to Hong Kong.

My father had been waiting for us at his apartment. I could tell by the way his body tensed that he was shocked at my appearance, but he tried not to show it.

"Stephen," he said, "it's good to see you." His eyes surveyed my feverish face and too-thin body before he hugged me and touched my wavy hair. My hair has always delighted him, because it isn't straight like most Chinese. Then he stepped back and said softly, "We will see that Michiyo makes her *sukiyaki* tonight."

Kobe was only slightly cooler than Hong Kong, and Michiyo watched over me as closely as Ching. My father worked long hours and couldn't get away to take me to Tarumi as he had hoped. Transportation had been interrupted all over China, and his business was hanging in the balance. The more Michiyo fussed at me to rest, to eat, the less I was able to do either. It was then I realized there wasn't any reason why I couldn't find my own way to the village of Tarumi.

This morning in Kobe, I rose early, dressed, and had finished packing before my father knocked gently on the door to awaken me. I packed lightly, bringing only one suit, comfortable clothes, several books, my oil paints, and two tablets of paper. My father promised to send me some canvases shortly.

The drive to the train station was quiet, my father asking only twice if I was feeling well enough to travel. Even my coughing had eased. When we arrived at the station, he suddenly turned around and asked, "Do you have enough money?"

"Yes, you've given me more than enough," I answered, my hand instantly feeling for my wallet in my jacket pocket.

"You know you can always reach me at the downtown number."

"I know, Ba-ba, I know," I said. It was something he had been telling me for the past two weeks.

"The most important thing is that you take care of yourself, rest, and don't tire yourself out with your painting." My father looked away as he said this, always awkward when it came to the subject of my painting, which he saw as a time-consuming hobby.

"I won't," I answered, knowing that my only solace in being exiled to Tarumi was that I would have more time for my painting.

My father excused himself to make sure my luggage was safely aboard the train. He had agreed to let me go alone only after he wired the servant at the beach house to be waiting for me at the station. I saw him slip a Japanese porter extra money to watch me on this short journey. He returned through the crowd, telling me to board and get settled. He grasped my hand tightly.

"I'll see you in a week or two," he said.

"You don't have to worry about me," I reassured him as I boarded the train. "I'll be fine."

I watched my father from the train window, a small man in his dark double-breasted suit and thin, rimless glasses, standing next to a group of Japanese children. My father usually seemed so short, but as the train pulled out and he lifted his arm to wave, I thought he looked tall in the fading light.

The train was half-filled with elderly Japanese men and women, and mothers with small children who exchanged conversation with one another in hurried whispers. They mostly spoke of their children from what I could understand, and I was relieved when we finally left the outskirts of the city and I could focus my attention on the fleeting landscape outside the window. It was greener than I remembered, with large pine trees waving against a sky so sharp and clear that I felt as if I could almost reach out and grab one of their long, spiny arms. My mother had taken us to Tarumi for two summers of our childhood. I still remember her complaints about the heat, and her elaborate silk-painted fan, as she moved the thick air in front of her in quick, short strokes.

After a while, I was hypnotized by the passing scene. My eyes felt hot and tired. It was the first time since leaving my family in Hong Kong that I had thought about being completely alone. With my father only a few hours away in Kobe, and my mother planning to visit me in a matter of months, I could only breathe in both the fear and attraction of facing the unknown.

A little girl walked down the aisle of the train staring in my direction. When I looked up at her and smiled, she bowed her head shyly, then rushed back to her mother. She reminded me of Pie, though Pie might have stopped and spoken to a stranger to satisfy her curiosity. She has always been my favorite, with her large round eyes and pigtails. Part of the reason I was sent to Tarumi was to avoid infecting Pie. As a small child, she was the one who was always sick. Her frailty was equalled only by her quick, sharp eye and teasing nature. She and Henry were constantly entangled in something, often leading to violent fights. It worried me at first, until I realized Pie was always intelligent enough to know when to stop.

After my illness was diagnosed, Ching tried not to let Pie get too near, but Pie refused to listen, poking her head into my room whenever she could. When Pie found out I was leaving for Japan, she slyly slipped into my room after everyone had gone to sleep. Ching always left a small light in the entryway for anyone who had to make a trip to the water closet during the night. In the stillness, Pie entered and whispered my name until I awakened. I knew immediately it was she by the smell of mothballs on her sleeveless, yellow silk pajamas with flowers embroidered on the front.

"What are you doing here? I asked, rubbing the sleep from my eyes and sitting up. I coughed, and was quick to cover my mouth.

"You're leaving with Ching tomorrow to see Ba-ba, so I've come to say good-bye," she answered. "I'll miss your handsome face."

"You shouldn't be in here, you might get sick," was all I could say. I could see Pie smile in the muted light from the hall. She threw her thin, pale arms around my neck and kissed me on the cheek. Her lips felt cool against my warmth. "Go now," I said. "I'll see you soon."

Pie reluctantly withdrew her arms and ran to the door. "I'll write to you," she said, closing the door and leaving me in darkness.

When the train blew its whistle and slowed down for the Tarumi station this afternoon, I waited until it came to a complete stop. All around me were the anxious movements of others gathering their belongings. The station itself was just a one-room wooden building set on a wooden platform. I looked about and saw several Japanese women in kimonos, waiting along with a couple of older men. I leaned back uneasily and searched my mind, unable to remember how Matsu, the caretaker of the beach house, looked. Our last visit had been years ago, and I only remembered catching glimpses of him as he went about his duties. I was afraid of him. Matsu had seemed old to me then, so I was surprised when my father said he would be the one waiting for me at the station today.

I waited, letting the others disembark first, then followed behind them. Some were greeted at once, while others scrambled off by themselves in different directions. I walked to the middle of the platform, put down my suitcase, and watched for any sign of Matsu, already preparing myself to find the beach house on my own. It was a warm afternoon and my shirt was wet down the length of my back. I tried to remember which direction the house was, but every road appeared vaguely familiar. The crowd was beginning to thin when out of the building came a heavyset man with close-cropped gray hair. Nervously, I watched him approach.

"Pao-Lin Chan's grandson?" he asked, stopping a few feet from me. He was dressed in baggy khaki trousers and a gray sweater. I felt skinny and small next to him, though I was a good foot taller.

"Yes, and you're Matsu-*san?*" I asked. He gave me several stiff bows, which I returned. Before I could say anything else, Matsu had taken my suitcase and begun to walk to the station. At the door of the shabby building, he stopped and stared impatiently, waiting for me to pass through first.

My father told me Matsu has lived alone and taken care of my grandfather's beach house for the past thirty years. After his parents died, he was given the choice either to join my grandfather's Hong Kong household, or stay in Japan by himself to care for the beach house. Matsu has worked for our family since he was a boy, and his parents worked for my grandfather before that. He appears about sixty, with weathered, umber-colored skin and a remote, impatient manner. He seems the type of man who's more comfortable alone, and it's not hard to figure out that he must be annoyed at my disturbing his tranquil world.

The road to the beach house was powdered with white sand and felt stifling in the hazy heat. It was late afternoon and the sun exerted its last burst of energy before disappearing into evening. We walked past a few bamboo-fenced houses, which increased in number as we continued down the road. I was sweating heavily by then. Matsu silently walked in his quick gait a few steps ahead of me, as if he were all by himself. I increased my pace, pushing myself to keep up. The farther we walked, the more fine sand lined the road. The salty sea air filled my head, and from beyond the dune came the steady surge of waves. In between, I felt consumed by the quiet, so different from the summers I had spent here surrounded by my family and the noise of playful children. This early autumn there didn't seem to be anyone else here, just me, Matsu, and a complete, white silence.

I was exhausted by the time Matsu stopped in front of one of the many bamboo-fenced houses and cleared his throat to get my attention. My lungs were burning and my legs weak. Matsu wasn't about to treat me like an invalid. Never once had he stopped, or even asked to see if I was all right. My mother and Ching would have fussed over me, made me rest every five minutes. "Stephen, you mustn't tire yourself out, rest, rest, go slowly," they would say, as their high-pitched voices pierced the air.

I watched Matsu put down the suitcase and proceed to unlock the gate. My grandfather's house stood on the right side of the road on the slight slope of a hill. Across the road was the path down to the beach. I remembered how Henry and I used to race down it during our stay here.

Matsu gestured for me to enter first. Stepping through the

bamboo gate, I found myself in the garden. The sweet perfumes were immediately intoxicating. A silk tree, still heavy with summer blossoms, and two large black pine trees shaded the house. An oval-shaped pond, with hints of movement that flashed orange and silver beneath its surface, dominated one side of the garden. It was surrounded by pale green moss. A wooden bridge arched across its width, and lines of odd-shaped, waterworn stones created two paths, one leading through the secluded garden right up to the front door, while the other disappeared around the back of the house. White sand formed soft beds in the crevices.

The house appears smaller than I remember, though it feels comfortable here, with a simplicity I could never find in crowded Hong Kong. On the left side of the house, there's a small verandah looking out over the pond. I like the straight and curved shapes of the tile roof with its projecting eaves; it all seems to harmonize with the surroundings.

We proceeded through to the *genken,* the entrance room, which had a wooden bench where shoes are to be removed. There were two pairs of house slippers neatly lined up. One pair was clearly worn, and next to them was a new pair that I slipped on. They felt cool and welcoming. The first summer we came to Tarumi, I asked my mother why we had to change our shoes before going into a house. She said it had to do with the Japanese custom of cleanliness, of not taking dirt from the streets into the house, and also because of the delicacy of the *tatami* mats lining the floor inside. It's a ceremony I found refreshing after arriving from the dirty streets of Hong Kong.

After I put my things away, Matsu led me out to the back garden where I took my first Japanese bath. On a wooden platform by the back of the house sat a wooden tub, a small black door open at the bottom of it, through which I could see coals in an iron container to heat the water.

While Matsu prepared the bath, he gestured for me to wash first. To one side was a stool, bucket, and a washcloth. I was embarrassed thinking I had to undress and wash in front of Matsu, but he went about heating the tub, ignoring me. I took my time taking off my clothes, then sat down on the stool, and began to soap and wash my entire body with the washcloth. From a barrel of cool water, I used the bucket to pour water over my head, rinsing over and over as I'd seen my father do. It felt good after the hot, dusty walk.

I stood up, feeling self-conscious as I walked toward the tub. I'd lost so much weight in the past few months, I looked no more than a skeleton. At my father's apartment, I had bathed quickly, too embarrassed to linger for a soak.

"The water's hot," Matsu said, not paying the least bit of attention to me. "Step in quickly. Then stay as still as you can."

I stepped up onto the wooden platform, then lifted my leg over the side and into the tub. I let the rest of my body follow as water splashed out over the rim. Steam rose, surrounding me with the sweet fragrance of cedar. There was a smooth touch of the wood under my skin. The water was very hot, but when I sat perfectly still as Matsu advised, my body calmed. Matsu stood to the side and almost smiled as I leaned back, letting the hot water embrace me.

SEPTEMBER 16, 1937

I fell asleep while writing after my bath last evening. I'd told Matsu I was only going to rest a short time on the bedding he had rolled out for me. He nodded his head with a look of relief. Wrapped in a light cotton kimono he gave me to wear, I fell into a deep sleep from which he did not disturb me.

When I awoke, this book still lay open across my chest. It took me a few minutes to recall where I was. On the floor across from me was a tray with a small pot of cold tea, and the snack of red bean cakes Matsu had brought to me when I arrived.

It's very early, but I already hear Matsu moving around in the kitchen, and the faint smell of something cooking reminds me of how hungry I am. I haven't experienced the hollowness of hunger for the longest time. Below my bedding, Matsu has placed several quilts to ease the hardness of the floor, but there's still a stiffness up and down my back as I stand up. The air tastes sweeter here, and my throat is dry, but the coughing has lessened and I feel almost healthy again.

I slide open my door. Matsu's in the kitchen in the back of the house, so I walk through the hall, taking stock of everything I had missed the night before. Beyond the *genken* there's a long corridor with two rooms on each side, separated by thin *shoji* walls, whose paper screens slide open to expose each room. The main room is a good size, lined with six *tatami* mats with clean lines. There isn't any furniture, and it smells musty from lack of use. There are two small recesses which I remember are called *tokonomas,* one where a simple scroll painting hangs with a basket of dried flowers beside it on the floor. The other has cupboards with sliding doors that hide the *zabuton* cushions which are taken out for guests to sit on. Matsu keeps the house immaculate. I can't help but think how ecstatic Ching would be at the lack of clutter. The last time we visited, Henry slid open the doors every morning and strewd the cushions all over the floor, as he jumped from one to the other pretending they were small islands. My father had remained in Kobe that time because of business, while my mother spent most of each day alone in the garden, shaded from the sun by a large, red-paper parasol.

Across from the main room is my grandfather's study, with a low-set black lacquered desk and a large, hand-carved ivory urn on the floor nearby. I enter the room that had always before been forbidden to the children. The room is light and cool, and I lay the palm of my hand on the mirrorlike surface of the desk. I look down to see my disheveled appearance: wavy unkempt hair, dark hollow eyes, the thin face with flushed cheeks and slight shadow of a beard. Except for my obvious weight loss, the feverish glow still gives me a deceptively healthy appearance in the dark lacquer surface.

My room is down the corridor, smaller and brighter than the main room. It seems especially true this morning when a white light comes through the *shoji* windows, which aren't shaded by so many trees. The light makes everything appear clear. The pale green of the *tatami* has a spiral design which corresponds to the fluid grain of the natural wood. The plastered walls are the color of sand. There's a low sitting table, cushion, and a *tokonoma* which houses a Chinese scroll painting of the jagged mountains of Guilin. It was painted by my grandfather, and I've admired it since I was a child. It's a pleasure to wake up to the sight of it.

Matsu prepared a breakfast of rice with pickled vegetables and miso soup. After a six-word conversation with him, which consisted of my poor Japanese and several low grunts from him, I grabbed my sketch pad and headed down to the beach. The cool wind of early morning sent a chill through me.

The road was empty. The thick, sweet smell of the late summer blossoms drifted through the air. I walked down the road to see some houses still asleep behind their bamboo fences. Others were just waking with movement from within. Through the cracks between the bamboo I could see a servant or two moving about. Many of the houses were already empty, or with only a servant like Matsu left to care for them. I wondered if Matsu had any contact with the other servants, or did he simply keep to himself? I tried not to think that it would be almost a year before Tarumi came alive again with families returning on vacation. Meanwhile, I'd have to adapt to the silence, put away all the noise and comforts of my family and friends in Hong Kong and Canton. It's harder than I imagined, to be alone. I suppose I might get used to it, like an empty canvas you slowly begin to fill.

The path was just as I remembered it, a narrow strip of sand threading down to a large, open beach. From the top of the slope I could see the empty stretch of white sand, divided by a large sand dune. The sea was blue-green and very quiet. As I ran down the path, my canvas loafers filled with sand, still cool from the night before. I struggled up and over the dune, then moved closer to the water, breathing in the salty air. I didn't want to lose the morning light, so I quickly settled down and opened my sketch pad to draw the ocean and surrounding mountains.

The sun felt hot and sticky against my back by the time I was mildly satisfied with what I'd drawn. I put down my sketch pad and felt hungry again. My stomach rumbled at the thought of Matsu's rice and vegetables. Matsu was certainly a good cook, even if he wasn't much of a talker.

I decided to go for a swim to take my mind off food. There was no one in either direction down the length of the beach, so I dropped my clothes on top of my sketch pad and walked quickly to the water. In my head I could hear my mother and Ching scream their disapproval as I plunged in. The sudden cold made my whole body tighten. With each stroke against the salty water, I felt a new surge of energy travel through my body. I swam back and forth, my arms thrusting forward with each stroke as I disrupted the calm of the sea with my furious motions. The coolness of the water felt good against my body. As I relaxed, a sense of freedom emerged which had been buried under my illness.

When my arms became too tired and my breathing labored, I simply lay back and floated. I could have stayed there forever, like a small child in a bathtub. Since returning to Hong Kong from my school in Canton, I'd spent most of my time in bed, too weak and feverish to do anything else. No one was allowed to visit, though Pie stuck her head in now and then. With only my mother and Ching as company, I missed King and my other friends at Lingnan University even more. I had been nothing but a prisoner in my own room.

My thoughts were suddenly interrupted by the sound of voices coming from shore. Instinctively, I lowered myself in the water. I was surprised to see two young girls on the beach. The taller of the two chased the other along the sand, laughing wildly. They didn't seem to notice me. At first I wanted to yell out to them, happy to discover other young people were living in Tarumi, but then I realized my clothes were on the beach. Watching them run up the dune, I kept very still until they were well out of sight.

When I returned to the house, Matsu was nowhere to be found. I quickly ate the bowl of cold *udon* noodles and fish cake he had left in my room. Later on I tried to keep myself occupied writing letters to my mother, Pie, and to King. I hoped he was still studying at Lingnan University. Three months had passed since I'd come home from Canton and my life as a student. I had no idea if my letter would ever reach him there, with the Japanese swarming all over China. In King's last letter to me in Hong Kong, he had said all was quiet in Canton and that the Japanese devils were currently leaving them alone. He ended his letter hoping I would use my "rest and recuperation" to perfect my art. King was one of the few friends I had who always understood how much painting means to me.

Matsu returned late in the afternoon carrying several magazines and small packages. He quickly took them to the kitchen, barely stopping long enough to give a slight bow in my direction. I followed him and stood in the kitchen doorway while he unwrapped his packages. The bloodier of the two contained a chicken, its head freshly severed, while the other was some sort of raw fish. At home, Ching forbade any of us to bother her when she cooked, including my mother who rarely entered the kitchen except to give last-minute instructions on what was to be served at her mah-jongg games.

Matsu finally looked up, no longer able to ignore me without being impolite. He shifted uncomfortably before saying his first full sentence since we met at the train station.

"Is there anything you need?" he asked. His hoarse voice vibrated through the small room.

"Yes," I replied, eagerly. "I wanted to ask you about some of the people staying around here."

Matsu looked away, a towel draped over the right shoulder of his worn gray kimono. He lifted up the chicken and continued to pluck out the brownish feathers.

"There aren't many people, only those in the village and some looking after houses. Summer is when the others come."

"But I saw two young girls at the beach this morning. Do you know if they live close by? Could they be the daughters of a servant?"

Matsu shrugged his shoulders. "Most of the young people left in Tarumi live in the village," he answered. He turned away and lifted a large clay pot onto the stove.

I waited until he turned around again before I asked, "Don't you ever get lonely here by yourself?"

I don't know what possessed me to ask Matsu such a personal question, but once I'd said it, I looked him in the eyes and waited for an answer. He didn't reply for a long time; he simply stood looking at me. Then he lifted his rough, thick fingers to his cheek and scratched it.

"There's always plenty of work," he finally answered.

15

"But what do you do when the work's done?" I continued to probe. "I suppose you have many friends here to pass the time with?"

Matsu's eyes narrowed. He looked me up and down suspiciously. "Why?" he asked.

I shifted uncomfortably, trying to find the right words to say in Japanese. "I just wondered. It seems so quiet here."

Matsu waited a moment, then let out a sharp laugh. "A friend here and there. Mostly, I work in the garden or read my magazines. I have a sister who sends them to me from Tokyo."

"You have a sister?"

"Does it seem so impossible for me to have a sister?" Matsu asked, clearly amused.

"No, of course not."

"I had two sisters, but one is dead now."

"I have two sisters and a brother," I said, realizing it was something he must already know. The few times our family came to visit, Matsu had helped us settle in, then quickly made himself scarce. I would have gone on telling him more about my family and friends, but Matsu cleared his throat and pointed to his clay pot on the stove. He picked up the chicken and turned away from me, but I didn't leave. Instead, I stayed and watched as he skillfully butchered the fowl. Matsu didn't look up or say another word. Still, it was a start.

SEPTEMBER 20, 1937

It was so warm last night I had a hard time sleeping. The moon was unusually bright, keeping the room awash in a hazy white light. Today I tried to draw, but nothing that made any sense found its way onto the paper. It was as if the dark charcoal lines were simply interrupting the whiteness of the sheet. I threw several away before I gave up in frustration. I tell myself I'll have much better results when I work with oil paints, but the canvases my father promised to send me from Kobe haven't arrived yet. He did send word that he wouldn't be able to come see me until next week. There also hasn't been any word from my mother and Pie in Hong Kong. I know it's been less than a week since I arrived, but it feels longer.

16

Matsu seems more receptive to my attempts at conversation, but we never get farther than what is already known. He acknowledges me with a slight bow of his head when we see each other during the day. At night, he spends most of his time back in the kitchen, or listening to the static sounds of his radio in the small room he sleeps in next to the kitchen. Matsu continues to surprise me. Usually he listens to pieces by Mozart or Chopin, which remind me of Pie and her White Russian piano teacher, or to the high female voice of a newscaster declaring "Shanghai's foolishness at not accepting the good intentions of the Imperial Army." Only once have I had the courage to ask Matsu what he felt about his country's victories in China. He was in the kitchen reading a magazine, as his radio blared from his room. He looked up at me, and simply said, "Japan is like a young woman who thinks too much of herself. She's bound to get herself into trouble." Then he looked back at his magazine and continued to read. I remained silent. Unlike me, he doesn't seem to need anything more. I guess all his years alone have left him comfortable with himself. We are slowly learning to live with each other.

There has been no sign of the two girls I saw my first day here. Every morning I go for a swim, hoping by chance another similar situation might bring them out. But it's been fruitless. Sometimes the house is so quiet I feel like the only noise that fills my mind is what I've created myself. Remembered conversations come back to me as if my friends and family were right here in the room.

SEPTEMBER 29, 1937

For the past week, I've endured all the quiet and loneliness like a blanket covering me until I'm well again. So I've simply resolved to become healthy through rest, exercise, and my painting.

Then this morning when I returned from my swim, I entered the garden gate to find Matsu carrying two wooden buckets of water to the silk tree. Instead of just giving me his usual quick bow, he paused and said, "A package came for you."

I don't remember if I said anything back to him. I ran into the house to find a large brown package of canvases leaning against the wall of my room, along with a letter from my mother and Pie lying on top of a stack of Japanese magazines. I grabbed the letter

17

and a few magazines, then headed back out to the garden, but Matsu was no longer there. The garden was definitely Matsu's domain and I felt his odd lingering presence in it. Every part of the garden seemed to have a sturdiness about it, even with its quiet grace.

It was a warm day, so I sat down near the pond to read my letter. The green moss was like a soft blanket. I felt like a child opening a long awaited present. The thin, blue papers went limp in my hands as I unfolded the pages to see the quick, strong strokes of my mother, followed by Pie's large, neatly written Chinese characters.

My mother spoke mostly of my health. Was I feeling better? Was I getting enough to eat? She would come to visit me as soon as possible. Anne and Henry would be returning to Hong Kong from school in Macao when the term was over in December. We would all be reunited then. She didn't believe the Japanese would ever have the nerve to enter Hong Kong. After all, it was under British sovereignty. Still, as I read her words I couldn't help but feel troubled.

Pie's words gave me much more comfort. She was first in her class, and was currently designing her own dresses for the dressmaker, inspired by *Poor Little Rich Girl,* the last Shirley Temple movie she had seen. The bulk of her letter was devoted to Anne's having fainted in Macao during one of the blackout procedures. Anne's teachers had to revive her with smelling salts and a shot of brandy. Pie said she would try it next blackout, just for a taste of brandy.

When I put down the letter I felt more homesick than I had in days. It was difficult to keep up with the war news so far away from everything. I had only been able to hear bits and pieces of the Japanese version from Matsu's radio. I was beginning to feel trapped behind this bamboo fence, which kept me separated from my family and the rest of the world.

I lay down on the cool blanket of moss and closed my eyes. I might have fallen asleep, but sounds outside the fence revived me. At first I thought it was Matsu, so I lay my head down again. Though he was nice enough to leave me some of his magazines, I was tired of trying to get the simplest conversation out of him.

But the sound of whispering voices grew louder. I sat up to see two shadows moving around on the other side of the fence. I tried to make out what was being said, but they spoke in hushed, hurried tones. I was about to get up when I felt something brush the top of my head. I looked up to see a shower of white petals fall in my direction, scattering on the ground around me, dropping like little boats into the pond. I jumped up and could hear two girls laughing aloud as I rushed to the gate. But by the time I swung the gate open, they were already running down the dirt road away from me. I yelled for them to stop. I only wanted to speak to them, but they continued to run, never turning back.

OCTOBER 5, 1937

Yesterday morning my father arrived from Kobe. He came unexpectedly, walking from the train station without telling us of his arrival. Matsu, who was outside tending his garden, greeted him first. When I heard Matsu's voice, which was unusually loud and excited, I wandered out from my room to see what was going on. At the front door, the brightness of the sun blinded me a moment before my sight adjusted to the figure of my father standing there, wiping his glasses. I ran up and threw my arms around him, almost knocking him down I was so happy.

"Ba-ba, why didn't you let me know you were coming? I would have met you at the station."

My father put his glasses back on and smiled. "I only knew myself at the last minute. There was so much work at the office, I barely made the train. Now, stand back and let me see what this fresh air has done for you."

I took a few steps back and stood up straight. "What do you think?" I asked.

"You still look too thin," he answered. Then, looking at Matsu, my father said teasingly, "Matsu, aren't you feeding my boy enough?"

Matsu walked over to my father rubbing his hands against his soiled pants. "He eats like a bird," he answered, picking up my father's suitcase and walking into the house.

* * *

Last night at dinner, my father drank *sake* and seemed relaxed as we ate rice, chicken, and pickled turnips in my grandfather's study. I was happy just having someone to speak to again.

"How are you feeling, Stephen?" my father asked. He lifted the small cup of *sake* to his mouth, so that just his eyes watched mine.

"I've been feeling well. The chest pains have disappeared and I'm coughing less," I answered.

My father brought down his cup and smiled. "And you're enjoying your stay here?"

"Yes, for the most part, but I miss everyone. It's rather lonely here."

"I know, Stephen, but it won't be for much longer. When you're well again, this period of your life will simply be a quiet memory."

I looked hard at my father, his graying hair and kind eyes, only to realize it had been a long time since I had so closely felt his presence. After Pie was born, she seemed to dominate my parents' attention. Then in Hong Kong, and even in Kobe, there were always family or business problems to keep us from really speaking to one another. But here in Tarumi it's different. Even the light is revealing; you can't miss the smallest nuance, the slightest sound. It's as if the world were concentrated into just these small rooms. I wonder if it appears the same for him.

OCTOBER 6, 1937

Today my father and I went down to the beach. It was still warm enough, so I swam while he sat on the sand in a wooden chair under a large yellow umbrella Matsu had set up. Wearing white slacks, a white shirt and hat, he looked nothing like the father I'm used to, dressed in severe, dark business suits. He appeared more like an acquaintance of our family, someone I hadn't seen in a long time.

I didn't swim very long before I was back sitting beside him on the beach. I felt like a small child again. We spoke of how it was when I was a young boy, and how I had always loved the water.

"Did you swim much as a boy?" I asked.

My father laughed and said, "I was afraid to put my head in the water. It was never easy for me as it is for you."

"You can't swim?" I asked, astonished at the fact that I didn't know. Usually when we came to Tarumi, it was Ching who brought us to the beach. She would sit on the sand screaming for us to be careful, hot and uncomfortable in her dark cotton tunic always buttoned up to her neck.

"I can float, just long enough for someone to come and save me," he then added.

"I'll teach you."

"Perhaps on my next visit," my father smiled.

I felt sad knowing our time together was coming to an end. He would have to be back in Kobe the following day. I fought back the sharp sting of loneliness returning as we sat in a comfortable silence.

"What's the situation like in Shanghai?" I asked, hungry for any news. "I don't hear much here."

"It's not good," my father answered, his face becoming serious. "Warplanes have bombed Shanghai incessantly. What the bombs don't destroy, the fires they start do. So many innocent lives have been lost." He paused, shaking his head. Then he looked at me and said, "I'll have some newspapers sent to you."

"What do you think will happen after they capture Shanghai?" I persisted.

"They will most likely keep moving south."

"Do you think they'll ever get as far as Hong Kong?"

My father lifted his hat and wiped his brow. "It's possible," he finally answered.

We stayed quiet for a while, each of us lost in our own thoughts.

"Can you tell me something about Matsu-*san?*" I suddenly asked.

My father squinted down at me. "What do you want to know?"

"Why has he stayed alone in Tarumi for all these years?"

"Tarumi has always been his home."

I spread my legs out on the warm sand. "But when he was young, didn't he ever want to see other places, raise a family of his own?"

My father laughed. "I can see you haven't gotten much out of Matsu, have you?"

"He doesn't say much," I answered.

21

"He never did. Even when I used to come here as a boy I re-member Matsu always keeping to himself, only at ease talking with his sisters. One of his sisters, the younger one, Tomoko, was very pretty and had caught the eye of many a boy."

"Did she catch your eye?"

"I was too shy to do anything." He smiled to himself. "Besides, I was the owner's son, and we were kept apart by class and cus-tom. Your grandfather and grandmother had other plans for me in those days."

"So you never had anything to do with Matsu and his sisters?" I asked, burying my foot in the sand, where I could still feel some coolness.

"We were children. Sometimes we'd play together when they came to help their father with the garden. Most of the time, they stayed at the house they lived in near the village."

"What was Matsu like at my age?"

My father leaned back and closed his eyes for a moment before answering. "Matsu was like a bull, his energy pent up, as if he was ready to break out at any moment. Why he never did, we'll never know. There were rumors that he loved a girl in town. She moved away, or married someone else. I'm not sure which. Then his sis-ter Tomoko suddenly died, and Matsu seemed to lose all his steam."

"You don't know what happened?" I asked, eager for answers.

My father shook his head. "I believe his sister had some kind of accident. By then, I was coming to Tarumi less and less and had only heard scant rumors of what happened."

"His other sister lives in Tokyo now," I said.

"She married and moved there."

"But why didn't Matsu leave here? What would keep him alone here all of his life?"

My father laughed at the urgency in my voice. "If you can get anything out of Matsu, I'll say you've accomplished quite a feat. He isn't the kind who will likely tell you his thoughts. Let's just assume he has found some sort of peace here in Tarumi, and leave it at that."

I kicked some sand away from me and remained silent. Matsu scared away most people with his aloofness, but I saw something more. He seemed to have a story no one had bothered to discover.

My father returned to Kobe yesterday. Matsu remained at the house, allowing me to accompany him to the station alone. As we waved good-bye at the train station, he was again the father I recognized in a business suit. Walking back to the house, I felt such an emptiness, I wanted to cry.

Matsu was in the garden. He was stooped by the pond grumbling to himself as he picked up the wet flower petals which had showered the garden every few days. I still hadn't had any luck meeting the two girls who threw them over the fence, but I knew it was just a matter of time.

Matsu looked up when he heard me close the gate. He was almost shy as he bowed and spoke. "Your *o-tōsan* is safely on his way back to Kobe?"

I nodded, then whispered, "Yes."

Matsu straightened. "I'm going to visit a friend who lives in a small mountain village near here," he said, his eyes avoiding mine. "I wondered if you would like to come with me?"

I looked at him and smiled, unable to conceal my surprise. "I would be happy to go with you!" I quickly answered before he had time to change his mind.

"Good, then we'll go after lunch," he said.

I watched Matsu turn around and walk back to the house, still clutching a handful of wet flower petals.

Yamaguchi was a small village in the mountains, Matsu said. He often visited to deliver supplies to a friend. We walked the two miles or so up a narrow, rocky, brush-lined dirt road. Ahead of us I could see the hilly slopes and large pine trees, which could easily cover up any signs of life.

"Yamaguchi is also called the Village of Lepers," Matsu said, as we walked slowly up the road. "When some of those who had the disease were no longer wanted by others in town, they took what few belongings they had and went up into the mountains, hoping to die peacefully. Away from the cruelties of the healthy."

"Aren't you afraid to go there?" I asked hesitantly.

Matsu walked straight ahead. I thought he wasn't going to answer, when he suddenly looked right at me and said, "The first time I went, I wasn't sure what to expect. After all, lepers from all over Japan found their way to Yamaguchi, simply hoping to be accepted, to be swallowed up by the mountain." Matsu looked down at the path again and then walked on. "I began to visit a friend there—someone from my youth. No one knew. I was young and healthy. And I remember being told long ago by a visiting doctor that there was nothing to fear. Leprosy wasn't a disease that could be spread by simple contact."

When Matsu's voice stopped, I realized he was several steps ahead of me and had turned to wait for me to catch up. I felt a shortness of breath as I drew in more air and let out several long sighs. "I'm fine," I said, increasing my pace and moving past Matsu up the hill.

"Maybe we should visit another day," Matsu said, raising his voice to make sure I heard.

I stopped and turned back to him. "I'm really fine!" I said, with such conviction that Matsu caught up, then continued up the path alongside of me.

The village of Yamaguchi stood in a clearing on the gradual slope of the mountain, hidden away by tall pine trees. Small wooden houses sat in a cluster like any other village. I stopped at the outskirts and let my eyes wander over the tranquil sight. From the distance, the villagers appeared just like Matsu and me. Men were gathered in small groups sipping tea and talking, while others worked in small gardens, and women sat mending clothes. Only with closer scrutiny did I begin to see that the houses were painstakingly pieced together with mismatched scraps of wood. And while some villagers had their heads and hands bandaged, others freely displayed their raw scabs and open wounds. I felt a strange curiosity, rather than fear. In China, lepers had always been feared and shunned. I had heard stories of how they were forced to live on the streets, left to beg or eat rats, while they simply rotted away.

I stood a long time taking it all in. When I finally came out of my trance, Matsu was studying my face with an unusual intensity. He continued to watch me and finally said, "You don't have to be afraid. I wouldn't have brought you here if there were any danger."

I smiled at his concern. "I'm afraid for them," I said, quick to cover my cough.

Matsu laughed, then pointed toward the far end of the village. "My friend's house is that way," he said.

We walked slowly through the village. There was a distinct smell of eucalyptus and something else medicinal. For the first time in my life I saw what it meant to be a leper, a disgraced one. They seemed to watch me with just as much curiosity. I tried not to stare, but I couldn't take my eyes off their wounds; the missing fingers and toes, the large, gaping holes in the sides of their faces, the mangled features that had once been noses and ears. It looked as if they were all wearing monstrous masks that I kept waiting for them to remove.

Matsu must have understood my thoughts. He suddenly stopped, turned to me, and said, "Most of them came to this village as young men and women. Now they are too old and set in their ways to move. Even though the Japanese government has acknowledged their situation and would gladly move them to better facilities. Good or bad, Yamaguchi has been their home."

I watched as Matsu then nodded and exchanged pleasantries with several of the villagers.

From some doorways I could also smell the strong, sweet aroma of tea which filled me and my parched throat with longing.

"Who is the handsome young man, Matsu?" one man asked, taking a few steps closer. His right arm was a gnarled raw stump which looked like it had been eaten away.

"The son of my *Danasama,* my master," Matsu answered, walking on without a pause.

I smiled at all of them self-consciously, then followed Matsu as if he were the master.

We walked to the far end of the village, where there were few houses and the pine trees thickened. Matsu slowed down as we approached a small, sturdier-looking house almost hidden among the trees.

"Who lives here?" I asked, catching my breath.

"A friend," Matsu answered. As he led me toward the house, I noticed how his steps lightened, his body relaxed, and he seemed almost young again.

I stood behind Matsu as he tapped three times on the door and waited, blowing air through his teeth to create a small whistling sound. I'd never seen Matsu so exuberant and was curious to see who lived there. Within moments the door opened just enough for a head, veiled in black, to peek out.

"Sachi-*san,* it's me," Matsu said, gently.

The woman stepped back and opened the door wider, allowing the sunlight to brighten the clean, spare, white room behind her. She looked away from Matsu toward me and held her place behind the door. "Matsu?" she said softly, watching me closely.

Matsu glanced back at me, then said, "This is Stephen-*san,* he's a friend."

"Konnichiwa," I said, smiling and bowing, trying to put her at ease.

The woman stepped back and bowed humbly. Matsu entered the small house, and with a slight wave of his hand urged me to follow. I did, anxious to know more about the timid woman who lived within it. The room smelled of the pine branches which sat in a vase on a low table in one corner. Next to the vase were two small, shiny black stones. Other than the table and a few cushions neatly stacked to the side, the room was bare.

"I didn't know you would come today, Matsu," the woman said, keeping her head bowed so low I couldn't see her face under the black scarf. Her voice was soft and hesitant.

"It was a nice day to take a walk. Anyway, since when do I need an invitation to visit you, Sachi?" Matsu said, teasingly.

Sachi laughed, looking down and away from Matsu.

"I will bring some tea," she then said shyly. She adjusted the black scarf so that it covered her face as she turned to leave the room.

"Is she?" I asked, without completing my sentence.

Matsu walked to the window and looked out. "Yes," he said softly, "she's a leper."

We stood so quietly for a few moments that the muted sounds coming from the kitchen filled the room. It was strange to be standing in a different house with Matsu, seeing him for the first time in a new light. He seemed gentler, less in command.

"This is a nice house," I finally said.

Matsu nodded his approval.

Sachi returned carrying a tray of tea and crackers. When we were seated on the cushions, I looked up to examine the face of our hostess. She was older than I had first thought, with a slender build and quick movements. When Sachi leaned forward to serve the strong green tea, her black scarf slipped a little from the left side of her face. Underneath I could see where the ulcers had eaten away her flesh, leaving white, scaly scabs, creating a disfigured mass as her half-closed left eye strained to open. When she saw my gaze, Sachi quickly looked down and re-covered the side of her face. As far as I could see, only her face and left hand seemed affected by the disease; her smooth, white right hand and fingers were untouched.

"More tea?" she asked, beginning to rise.

"Please," I answered, my face flushed and embarrassed.

Matsu rose quickly before her and said, "Let me get it," disappearing into the kitchen before Sachi had time to say anything. Very slowly, she lowered her body back down onto the cushion and turned just enough so that only the right side of her face was exposed to me. While the left side of her face had been devastated, the unblemished right side was the single most beautiful face I'd ever seen.

"I hope we're not disturbing you," I said, my voice sounding young and eager.

Sachi shook her head. She turned a bit more to get a good look at me with her one good eye. "I don't have many visitors, only Matsu-*san*. Often years will go by without my seeing a new face. I am honored to have you visit."

Then I was the one who seemed shy, not knowing what to say to this very beautiful woman. It seemed we already had something in common in our loneliness. I tried to imagine what Pie would do in my situation, but realized she might just ask to see what was under the black scarf.

Sachi must have sensed my discomfort, because she was the one to continue the conversation. The words flowed from her with ease. "The last time Matsu came, he told me you were staying at the beach house for a while," she said.

27

"I haven't been well. My parents thought it might be better for me to be away from Hong Kong and my younger sister while I'm recuperating. They're hoping the fresh air of Tarumi will help me."

Sachi pulled the black scarf tighter across her left side. "Yes, Tarumi can be a cure for some, and a refuge for others."

"What's a refuge?" Matsu asked, walking heavily out of the kitchen, carrying a pot of tea.

Sachi looked toward him and smiled. "The beauty of Tarumi," she answered. She quickly rose from her cushion and bowed her head. "Matsu, let me see if I need anything for the garden."

We both watched in silence as Sachi slid open the *shoji* door and disappeared.

By the time we were ready to leave Sachi's house, it was late afternoon. I was filled with tea and crackers, happy that Sachi had relaxed and grown comfortable in my presence.

"I would be honored if you would come and visit me again," Sachi said. She stood at the door and pulled her scarf closer to her face.

"I will," I smiled. I glanced toward Matsu.

"There's no need to wait for Matsu," she said. "You are always welcome."

I bowed, and said, *"Dōmo arigatō gozaimasu."*

Matsu watched us and smiled. Then before he turned to leave, he gently touched Sachi's arm.

Matsu and I walked through the village saying very little. The same villagers sat playing cards or smoking in small, scattered groups. They were less interested in us this time, though Matsu lifted his hand and gestured to several of the men along the way. Our walk back down the mountain was quick and quiet. Only when we reached the beach road that led back to the house did I gather the courage to speak.

"Sachi-*san* is very nice," I said.

Matsu nodded his head in agreement, then added, "She was

once one of the most beautiful girls in all of Tarumi, perhaps all of Japan!"

"How did she catch it?" I asked hesitantly.

"The leprosy?" Matsu shook his head. "It was like a wildfire back then. It couldn't be stopped once it began."

"When did it happen?"

Matsu slid his hand through his short gray hair. I watched his brow wrinkle in thought, as sweat glistened and slowly made its way down the side of his face. "It must have been at least forty years ago or so when it first appeared in Tarumi," he finally answered. "I don't know what brought the cursed disease to us. We had never seen it before, but maybe it was always incubating, waiting like a smoldering fire to spread out. One day, it began to show its ugly face and there was nothing we could do. The disease chose randomly, infecting our young and old."

"My father never told us anything about it."

"He never knew," Matsu continued eagerly, as if it was a story he'd long held inside and could finally unleash. "It was kept quiet among the local villagers. After all, Tarumi was a place for outsiders to come on holiday. If they'd heard about the disease, no one would return. We didn't want to frighten anyone away until we knew more about it. At first, no one had any idea what was happening, then a few more became infected with the scaly patches. It first appeared like a rash, only it wouldn't go away. Within months, it began to eat up the victim's hand or face." Matsu paused and swallowed. "Fortunately, there was a young doctor visiting Tarumi who tried, without much success, to reassure us that the disease couldn't be spread by simple touch. We wanted to listen and learn, but those first few months were like a bad dream. Every day people awoke, afraid the leprosy would claim them. Some of those suffering from the disease quickly left the village, while others ended their lives, hoping not to dishonor their families."

"Was your family all right?"

Matsu was silent. The road had become familiar again, with bamboo-fenced houses and trees. We were almost home. I could smell the salt from the ocean and feel its mist on my face. I waited for him to go on.

"It took my younger sister, Tomoko," Matsu finally said.

I hesitated, remembering what my father had said about her accident. I wanted to know more, but Matsu had quickened his pace as we neared the house. Instead, I asked, "Why did you take me with you to Yamaguchi?"

Matsu slowed, then turned to face me before he answered, "So you would know that you're not alone."

OCTOBER 21, 1937

Everything has changed between Matsu and me since we've visited Sachi. It's as if the awkwardness has disappeared and we share some precious secret. It's not that we speak a great deal more, but the silence no longer seems intimidating. Once in a while, I even catch Matsu glancing my way, a smile just barely visible on the corners of his lips.

Last night after I'd finished eating in my room, I walked back to the kitchen to find Matsu still sitting at the wooden table. A high, scratchy voice coming from his radio had just declared another Japanese advancement in their struggle against Shanghai. Matsu leaned over and played with the dial until a Bach concerto filled the room. He seemed oblivious to my presence.

After I listened for a while, I softly said, "Excuse me," to let him know I was there.

Matsu turned to me, startled for a moment.

"Will you be going to Yamaguchi soon?" I asked.

Matsu laughed and relaxed. "So you want to see Sachi-*san* again, do you?"

"Yes," I quickly answered, embarrassed that my curiosity was so apparent.

Matsu laughed and rubbed his thick hands together before he said, "I suppose it does Sachi good to see a young, handsome face now and then. Unfortunately, she has had only mine for too long."

"You have a strong face. A face someone doesn't forget."

"Like a monster," Matsu added.

"Like a samurai," I said.

Matsu opened his mouth as if to say something, but quickly swallowed the words before they came to his lips. I waited a few moments, then turned to leave. I already knew from the month I'd been here, Matsu had little more to say. It was always the same, conversations would simply end as they began. Matsu felt most comfortable when he spoke about his garden, and was most abrupt speaking of himself.

I was barely out of the kitchen when I heard Matsu's voice rise above the music. "We'll go again at the end of the week."

"Thank you," I said, happily.

I was grateful that Matsu understood. Sachi was definitely someone I wanted to know better. From the moment I met her, she had instilled a sense of richness and mystery in Tarumi. Her once-beautiful face had even appeared in my dreams, the sadness half-hidden under her black scarf. I wondered how long she'd been living alone in the mountains. Had Matsu always loved her? Did Sachi love him? These questions occupied my mind, and made her all the more enticing.

This morning I decided to paint the view of the garden from my grandfather's study. When I first arrived in Tarumi, I wondered how Matsu could spend so much time in the garden. But the more time I spend here, the easier it is to see there's something very seductive about what Matsu has created. Once, when I asked him to name a few blossoms for me, the words "Kerria, Lespedeza, Crepe Myrtle" seemed to flow from his lips in one quick breath.

The garden is a world filled with secrets. Slowly, I see more each day. The black pines twist and turn to form graceful shapes, while the moss is a carpet of green that invites you to sit by the pond. Even the stone lanterns, which dimly light the way at night, allow you to see only so much. Matsu's garden whispers at you, never shouts; it leads you down a path hoping for more, as if everything is seen, yet hidden. There's a quiet beauty here I only hope I can capture on canvas.

After breakfast, Matsu went to work in the back garden behind the house, so I carried my paints, a canvas my father had sent, and a makeshift easel into the study. I carefully pushed my grandfather's desk aside, then slid open the *shoji* doors that faced the front garden. The bright white light filtered in through the trees, leaving a sway of ghost shadows on the walls. I felt a burst of energy in my body as I ran across the hall to the main room and slid open its doors, so that the entire front of the house opened up to the garden. I breathed in the sweet air without coughing, filled with an urgency to paint. It was the first time in so long that I had felt any real energy return to me. From one full tube of oil paint and then another, I squeezed out large daubs of blue and yellow onto a wooden tray that served as my palette. The sharp, tinny smell filled my head. I looked outside to the quiet beauty, wondering how it would fill the blank canvas. My brush had just touched the white surface when I heard Matsu's quick, shuffling footsteps come from the back of the garden. He stopped abruptly when he'd seen what I had done.

"What are you doing?" Matsu asked accusingly.

In my excitement, I hadn't thought to ask his permission before opening up the rooms. "I wanted to paint the garden. I hope it's all right—" I answered.

Matsu stood silent for a moment. His mouth remained slightly open, as if surprised to see the two rooms in such a different light.

"Do as you wish," Matsu finally said, disappearing around the side of the house.

After Matsu left, I began to paint. I didn't want to lose the light which had already begun to change. I painted with a vengeance, and might not have stopped at all if Matsu hadn't returned with a covered tray of lunch. I wanted to apologize for not asking him earlier if I could use the study to paint, but I was so involved I just kept working. He set the tray down on my grandfather's desk without saying a word. The next thing I knew he was gone.

When I finally lay down my brush, I stepped back to see that the garden was slowly emerging on the canvas. I felt happier and healthier than I'd been in months. My eyes wandered from the canvas to the tray Matsu had left on the desk. Under the lacquer cover was a bowl of noodles sprinkled with green onions and thin slices of fish, a rice cake, and tea. I was so hungry I picked up the bowl and began slurping up the noodles. It took a few minutes before I realized there was something else lying on the tray. A long, slim, black-lacquered box lay next to my cup of tea. I swallowed another large mouthful of noodles before investigating the black box. I lifted off the shiny lid to find three very expensive sable paintbrushes. Picking up one, I fingered its smooth, soft tip, thinking how well it would stroke against the canvas. I wondered where Matsu could have found such beautiful brushes. I examined the other two before placing them all back into the black box. When I finished my noodles, I picked up the lacquer box and went to look for Matsu. He wasn't in the kitchen, so I stepped outside. I found him in the back garden, carefully planting a small black pine. His thick body was bent over, so he couldn't see me watch him pat the dirt in place, then mumble some inaudible words to the plant. He was as gentle with it as with a small child.

"These are beautiful brushes," I said, as I held the black box out toward him.

Matsu turned around and raised his hand against the sun to see me. "I thought you might like them," he said. "They belonged to your *ojī-san*."

I lifted the lid off of the box. "They're new. Didn't my grandfather ever paint with them?"

Matsu laughed. "Your *ojī-san* had more brushes than he knew what to do with. He often painted when he came to Tarumi, but he only used one or two old brushes. He would usually sit half a day away looking through art books and catalogs. He liked to buy beautiful things simply to have them. I found those in his desk many years ago. I thought you might make better use of them."

"Thank you," I said, "I'll try."

I stood gazing down at the young pine he'd just planted. When I looked back up, our eyes met for just a moment before Matsu turned away.

OCTOBER 29, 1937

I painted a little today, then stopped. The painting's almost complete and part of me wants to save it, savor the last few strokes like precious drops of water. The thought of water was a reminder that it'd been days since I'd gone down to the beach. Since we visited Yamaguchi and I began to paint again, I'd barely left the house.

I went to tell Matsu I was going down to the beach, but I couldn't find him anywhere. For a moment I thought he might have gone to visit Sachi without taking me along as he promised, but I knew he was nearby when I saw his garden tools still spread out in the garden. I left a note for him on the kitchen table.

The path down to the beach felt like a familiar friend. I kicked off my shoes and walked slowly across the white sand and over the dune. Everything seemed in perfect focus. The air carried a sharp coolness to it, awakening me. The sky was a pale blue with small patches of clouds that resembled islands. Even the sea was calm. Small waves lapped in and out mechanically, clear as glass.

I fell limply onto the sand. As always the beach appeared to be all mine, so I began to undress for a quick swim. I had just taken off my shirt when I heard the sounds of laughter I'd been waiting for weeks to hear. In the near distance, I saw the two girls slowly walking toward me. The nearest I had come to them was when they had thrown flower petals into Matsu's garden. As they approached, I remained sitting on the sand, half-hidden behind the tall beach grass. My heart was pounding, yet I didn't move a muscle, hoping to blend in to the sand like a chameleon. I decided I'd only show myself when they were too close to run away. I suddenly thought back to Canton, back in school where so many girls had been afraid to approach me. They would whisper and giggle, never daring to speak to me. My friend King had his own explanation.

"They're afraid of you," he once said. "You're too good-looking. They don't trust someone as good-looking as you, which is a lucky break for us ugly ducklings!"

I was determined to prove King wrong. I sat perfectly still, watching them bob back and forth against one another as they walked. They reminded me of my own sisters as they talked and shook their heads in laughter.

It was the shorter of the two girls who first caught sight of me. She wavered a bit, then tugged anxiously on the sleeve of the taller girl. They stopped. I quickly put my shirt back on and stood up, waving in their direction. After a moment's hesitation, the taller girl began to walk toward me, closely followed by the other.

I searched my mind for all the right Japanese words with which

34

to introduce myself, but simply bowed and said, *"Konnichiwa,"* when they were close enough to hear.

My greeting was returned with giggles. The two girls glanced at each other, before they turned back to me and bowed quickly.

I could see the taller girl was the older of the two, her face narrower and her giggling more controlled. She eyed me with a shy, yet inquisitive glance. They shared some resemblance, but the shorter girl had a fuller, younger face. She probably wasn't much older than Pie, who at twelve always seemed much older than her age.

"Hajimemashite. How do you do. My name is Stephen Chan," I said, bowing deeply again, careful not to do anything that might frighten them away.

The taller girl returned my bow and said, *"Hajimemashite.* My name's Keiko Hayashi, and this is my sister Mika." Mika looked away from me to her sister, then began to pull on Keiko's arm.

"I wonder if I could have the honor of speaking with you for a moment," I said quickly, hoping they wouldn't run off so soon this time.

Mika had apparently made up her mind to leave, but Keiko hesitated, then planted her feet in the sand against her sister's urging.

"Do you live around here?" I asked, my Japanese halting but polite.

Mika giggled.

But Keiko nodded her head, and in a clear, high voice answered, "Yes, we live in the village."

"I think I've seen you around here before," I said, focusing my attention on Keiko.

"Yes, it's possible, we often walk out to the beach," Keiko answered. She shook off Mika's grip. She had a pleasant, pretty face and spoke with assurance.

"Are there lots of young people around here now?" I continued.

"Not many. A few families in town," she answered. "Most of the young men have joined the army, while the others move to the city as soon as they can."

Mika began tugging at her arm again, then whispered something quickly to Keiko, who nodded her head.

"We must go," Keiko said, glancing shyly up at me.

"Can we talk again?" I quickly asked.

Keiko bowed but said nothing more. In the next moment, she and Mika were running back to the dunes and away from me. I waited until they were completely out of sight and their voices had faded in the cool, calm air. Then I turned around and ran to the water, forgetting to take off my clothes.

Once I was safely back in the garden, I took off my wet clothes and left them in a heap by the front steps. By the time I put on dry clothes, I found Matsu in the kitchen cleaning a fish and humming to himself in a relaxed, happy manner I was unaccustomed to. It wasn't far from what I felt myself after finally making contact with Keiko and Mika. At least I knew they weren't a figment of my imagination. During the height of my illness in Hong Kong, I would sometimes see spirits that couldn't be explained or identified. I was frightened by these apparitions, though they always approached me as harmless young children. I wanted an explanation as to why they stood quietly by, watching me. I would be in my room or sitting in the warm sun of the courtyard. These spirits would be there one moment and gone the next. I felt them waiting, and I wondered if it could be true that they would soon take me with them. Ching said it was the fever, and my mother blamed it on the tricks of a creative mind. "You're more sensitive," she would say. "The spirits are more alive for you." She told me to ignore them and they would soon go away. I tried not to pay attention to them, but the spirits only left when my health improved. Until now, I didn't dare let myself think that these ghosts had returned.

"How was your swim?" Matsu asked, hearing me approach.

"It was great," I answered. "I finally talked to the two girls I told you about."

"So they do exist."

"They live in town."

Matsu turned around to face me and smiled. "Did you tell them to stop throwing flowers into my garden?"

"I forgot," I confessed.

Matsu laughed. "Were you so captivated by them?"

"I barely got to say anything before they ran away again."

"They'll be back," Matsu said, matter-of-factly.

"I hope," I said, more to myself than to Matsu.

"How could they resist a handsome young man like you?"

I laughed, "They have, until now."

"It's part of the game," Matsu said, "you'll see."

I was about to ask Matsu how he knew so much about the strategies of two young girls, but before I could, he cleared his throat and said, "Sachi has sent a note inviting us for lunch. Are you free tomorrow, or will you be meeting your new friends?"

"What time should I be ready?" I asked.

Matsu laughed. "We'll leave before noon."

OCTOBER 30, 1937

I was up early this morning, too excited at the thought of seeing Sachi to sleep. I lay in bed and waited for the first sounds of Matsu preparing breakfast in the kitchen before I got up, and dressed in a clean white shirt and my beige cotton slacks. When I slid open my door, the delicious smells coming from the kitchen were not those of our usual salted fish or pickled vegetables.

The doorway of the kitchen had become my usual place to stand since the kitchen wasn't large and I didn't want to get in Matsu's way.

"What smells so good?" I asked.

"Bacon and eggs," he answered, without looking up from his frying.

"How do you know how to make bacon and eggs?"

Matsu turned to me and smiled. "How do you want your eggs, scrambled, sunny-side up, or over-easy?"

"Scrambled," I quickly answered. It seemed like a long time since I'd eaten bacon and eggs. Before my illness, when all of us were home from school on vacation, my parents would often take us to Western hotels for brunch. The long tables held something special for each one of us. Pie would race through her entrees so she could get to the miniature cream puffs and puddings, while Henry and I concentrated on the bacon and sausages, and Anne nibbled on the salads.

"Your *ojī-san* always had his over-easy."

"My grandfather liked to eat eggs?" I asked.

"When he was here, he'd have three eggs every morning, and strong European coffee he brought with him from Tokyo."

"How old were you when you began working for my grandfather?"

"I wasn't much older than you are now. My family has always taken care of this house. Even when we were young, my sisters and I ran little errands and I helped my father take care of the garden. When my parents became too old, I took over for them," Matsu answered.

I watched as he cracked two eggs into a clay bowl, mixed them thoroughly, and poured them into a hot skillet.

Then while the eggs were cooking, he laughed hoarsely and continued, "The first time I made your *ojī-san* his breakfast, I was afraid I couldn't make his eggs the way he liked. I must have gone through half a dozen eggs before he came into the kitchen and showed me how he wanted them cooked."

"I never knew much about my grandfather. He died before I had a chance to really know him. I only remember his carved cane and the tall hats he wore."

"Your *ojī-san* was a very good-looking, intelligent man. He knew what his assets were and sometimes liked to flaunt them." Matsu paused, then quickly added, "But never in a way that offended anyone. Everyone in Tarumi liked your *ojī-san*. He was a very generous man."

"Did he come here often?" I asked, thinking of my own father's infrequent visits.

"Once a month, or whenever the import business brought him back to Japan. Unlike your *o-tōsan,* who is more serious about his work, your *ojī-san* seemed to relax immediately once he was here."

Matsu scooped up some scrambled eggs, laid three pieces of bacon beside the eggs, and placed the plate on the wooden table.

"Eat," he said.

I pulled out a wobbly wooden stool from under the table and quickly sat down as ordered. Matsu filled a plate for himself and sat down next to me. He leaned toward the counter and brought back a pot of tea, filling the two cups in front of us. Then he waited for me to begin to eat first. I picked up a strip of bacon and took a big bite.

"It's very good," I said, savoring its smoky taste. "How did you get it?"

"I have a friend who can get me anything I need, including bacon," Matsu laughed.

"It's delicious."

Matsu nodded, then began to eat his own food with pleasure. At first it felt strange to be eating in the small, crowded kitchen with Matsu, but it didn't take more than two mouthfuls before I was perfectly at ease.

It seemed like a good time to bring up another subject that had been on my mind. "Would it be all right if I took something to Sachi-*san?*" I asked. "Just a small gift to show my appreciation."

I watched Matsu chew his food in thought. It felt like forever until he looked up and said gently. "It isn't necessary. It would only embarrass her."

"It'll just be something small," I said.

Matsu cleared his throat and didn't say anything more. I took the gesture to mean yes, but knew better than to stress the point.

Matsu said very little during our walk to Yamaguchi. I wasn't sure if he was upset at my bringing something to Sachi, but he had smiled his approval when I showed him the charcoal sketch I'd drawn down at the beach after breakfast. I had hoped to run into Keiko and Mika again, but the beach remained empty.

When the road ended, we followed a dirt path that gradually wove its way up the mountain. Since the path was too narrow for two to walk comfortably, I followed Matsu, who remained lost in his own thoughts. Nothing seemed to deter him, while I jumped over rocks and overgrown shrubs along the way. Matsu walked ahead, sure-footed, turning back only once to see if I was still there. Under one arm, he carried several newspapers and magazines. And in the other, a package wrapped in brown paper. He never even noticed when I stopped to catch my breath.

When we reached Yamaguchi, the village was relatively quiet. Most of the villagers were inside eating lunch. I could see shadows move about darkened doorways as we walked by.

Once in a while, a gruff, loud voice acknowledged our presence with a spirited hello. *"Konnichiwa,* Matsu-*san,* come join us for something to eat!"

Matsu lifted his arm to wave his regrets as we continued walking.

I felt a twinge of nervousness when Sachi's house came into sight. I carried the rolled-up charcoal sketch in my sweaty hand. It wasn't my best work, but I thought I'd captured some endless, serene quality about the sea which I hoped Sachi might appreciate.

Matsu knocked on the door and waited. I expected to see the same shy smile greet us from under her black scarf, but a few moments passed and no one answered. Matsu took a step back and knocked louder. When there was still no answer, he turned to me and said calmly, "She must be in the garden."

I followed Matsu as he walked down a stone path which led around the side of the house to the back. He swung open a tall bamboo gate and stepped to the side, allowing me to enter first. In place of the greens, browns, and flashes of color which punctuated Matsu's garden, the spareness of Sachi's garden stunned me. There were no trees, flowers, or water, only a landscape made of sand, stones, rocks, and some pale green moss which covered the shaded areas. I took a few minutes to take it all in. On the rugged, sloping earth, Sachi had created mountains from arranged rocks, surrounded by gravel and elongated stones flowing down like a rocky stream leading to a lake or the sea. The flat surface of water was formed by smooth round pebbles, raked in straight and encircling lines to suggest whirlpools and waves.

"A dry landscape," I whispered aloud.

"It's called *kare sansui,"* Matsu suddenly said. Only then did I even remember he was behind me.

"It's beautiful," I said, amazed at how the different light and dark stones could create such texture and illusion.

"Where did Sachi go?" Matsu asked, talking more to himself than to me. "She would have liked to have shown you the garden herself."

"I'm sure she'll be back soon," I answered. It was the first time I saw him so disturbed.

Matsu quickly walked back to the front of the house, but I

couldn't move. I took another long look at Sachi's garden before I turned around and followed.

Matsu had already begun walking to the village when, in the distance, I saw Sachi hurrying toward him. Her dark blue kimono swept across the dirt as she walked. Matsu stopped and waited, as she approached and bowed. He reached over and took her packages as they walked back to the house.

"*Sumimasen,* please excuse me for being late," bowed Sachi, as they approached me. With one hand Sachi held her scarf close to the left side of her face.

I returned Sachi's bow and smiled. "We haven't been waiting long."

"Tanaka-*san* asked me if I would bring him some old newspapers. I didn't realize it would take so long," Sachi continued to apologize. "Most of the food has already been prepared."

"There's no hurry," I said. "Matsu made a big American breakfast this morning."

Sachi turned to Matsu and said, "Ah, your eggs!"

Matsu laughed aloud. "Sachi likes her eggs scrambled as you do."

Sachi smiled shyly, pulled her scarf closer, and hurried into the house saying nothing.

Once again I was taken aback by the simplicity of her world—elegant and uncluttered. Matsu handed Sachi the newspapers and magazines, then took the rest of the packages to the kitchen.

"This is for you," I said. I handed her the soiled, rolled-up drawing, wishing I had wrapped it in another piece of paper.

Sachi bowed timidly. *"Dōmo arigatō gozaimasu."*

"I hope you'll like it."

Sachi smiled, but hesitated to unroll the paper in front of me.

"Please," I said, nodding my head.

She turned away from me and unrolled it slowly. When she saw that it was a charcoal sketch of the sea, she quickly turned back to me and bowed again, exposing the scarred side of her face. "I am very honored."

41

"It's just a quick sketch I did this morning. I wanted to bring you a token of my appreciation."

"You have brought me more than that, you have brought me the sea," Sachi said, her voice tight with emotion.

I didn't know what to say, and was saved when Matsu, lifting up his brown package, said loudly from across the room, "And I have brought you a chicken!"

Sachi and I laughed, as she carefully rolled up my sketch and placed it on a table. Her hand patted it gently just once before she turned back to me.

We ate lunch at the low table in Sachi's dining room. She had prepared fish cake, rice, thin slices of raw fish, marinated eel, and pickled vegetables. It all came in a black *bento* box, divided into separate sections. While Matsu and I ate, Sachi nibbled at her food, poured tea whenever we had sipped from our cups, and was ready at any moment to go back into the kitchen for more food.

"It was a wonderful lunch," I said, bowing my head in appreciation.

"I'm happy that you could come," Sachi said. She slowly rose to collect the empty boxes.

"Let me help you," I said.

"I'll take care of it," Matsu suddenly interrupted. "Sachi, why don't you take Stephen-*san* out to the garden."

Sachi glanced down at me and said, "If you would like to see the garden, I would be honored to show you."

I stood up quickly and felt a stiffness along my legs as I stretched my muscles. "I would love to see your garden."

I followed Sachi, as she slid open the *shoji* door that led out into her garden.

"It's wonderful," I said, even more intrigued than the first time I'd seen it. The sun was overhead, which lightened the color of the rocks, setting them aglow.

"I could not have done it without Matsu's help," Sachi said. "Many years ago, when I first came to Yamaguchi, the possibility of having a life had all but vanished. Matsu was the one who insisted I have a garden."

"And you created this?"

"With Matsu's help. He showed me that life is not just from within, it extends all around you, whether you wish it to or not. And so, this garden has become a part of my life."

I wanted to say something back to Sachi, but the words were caught in my throat. Her garden was a mixture of beauty and sadness, the rocks and stones an illusion of movement. What could she have possibly done to deserve such a fate? Didn't her family ever try to help her? I looked at the slim, shy woman standing in front of me and wanted all my questions answered, but I kept quiet and could only hope the answers would be given to me in time.

"If we invited Sachi-*san* to the house, would she come?" I asked Matsu on our way back down the mountain. I held my jacket tightly closed against the cold wind. The branches and twigs snapped beneath our feet as we walked. He was just a step ahead of me and in a good mood.

Matsu cleared his throat, slowed down, and turned to me. "She hasn't left Yamaguchi in almost forty years. In the beginning, I tried to get her to come down, but she was too ashamed."

"Didn't her family care what happened to her?"

"Her family gave up on Sachi a long time ago."

"They disowned her because of the disease?" I asked, flushed with anger.

Matsu shook his head, then said, "It wasn't so simple. It was a question of honor. Once she became afflicted with the disease, it was Sachi who chose not to dishonor her family any more than she had."

"What?"

"It was her choice."

"But why?"

"She saw no reason for them to suffer her shame."

"Do you think she might come down now?" I dared to ask.

"Again, it will have to be her choice," Matsu said, picking up the pace and moving farther ahead of me.

I completed the painting of the garden this morning. Finishing it was like saying good-bye to my family again and being cast adrift on some endless sea; I felt that empty.

"It's finished," I called out, when Matsu came into the house. A small replica of his garden sat propped on the easel drying. I stood by the painting, eager for some kind of reaction from him; a simple smile of recognition, or at the least, a lingering gaze. Instead, Matsu stepped into the room wiping his mud-stained hands with an old rag. He took no more than a moment to glance at the painting, then grunt his approval before he turned to leave again.

My fingers closed tightly around one of my grandfather's brushes. The strong, sharp smell of the paints filled the room. Then, as if he knew my thoughts, Matsu stopped and turned to ask, "I have to go into town now, would you like to come along?"

"I'd love to go," I answered. "Just let me finish cleaning these brushes."

It was strange to think that two months had passed without my having seen the small beach village. Yet, even when we came to Tarumi as children, we seldom left the house and beach. It was always Ching or the other servants who walked the mile back and forth to buy food and whatever else was needed. I never thought of it as much more than a few scattered buildings, but now the prospect of seeing the village seemed like a good way to spend the afternoon.

Tarumi was not far from the train station, lying in the opposite direction of our beach house. When Matsu and I approached the small station and worn tracks, a train had just pulled in. People had begun to disembark as we walked toward town. I felt their stares follow me. I knew it was not only because I was a Chinese face in their village, but I also realized there were very few young men in Tarumi. Most of the women were dressed in dark, padded kimonos, but a few younger girls had on Western dresses and coats. I was mesmerized being around so many people again; the subtle sweet and sour odors of perfume and sweat, the high and low of different voices. If I closed my eyes, I could almost pretend I was back in Kobe.

Tarumi looked tired and faded in the gray light. The buildings which lined each side of the dirt road were built of dingy brown wood. The village consisted of a store, post office, and teahouse. Their large, bold characters were carefully painted on signs above each building. Farther down the road were smaller houses where the townspeople lived. Bits and pieces of their lives could be seen in the bicycles and toys leaning against the mismatched bamboo fences. Dogs roamed freely down the road, as the bobbing figures of women and children walked back to their houses. I couldn't help but wonder which house belonged to Keiko and Mika.

"Come this way," Matsu said.

I followed him across the road to the teahouse. At the door we were greeted by a thin man with a white towel draped over his shoulder. His eyes were dark and sharp, and I watched as he lifted his right hand against the dull light from the street.

"*Matsu, konnichiwa!* I wondered when you would stop by," he bowed.

"Did you think I would forget, Kenzo?" Matsu answered.

"No, not you Matsu," he said, with an almost childlike enthusiasm.

Matsu turned, grabbed my shoulder firmly and pulled me forward. "This is Stephen-*san,*" he said. "And this is Kenzo-*san,* he makes the best rice crackers in all of Japan. He's also the man who gets me bacon and whatever else I need."

Kenzo and I bowed to each other.

"Come, come sit down," Kenzo said, leading us to a table at the back of the large room.

When my eyes adjusted to the dim light inside, I noticed that besides us, there was a lone old man sitting in the far corner. The neat rows of tables were separated by simple wood panels, while sturdy wooden beams ran across the ceiling. The room felt comfortable and inviting.

"The usual for you, Matsu?" Kenzo asked.

Matsu laughed. "I didn't walk all this way just to visit with you!"

Kenzo turned around and disappeared behind a doorway covered by two long panels of blue fabric. On each panel was printed a large white character, which when read together meant, "Great Harmony."

"Is he an old friend of yours?" I asked.

"One of my oldest," Matsu replied, his hand moving across his rough cheek. "Kenzo and I grew up together. This teahouse belonged to his family." He smiled, as if the memory pleased him. "I remember the morning we first met. Kenzo came to your *ojī-san*'s house while I was working with my father in the garden. Unlike me, Kenzo had always been very popular. He was the last one I had ever expected to see. I remember being covered in dirt. I barely said a word. Kenzo stood so straight, dressed in clean, starched clothes. Even as a boy, he was very proud and self-assured," Matsu said.

"What did he want?"

"He came to ask me if I had time to work on his father's garden. I was so surprised, I only mumbled that I would stop by his house and take a look. In the end, I didn't accept his father's job. My own father wanted me to spend more time on my studies. But soon afterward, Kenzo began to speak to me at school and we became good friends."

"Is that the same time you met Sachi-*san?*" I asked.

Matsu shook his head. "Sachi was already the best friend of my *imōto*, Tomoko. They were very popular. Most of the time they were off whispering and laughing, never paying much attention to me. It must have been hard for anyone to believe that Tomoko and I were from the same *ryōshin.*"

"I guess you were the strong, silent type," I teased.

"I was invisible to them," Matsu said, softly.

I looked down and didn't know what to say. "Kenzo-*san* seems very nice," I finally said.

"Kenzo was smarter than all of us. He should have gone off to the city like the others. He would be a rich man by now if he had."

"Why didn't he leave?"

Matsu coughed and rubbed his cheek again. "As far back as I can remember, Kenzo's father was always sickly. Being the only son, he felt it his responsibility to care for his mother when his father finally died. We were about seventeen at the time."

I was about to ask Matsu why he hadn't left Tarumi, when the panels of blue cloth parted and Kenzo returned carrying a tray. He placed it on the table and carefully distributed a bowl of rice crackers, a large brown bottle of beer for Matsu, and a pinkish colored cold drink for me.

"*Dōmo,* Kenzo," Matsu said, with a nod of his head. Then Matsu gestured for him to take the seat next to me.

Kenzo took the towel from his shoulder and wiped up the water beading on the table. He leaned over and arranged the bowl of rice crackers so that it was exactly in the middle of the table. When he slipped into the chair next to mine, he brought with him the oily smell of cooking, mixed with tobacco smoke.

Matsu had already poured out his beer, quick to drink down half a glass in one large swallow.

Kenzo pointed to the glass in front of me. "*Dōzo,*" he said, watching me.

I smiled and bowed my head. The glass felt wet and cold in my hand as I sipped the pinkish drink. It tasted sweet and flowery. "It's good," I said, politely.

Kenzo smiled and turned to Matsu. "You see, the young man has good taste!"

Matsu laughed. "What do you expect, he's just trying to be polite."

"It's good," I said again, not quite understanding what was going on between them.

"You see, not everyone agrees with what the mighty Matsu-*san* thinks!" Kenzo said.

Then, before anything else was said, both Matsu and Kenzo burst into laughter.

"Kenzo has been trying to get someone to like that drink of his for the last twenty-five years," Matsu explained. "He has tried everyone in Tarumi, with no luck."

"Don't listen to him," Kenzo said, as he wiped away a new water mark left by Matsu's bottle of beer. "He has always been jealous of me."

"He's crazy," Matsu laughed, lifting his thick fingers to the side of his head.

I took another swallow of the too-sweet drink. Each sip let me know something new; it tasted more and more like flowers, with a strong scent of roses.

"What's in it?" I asked Kenzo.

But it was Matsu who laughed and answered, "It's his secret recipe that no one wants."

Kenzo made a growling sound in his throat, but didn't say anything.

In the dim tearoom, I once again saw Matsu as if for the first time, like someone I didn't know, light and playful. I imagined they knew each other's every move. Matsu was always the one who made the water marks, while Kenzo dutifully wiped them up.

I listened while their low, rough voices filled the open room.

"Did you hear our troops have captured Soochow? Muramoto-*san* just came to tell me the news," said Kenzo. "Shanghai is as good as taken!"

Matsu looked over at me and then answered abruptly, "In times of war, there are always rumors."

My heart sank with the news. I was grateful when Matsu changed the subject and spoke of the weather, business at the teahouse, his garden. My own thoughts began to take over. I knew deep inside that it was true that Shanghai would soon fall to the Japanese. Then they would continue south, destroying everything that stood in their way. I tried to change my thoughts, thinking how there might be a chance of my running into Keiko and Mika if I went for a walk. I was just about to excuse myself when Kenzo's questions drew me quickly back into their conversation.

"Have you seen her?" Kenzo asked.

"A few days ago," Matsu answered. "She's doing very well."

"Did you bring her the chicken?"

"Yes."

"Did she ask about me?"

Matsu drank down the remainder of his beer. "No," he said quietly. "But she gave me this note to give to you."

Kenzo's face lit up. He quickly reached across the table and snatched the note from Matsu's hand, placing it carefully into his shirt pocket.

"It's rosewater," Kenzo whispered to me as we stepped out into the cool air. "Just a drop."

I laughed and bowed, thanking him for the drink.

"What lies is he telling you?" Matsu asked.

"It's a secret," I answered.

Kenzo smiled, then looked toward Matsu. "You'll tell me if she needs anything?"

"Of course," Matsu said.

Kenzo bowed and put his hand over his shirt pocket to make sure the note hadn't slipped out. He stood just a moment at the doorway of his teahouse, then disappeared back inside.

"I need to get the mail," Matsu said, as I followed him back across the road toward another building.

"Does Kenzo know Sachi?" I quickly asked.

Matsu slowed down and turned to face me. "Tarumi is a small place. We all knew each other when we were young."

"Then why doesn't Kenzo go to visit her?"

"When we were young, Sachi cared a great deal for Kenzo, but the disease changed everything. After she left for Yamaguchi, she would no longer see him."

"Just like she wouldn't see her family?"

"Yes."

"But, she allowed you to visit her?" I asked, not knowing if Matsu would give me an answer.

"At the time," Matsu paused, in thought, "it was easier for Sachi to see someone she didn't care for." His face was expressionless, as he turned and walked quickly into the post office.

It never failed to amaze me how much one post office was like another in different places, even if every other custom varied. Tarumi's post office was identical to ones I'd seen in Hong Kong and Canton. A small, wiry man sat behind a caged window and became the messenger of words. The bare room was crowded with people who waited in line and whispered in low voices. Matsu gestured brusquely for me to wait while he went to collect the mail. I watched him hurry to the back of the room, down a narrow hallway, and stop halfway at what must have been his box.

I hoped I hadn't offended him by asking too many questions. When he returned, Matsu didn't say anything, simply handing me an envelope which had my name on it.

NOVEMBER 20, 1937

The weather had changed drastically this morning. I could tell right away just by the heavy smell in the air. The sky was a dreary gray that hung so low and thick it felt suffocating. Matsu kept looking out the back door and up at the sky with such an intensity, it seemed as if it were night and he was looking for a particular star. He then mumbled something I couldn't hear and returned to the table saying nothing.

After breakfast, I went out to the garden and read my mother's letter over again. I had hoped that something overnight might have changed its contents. In it, she asked if I'd known anything about a woman my father was keeping in Kobe. The shock and disbelief I felt yesterday now gave way to a stabbing pain that moved through my body as I faced her words again.

> "I have always known that there might be someone else," my mother wrote. "A man can't be so far from his family without seeking comfort elsewhere. In this I have never found fault in your father. He has always provided us with everything we needed. What he does during his life in Japan has always been his own business. But I have just learned through Mr. Chung at The Royal Hong Kong Bank that your father has been withdrawing large sums of money in the name of a woman residing in Kobe, Japan. Mr. Chung felt the need to tell me when your father asked to borrow against our Hong Kong house. It has been a great shock to me, Stephen. But my first concern must be for you children. Now that you are getting better, perhaps you should just return to Kobe early. You're old enough to understand these things, and you've always been the closest to your father. Maybe you can find out what this is all about."

There was little more to her letter, other than small formalities. Everyone in Hong Kong was fine, and Pie would write soon.

I sat, stunned by her words each time I read them over again. I swallowed hard and let my eyes wander away from her straight, neatly written characters. I knew my mother's even tone masked the embarrassment she must have felt, and part of me wished I could be in Hong Kong to comfort her. I tried to imagine my mother after she first heard the news. She might have been standing on the front balcony of our house, overlooking the Hong Kong harbor, her fan moving the heavy air from side to side, her other hand raised to block out the sun's glare. From the courtyard, the high, whiny voices of our servants could be heard, while Pie might be running in and out asking her question after question. All the while, I knew my mother could only have one thing on her mind: Who was this woman who had stolen my father's love?

I put the thin sheets of paper back into the blue envelope and closed my eyes. The wind had begun to blow, stirring the heavy air. I wanted to cry. My mother was wrong, I didn't feel old enough to understand any of it. My father never told me of another woman in his life. He was simply the man who wore immaculate dark suits, worried about my health, and sat on the beach waiting for me to listen to his calm voice. I never saw him give money to other women. I only knew one thing for sure, I wasn't ready to leave Tarumi yet.

The wind started to blow harder by late afternoon. I sat at my grandfather's desk trying to write a letter back to my mother when I heard the angry wind whistling through the house. It rattled the *shoji* walls and shook the floor beneath me. Matsu had disappeared after lunch without saying a word about where he was going. At the time I was happy to be left by myself, but as I stood up, I felt the floor vibrate and I began to worry.

All of a sudden I heard Matsu calling from the garden. I went to the front door and saw him hurrying through the garden to the house.

"A big storm is coming," Matsu yelled. He came into the *genken* and told me to follow him.

In a small storage space next to the kitchen, Matsu began pulling out several large wooden boards. "These slide into place in front of the *shoji* panels," he said, pushing one toward me.

We placed the wooden panels over the front *shoji* windows first. It began raining and the wind had increased so we could barely walk straight. I couldn't imagine Matsu having to do this by himself. We moved as quickly as we could around the house, until all the *shoji* panels were covered and the house appeared entombed. We were soaking wet, running around securing everything we thought might be washed away. When I stopped to catch my breath, I could hear the ocean rise up and crash against the road in front of the house.

Matsu stood at the open gate, watching the waves thunder up and over the dunes onto the road. "Do you think it'll come any closer?" I shouted.

"It has before," he answered.

"What should we do?"

"We'll wait and see. Sometimes the storm just dies down," Matsu said, turning back to watch the road.

It seemed like the storm would last forever, as it steadily grew in strength. The wind and rain continued, and the noise of the violent sea was deafening. With a wire net, Matsu carefully scooped up his fish from the overflowing pond into a wooden barrel. I watched as the waves crept closer and closer to the house, sliding under the bamboo gate and into the garden. Each time a wave receded, it left a foamy white line marking each advancing step.

"The waves are getting stronger," I yelled over to Matsu.

He nodded his head in acknowledgment. "You better go into the house," he yelled back, working frantically. I started toward the house, then stopped and turned quickly back to help Matsu catch the last of his fish. Just then the first wave crashed over the fence, drenching us. I saw several of his fish washed out of the barrel, squirming on the dirt. The next wave was even more powerful, and the one after that roared over the bamboo gate so fast and strong that neither of us had the chance to hang on. The wall of water swept us both off our feet, knocking us solidly against the house. I hit the house so hard the air was knocked out of me. I tried to get up, but the next wave slammed me back down before I knew what was happening. I grabbed onto a post by the *genken* and tried to stand up again. I could hear Matsu yelling to me, but he sounded strangely far away, like we were already lost, deep under the water.

NOVEMBER 24, 1937

I woke up lying naked in my own bed. I opened my eyes to the dim light of a flickering oil lamp. My wet clothes were on the floor next to me. As my head cleared, I remembered the last thing I felt was the strong punch of the rushing water and then nothing; blackness. It was just a miracle that the house still stood, somehow having survived the crashing waves.

When I tried to raise my head, I felt an intense pounding that forced me down again. I closed my eyes until the throbbing quieted, then opened them cautiously, hopeful that the gradual light wouldn't hurt my head.

The boarded *shoji* windows gave no hint as to whether it was day or night. The house was completely still. There were no sounds of Matsu anywhere. Outside I could hear rain falling, but the fierce winds seemed to have died down. The strong, sweet and sour odor of the dank *tatami* mats filled the room. All I wanted was to steady myself enough so that I could get up and see what was going on.

Very slowly, I moved my feet from the futon to the *tatami* mats, and with all the strength I could muster in my arms, gradually pushed my upper body into a sitting position. My head began to pound again. I gently rubbed my temples, still sticky with salt from the ocean. Behind my right ear I could feel a good-size bump.

It was the sound of voices that reached me first, followed by footsteps that entered the *genken*. I recognized Matsu's voice immediately, but the other was barely audible. From the ease of Matsu's words, I could tell it was someone he knew well. The sound of footsteps continued down the hall until the shadowy figures stopped in front of my door.

"What are you doing?" Matsu's voice boomed across to me as he slid open my door.

I smiled weakly up at him as he stood in the doorway. Across his left cheek was a long, white bandage.

"Are you all right?" I asked.

"That's what I was wondering about you," he laughed. He touched his bandaged cheek.

"My head hurts," I said, holding myself steady.

"You were knocked out when you were thrown against the house by a wave. It felt stronger than a *tsunami,*" Matsu said, stroking his cheek again.

I lifted my weak legs back onto the futon and quickly covered my nakedness.

"Someone's here to visit you," Matsu smiled.

Only then did I remember that there were two voices that had entered the house. I looked up just as Sachi stepped out from behind Matsu.

"Sachi-*san!*" I said, surprised. In the flickering light, I caught a slight smile from behind her scarf. I tried to sit up again as the throbbing in my head became stronger.

Sachi bowed. "I decided to come down when the storm finally passed," she said. "We were hardly touched in the mountains. But I remember from my childhood how violent the waves can become."

"Thank you." I swallowed hard and felt dizzy and feverish.

"I was worried about you and Matsu-*san,*" Sachi continued. She turned around and glanced shyly at Matsu.

"I'm very honored by your visit," I managed to say, lowering myself gently back down. I strained to keep sight of Sachi. I breathed in the pleasure of having her so close by, knowing it was the first time she had left Yamaguchi in forty years. I mumbled something about how long she was going to stay, hoping she would never leave, but my head began to pound so hard I could barely keep my eyes open.

"Do you think we should send for the *isha?*" I heard Sachi whisper.

I suddenly wondered if Tarumi even had a doctor. I wanted to say something more, but it took too much energy to tell them I just needed to close my eyes for a little while.

"He needs to rest," was the last thing I heard Matsu say.

* * *

When I woke up again, a white light came through the *shoji* windows and filled my room. My eyes strained against the brightness. The house was quiet. I looked around slowly until all the past events filled my mind. My vivid recollection of the storm quickly gave way to the letter from my mother, my father's infidelity, and finally, Sachi's visit. I suddenly wondered if Sachi's presence had been a hallucination. If it wasn't a dream, had she already returned to Yamaguchi? Or was it possible that she was still here? With a sudden burst of energy, I sat up.

A tray with cold tea and crackers sat by my bed. I was so thirsty I reached for the cup and drank down the tea, wanting more. I still felt a bit dizzy and my face was hot and flushed, but the pounding in my head had stopped.

Slowly, I stood up and stretched. My back felt sore from lying so long on the futon. I pulled on a pair of pants and a shirt and walked slowly to the kitchen, but no one was there. I wondered if Matsu was in the garden, or if he had gone to town. Maybe he had taken Sachi back to Yamaguchi. I only hoped she had really come.

The bright sunlight hurt my eyes as I stood in the *genken* and looked out. As my eyes adjusted to the light, I was shocked to see that Matsu's beautiful garden was now only a memory. Seaweed and sand covered everything, while debris and branches lay everywhere. The wooden bridge that stood over the pond was nowhere to be seen, and most of his best pines were torn from the ground, lying lifeless in the muddy mess. A thick, pungent smell of salty fish and earth filled the air.

While I surveyed the garden in disbelief, I heard a movement and looked up to see Matsu carrying two wooden buckets from around the back. The once-clean bandage on his left cheek was now soiled a dingy brown.

"Ah, you're finally up," Matsu said. "I thought you might sleep another day away."

"How long have I been out?" I asked, rubbing my head and feeling the throb of the bump.

"It's almost the end of the second day. You came around once or twice, but most of the time you've been unconscious. Sachi wanted me to get the *isha,* but he has been tending to other injuries farther down the coast." Matsu put down his buckets and said seriously, "You had us very worried."

"It's just a bump," I said, reassuringly. "Is Sachi still here? I thought maybe she was just a figment of my imagination."

Matsu laughed. "Sachi-*san*," he yelled, "look who has finally risen from the dead!"

In the next moment, Sachi appeared from around the back of the house. She pulled her dark scarf tighter around her face and happily bowed several times upon seeing me.

"Stephen-*san*, I am very happy to see you are feeling better," she said.

"I thought you were just an illusion," I said.

Sachi smiled. "As you can see, I'm really here. I came again this morning, hoping you would be better."

"Thank you, I'm very honored." I bowed my head, but stood straight up again when I felt the throbbing return.

Sachi looked away, embarrassed. "Matsu has also needed help with his garden."

"The storm has destroyed it," Matsu said. He pointed to his favorite silk tree which lay uprooted.

"I'm sorry," I said hoarsely.

"It's nothing that can't be replaced," Sachi said quietly.

"Can I help?" I asked. I took a step down and leaned weakly against the *genken*.

"Don't worry about the garden," Matsu answered. "The first thing you need to do is get your strength back."

"What better way to get my health back than to work in the fresh air," I argued.

Then Sachi turned to Matsu and softly said, "I remember a time when you told me working in the garden would give me back my life."

Matsu glanced over at Sachi, scratched his head in thought and said, "Only light work then, until you're better."

NOVEMBER 30, 1937

Every day Sachi comes down from Yamaguchi so early she's already hard at work in the garden by the time I've gotten up and eaten. She must start out when it's still dark, arriving here just as the morning light fills the sky. She doesn't leave again until the sun goes down and she can disappear into the hazy gray just before dark. Matsu usually accompanies her back up the mountain. When he returns, there's a calmness to him I know only Sachi can give.

Sachi and I are becoming good friends as we work in Matsu's garden. Yesterday and today we replanted some pines and cleaned the pond. Matsu finished building a new bridge for the pond, then went to the village for some new fish to fill it. I asked him to mail a short, noncommittal letter I had written to my mother. I told her briefly about the storm, my relapse, and how I would write her a more complete letter soon. The only thing I let my mother know for certain was that I needed to rest in Tarumi a while longer, and that I would try to speak to my father soon. But just the thought of facing my father made me feel sick to my stomach.

Each day I work in the garden with Sachi, I feel stronger. The headaches lose their urgency once my hands dig deep into the cool, dark soil and I smell the damp dirt and pine. Even the cold wind of approaching winter makes me feel more alive.

"How does it feel to be here?" I asked Sachi this morning.

She was on her knees planting moss by the pond. Matsu's newly built wooden bridge sat to the side. Its fresh cedar smell filled the chilly air. She pulled her scarf closer to her face and turned toward me. "It feels like a dream to be living this life," Sachi answered. "I'm always waiting for the moment I wake up."

"I wanted to ask you to visit us," I said, digging a hole large enough to fit a small pine Matsu wanted us to replant.

"It took a storm to bring me down from the mountain," Sachi continued. She turned back to her work and started digging the hole I'd begun deeper.

"Did you ever think of coming down before?"

Sachi hesitated. "Matsu had asked me before."

"But you never came?"

"I didn't have the courage."

"Why now?" I asked. I continued to work, not daring to look in Sachi's direction.

"It was for you and Matsu that I came, not for myself."

I could feel my heart beat faster. "I'll never forget your kindness," I said, as I glanced over at her.

Sachi smiled and remained silent.

"Don't you ever miss your family, or your old friends like Kenzo-*san?*" I blurted out after a long pause. Even as I said the words, I immediately regretted asking her such a personal question.

Sachi slowly stood up and dusted off her dark brown kimono. She pulled her scarf closer to her face and looked at the gate. I imagined Matsu coming through the gate right at that moment, angry and dishonored by my rudeness.

But before I could say anything else, Sachi turned and looked directly at me. "So you have met Kenzo," she said, pausing again in thought. "He was a difficult friend to lose, but the time for missing has long passed. I have many new friends in Yamaguchi. And there has always been Matsu."

"I'm sorry for asking." I quickly stood up and bowed to her. "I know it must have been difficult."

"I am honored that you cared enough to ask," Sachi said. Then she turned and pointed to Matsu's newly built wooden bridge. It was an exact replica of the original, its ascending and descending curves forming a perfect arch. "Matsu once told me the bridge represented the samurai's difficult path from this world to the afterlife. When you reach the top of the bridge, you can see your way to paradise. I feel as if the past few days have given me a glimpse of that. To simply live a life without fear has been a true paradise."

I touched the bridge which stood half the height of my body. Suddenly I couldn't wait to see it back in its place over the restored fish-filled pond. I didn't know what to say.

We stood a moment in awkward silence until Sachi sighed, and pointed to a pine tree lying on the ground. "Let me help you with that tree," she said.

Together we carefully lifted the uprooted pine and placed it gently back into the hole we had dug. I shovelled the dirt back in, while Sachi dropped to her knees and patted the loose earth back into place.

"Do you think it will live?" I asked.

"No one knows this garden better than Matsu," Sachi answered. "It won't be long before it looks just like your painting again."

"You've seen the painting?"

"It was the first thing Matsu showed me. He is very proud of you."

"He never said a word about it to me," I said.

Sachi looked up and smiled. "With Matsu, everything is in what he does not say."

Sometimes, when Sachi is at work and not paying attention, her scarf slips just enough so I can see the white, puckered scars on the side of her face. I find myself wondering what these scars must feel like; the translucent lines spreading like a map across the side of her face. It seems the more I see them, the less effective they become in their power to frighten and repulse me. She's still very beautiful. I want to tell Sachi this, but I'm afraid it will only embarrass her, send her back into hiding.

Matsu's definitely happier with Sachi around. There's a gentleness about him when he's with her. They speak in low tones, and he's always making her laugh. "Little *hana*," he calls Sachi, when she laments that he has lost all his autumn blossoms. She's the only flower that matters to him. Sometimes, I wonder how their lives would have been if the disease hadn't claimed Sachi. Would they be married and living happily in Tarumi? Would Sachi be married to Kenzo? Would Sachi have left Tarumi like so many others and found a new life elsewhere? Perhaps Sachi is right, the door to the past should be closed.

The news of the present continues to hang heavy. While we were happily eating lunch in the kitchen, the music from Matsu's radio was abruptly interrupted by an announcement: "Japan's most honorable Imperial Army has finally succeeded in convincing Shanghai to accept its protection."

Matsu looked over at me and I could see his smile slowly leave, as he pressed his lips tightly together. Sachi looked down and remained silent. It felt as if the noodles I'd just eaten were lodged at the bottom of my throat and I had no voice.

* * *

My spirits were lifted this evening when I saw Keiko again. After Matsu left to walk Sachi back to Yamaguchi, I tried to keep my thoughts off the war in China by working in the garden. I first saw shadows between the slats in the bamboo fence. Then I heard low whispers, which stopped at the front gate. I stood perfectly still, and waited to see what they would do next. There were more whispers and then I heard the shuffling sound of someone leaving. I was just about to open the bamboo gate, when a tapping sound came from the other side. I swung it open to find Keiko alone, standing there in a blue kimono and padded coat.

"Konnichiwa," she bowed.

"Konnichiwa, Keiko-*san,"* I said. "Where is Mika?"

"She had to return home," Keiko said timidly. "We heard that you were not well, and wanted to bring you something." Keiko handed me a black lacquer box tightly wrapped in maroon-colored cloth.

I bowed. *"Dōmo arigatō gozaimasu.* Won't you come in?"

Keiko shook her head. "No, *dōmo,* I must return home."

She turned to leave, but before she did, I asked, "Can we meet again to talk? We never seem to have enough time."

"Tarumi is very small, I'm sure we will see each other again," Keiko answered. She kept her gaze directed toward the ground.

"I thought maybe we could set up a time," I continued.

Keiko looked up shyly. "Perhaps tomorrow morning, down at the beach where we first spoke," she said. Then she bowed quickly and started down the dirt road to town.

"What time?" I asked.

Keiko stopped and turned around. *"Ju-ji,"* she called back. She hesitated a moment, gave a small wave, and continued walking.

"I'll see you at ten o'clock," I said, but I wasn't sure if she had heard me as she hurried down the road.

I could barely wait until Matsu returned home. I was already lying in bed when I heard him come into the *genken.* Before he reached the kitchen, I slid open my door and handed the black lacquer box to him.

"What is it?" he asked, surprised.

"A get-well present from Keiko-*san,* one of the girls I told you about. I'm going to meet her tomorrow morning. Would you like some?"

Matsu opened the box and smiled. "Homemade *yokan.* You must be quite special to this girl," he teased.

"She's just one of many," I laughed.

Matsu picked up one of the rectangular red bean cakes and put it entirely into his mouth. He chewed it slowly and swallowed. "Very good," he said with a wink.

"Has Sachi ever made you *yokan?*" I asked.

Matsu laughed. "I think you should ask if I have ever made Sachi *yokan?*"

"Have you?"

"I would not have dared."

"Why?"

"Sachi might have given it back to me then."

"Then, but not now," I added.

Matsu smiled. He quickly snatched another *yokan* from the box and handed it back to me. "You better get some rest for your big date tomorrow."

All of a sudden I remembered Sachi would be coming down. "What about Sachi?" I asked.

"I think she can stand my company for one morning," Matsu reassured me.

"Maybe for just one morning." I smiled, closing the black lacquer box.

December 1, 1937

Matsu and Sachi were already at work side by side in the garden when I woke up this morning. With their backs to me, I stood in the *genken* watching them as they moved up and down in their own rhythm. Sachi seemed to be struggling with something in front of her, as her scarf slowly slipped down from her head to her neck and shoulders. For the first time I could see the streaks of gray that ran through Sachi's dark hair and a hint of her pale, white neck. Matsu leaned over to help her, then whispered something that made Sachi laugh. I realized how good she must feel, to

61

live a normal life and not have to hide among the wounded. It seems unfair that so much time had passed with their being apart.

I stepped down from the *genken* and quickly surveyed the garden. It was slowly returning to its former beauty. Many of the pine trees had been replanted, most of the debris cleared away, and Matsu had replaced the new cedar samurai bridge over the pond. But this time it felt different. Sachi provided a deep richness that made the garden almost hum.

"Ohayōgazaimasu," I called out to them.

Matsu turned around. Sachi quickly stood, covered her head, and bowed before she returned my greeting. Matsu lifted his hand as if to wave, then pointed to the house to tell me my breakfast was in the kitchen.

"I'm not hungry," I said, as I walked toward them.

"Ah, too many *yokan*," Matsu teased.

"Yokan?" Sachi repeated.

"A get-well present from the girl he's meeting this morning," Matsu said, before I had a chance to say anything.

Sachi nodded her head and smiled. "A young man like Stephen-*san* should have many such friends."

"I won't be very long," I said.

Sachi bowed again. "We will be here," she said.

Matsu smiled and returned to work. He motioned for Sachi to hold on to a young silk tree as he unwrapped the burlap around its roots, and together they placed it into the earth. It was only then that I realized they might enjoy not having me around.

I was down at the beach before Keiko arrived. It had crossed my mind more than once that she might not show up, but I pushed the thought away and waited patiently. The air was sharp. For the first time in a week, the sun struggled weakly through the gray clouds. It left a strange bright light on the sand, still littered with remnants of the storm. I began to walk, sidestepping pieces of seaweed, branches, and large depressions still filled with saltwater. The air smelled of salty, dried fish. The waves came in calmly, slapping the sand so lightly it seem impossible they could have ever caused so much damage. I turned and looked out to the sea, shading my eyes from the glare. The blue-gray water mirrored the sky, and like it, went on and on.

A distant crunching sound caught my attention. When I looked up in the direction of the sand dune I saw Keiko, dressed in a dark blue kimono with light patterns on it. Her wooden sandals kicked up white sand and the wide sleeves of her kimono flapped in the air as she hurried to me. I was relieved to see that Mika wasn't with her.

"*Konnichiwa,* Stephen-*san,*" she said, bowing. Her waist-length hair was tied back to expose her delicate, flushed face. The patterns on her kimono were white circles.

I smiled and bowed. "*Konnichiwa,* Keiko-*san.* I hope you didn't have to rush."

Keiko brushed some sand off her kimono, bowed again, and said, "I am very sorry to be late."

"I'm glad you could come."

"I had to make sure Mika . . ." she began.

"I hope Mika is well," I said, realizing that it was probably rare for them to be apart.

"She is very well," Keiko said, suddenly laughing. She raised her pale hand to cover her mouth.

"What's so funny?"

"Mika is at home doing the laundry. This morning I made a bet with her that she wouldn't be able to keep quiet for five minutes, and she'd have to do the wash alone."

"And she spoke?"

"Only a moment later," Keiko laughed. "It was my one chance to get away alone."

We took a walk along the empty beach. At first, Keiko was anxious that Mika might find us, but it wasn't long before she relaxed enough to stop looking over her shoulder. When she did look away, I stole a glance or two at her smooth, pale skin, straight nose, and dark eyes. Keiko was quite tall and, when she wasn't bowing or looking down, stood somewhere between my chin and nose. If King could only see me now, he would be more than glad to trade places with me.

"I really enjoyed the *yokan*," I said.

"I hope you are feeling better, Stephen-*san*," Keiko said, her eyes focused on the sand in front of us.

"Yes, much better. I've been helping Matsu in his garden."

"I have heard that Matsu-*san* is a master of gardens."

"Yes, he is," I said, proud that Matsu was known in the village for his art.

After a moment of silence, Keiko glanced shyly in my direction and asked, "What is it like to live in a big city like Hong Kong?"

"It's noisy and crowded, but between the movie theaters and restaurants, there's always something to do."

"Do you miss being there?"

I looked at her and smiled. "Sometimes, but not right now."

Keiko looked away, embarrassed. In our silence, I could hear the measured squawking of the sea gulls. We walked along the beach until she stopped and asked, "Can we sit for a moment?"

"Of course," I said.

We sat down on the white sand that was still damp and cool. I threw aside large pieces of tubular seaweed, and wished I'd thought of bringing something to offer her to sit on.

"Are you comfortable here?" I asked.

Keiko nodded her head and gazed out to the sea. "It's always very beautiful after a storm. So calm and serene after all the destruction. We were very fortunate this time. The storm barely touched the village."

"We don't have much control over nature," I added, remembering some of the typhoons that had pounded Hong Kong. They swept in gradually, only to leave uprooted trees, debris, and even fragments of makeshift squatter houses scattered across the island.

Keiko smiled. "It's a reminder of the strength we all have within us. Many years ago, my parents told me of a storm that had destroyed much of the original Tarumi village. The villagers argued over where to rebuild, afraid that another storm would simply destroy the village again. Only one fisherman stood up and refused to move anywhere else, believing the best fishing was right here. He said that each storm would only serve to make them stronger if they carried the memory of its strength with them, and

64

used it to prepare for the next storm. Tarumi has stood here ever since."

"Have you always lived in Tarumi?"

"Mika and I were born right here. My older brother was born near Kobe."

"You have an older brother?" I asked, surprised by the fact.

"Yes," she smiled. "Do you have any brothers or sisters?"

"I have two sisters and a brother. My older sister and younger brother are studying in Macao, and my youngest sister is in Hong Kong. Mika reminds me of her."

Keiko suddenly turned around and looked behind her. "I should be going back now. My family will be wondering where I am."

We got up and brushed the sand from our clothes. The damp sand had left a wet stain on the seat of my slacks that I hoped Keiko wouldn't notice. I stepped back and let her walk ahead of me.

"Where is your brother now?" I asked.

Keiko looked away, hesitated a moment, then said, "He is with the Japanese army in China."

Then we both kept silent. I wondered if her brother was in Shanghai, celebrating their victory after months of fighting. I turned to see if there were any signs that Keiko might have felt the same thing. I thought I saw her shudder, but she simply wrapped her arms around herself for warmth. Then she gradually picked up the pace, her face serene, her eyes focused in front of her, giving me no hints as to what she thought.

I walked Keiko halfway back to the village until she stopped, bowed to me, and said, *"Dōmo arigatō gozaimasu,* Stephen-*san,* but I will walk the rest of the way from here."

"Are you sure?" I asked.

"I think it would be wise," she smiled.

"Are you afraid to be seen with me?"

"My father is very old-fashioned," Keiko answered.

I quickly asked, "Can we meet again?"

"I imagine we will," she answered. Her eyes avoided mine.

"I look forward to it," I said, bowing.

Keiko glanced up for a moment, smiled shyly, then said, *"Sayonara,* Stephen-*san."*

Before I could say anything else, Keiko quickly turned around and continued down the road that led back to the village. At that moment, I realized how much I wanted to see her again. I bit my lip to stop myself from calling out her name. Instead, I watched Keiko disappear down the road, a small cloud of dust rising up behind her.

By the time I walked back to the house, it was past lunch and my stomach was rumbling with hunger. I was eager to tell Matsu and Sachi about my morning with Keiko. I expected to find them both hard at work in the garden, but when I entered the gate, the garden was empty. There was a breath of quiet before I heard loud voices coming from the house.

I knew something was wrong when I reached the *genken.* There was a voice other than Sachi and Matsu's coming from the kitchen. I could barely catch all the words, spoken in obvious anger. I moved quietly down the hall and stopped in front of my room.

"What other lies have you been telling me?" the voice shouted.

Then Matsu's voice answered, "We never lied to you, Kenzo."

"You never spoke the truth!"

"Please, Kenzo-*san,* you don't understand," I heard Sachi's voice pleading.

I moved closer to the kitchen doorway, careful to stay in the hallway and out of sight. I could see Sachi pull her scarf closer, as she huddled next to Matsu. Kenzo's thin, angry face was crimson as he stood across from them. He looked nothing like the calm, gracious man I had met at his teahouse.

"I understand perfectly," Kenzo yelled. He moved his arms through the air in frantic motions.

"Kenzo," Matsu said, stepping up to him.

Without warning, Kenzo lunged forward and pushed Matsu back. Matsu staggered a bit, then caught his footing, but did nothing. He was much broader and stronger than Kenzo, and could have easily defended himself, but Matsu simply stood still. This seemed to anger Kenzo more. He clenched both of his fists and a deep groan rose from down inside him. Then, all of a sudden he turned to Sachi and tore the scarf away from her face. Sachi let out a small scream as her scarf dropped to the floor. For a split second, they all stood frozen; the white, puckered scars magnified in the bright light.

Kenzo stepped back. "You really are a monster!" he roared. He began to laugh hysterically.

Sachi turned away from Kenzo and quickly picked up the scarf to cover her face. I gripped the door frame tighter. I wanted to do something to help her, but I knew it was not my place. Swallowing hard, I waited to see what Matsu would do.

"A monster!" Kenzo shouted.

Then Matsu regained his voice. "You are the monster," he said, his voice low and threatening. He stepped forward and shoved Kenzo into the back door. Kenzo's body slammed hard against the door as he grabbed his shoulder.

"Matsu!" Sachi screamed.

But he continued to move closer to Kenzo. Matsu grabbed Kenzo by the shoulders and threw him out the door. He fell clumsily down the wooden steps and onto the dirt. Then Matsu stood at the door, not moving. I stepped forward, just far enough to see Kenzo quickly pick himself up off the ground.

"To think I wasted all these years on a monster," Kenzo yelled, backing away from Matsu. "Now I understand everything! She's all yours, Matsu, no one else would want her!"

Matsu didn't say another word as he shielded Sachi, who stood behind him. She was crying softly, as she pulled the scarf tighter across her face.

I quickly stepped back into my room and leaned heavily against the wall, as if I had just taken the blows given to Kenzo. I didn't want Sachi to know I had witnessed her shame. If she did know, she might never be able to face me again. I wanted nothing more than to tell her how beautiful she was, to let her know she didn't have to hide from anyone, especially not from someone as cruel as Kenzo. But I knew my words would be a waste of time. They would mean nothing to her now, just as Kenzo's words meant everything. So I hid from them, until I heard their footsteps move through the house, and Matsu's soft words grew more distant. I swallowed hard and felt an emptiness, knowing in my heart that Sachi was returning to Yamaguchi and wouldn't be back.

DECEMBER 2, 1937

"Sachi has returned to Yamaguchi," was all Matsu said, when he returned yesterday. Then he went back out to his garden and began planting more moss around the pond.

It wasn't until we ate our dinner of rice and marinated eel that he suddenly looked up and remembered to ask, "Did you see the girl this morning?"

"Yes," I answered. "We had a nice time."

Then a silence so thick filled the kitchen, I could hear my chopsticks slide against the side of my bowl. I looked around the small kitchen, which held no signs of what had happened that afternoon.

Matsu set his bowl down and rubbed his chin. He had eaten very little and appeared restless. I thought it better to stay out of his way and keep quiet.

"There was trouble here this afternoon," he suddenly said. His voice sounded low and tired.

"I know."

Matsu looked at me, his eyes opening in surprise. "You know?"

"I came back and heard your voices. I didn't know it was Kenzo until I heard the yelling."

Matsu shook his head slowly. "Good, then I won't have to explain to you why Sachi won't be visiting us again." He leaned forward on the wooden table. "Kenzo rarely comes out to the house, but he forgot to give me a letter for Sachi, so he decided to bring it himself. We were in the garden working when he came through the gate. We thought it was you returning, so Sachi made no move to hide. By the time I realized it wasn't you, it was too late. Kenzo didn't immediately know it was Sachi. He stood for a moment, as if surprised that a woman would be with me. It was Sachi who stood and bowed, addressing Kenzo by name. At the sound of her voice, I saw the light of recognition appear in Kenzo's eyes. He took a step forward, then stopped, and whispered her name.

When Sachi bowed again and nodded her head, Kenzo simply stood speechless. It was Sachi who asked him into the house for tea."

"What did you say?"

"What could I say? I had led Kenzo to think Sachi would never step foot out of Yamaguchi. It had been the truth until the storm brought her down."

"Why does Kenzo still have such strong ties to Sachi?" I asked.

Matsu didn't answer. Instead, he stood up and walked over to the small cabinet above the wooden basin. He took down a bottle of whiskey and a glass.

"They were once engaged to be married," he finally answered. "Sachi was the only girl Kenzo ever loved. I was his best friend and his go-between when the disease came. At first he didn't have the courage to face Sachi, but later when he realized how much he loved her, his family had forbidden him to go to Yamaguchi. So I became their only link."

"What about your feelings?" I dared to ask.

Matsu poured the whiskey into the glass and took a large swallow. When he spoke again, his voice was tight. "Kenzo has been my best friend since we were young. If I felt anything for Sachi, he was never supposed to know."

"But after all these years," I said.

"I've never seen Kenzo so angry. In all the years we've known each other, there's never been any anger. I have misled him, dishonoring myself and our friendship," Matsu said as he emptied his glass.

"Why didn't he just go to see Sachi himself after his parents died?"

"It was too late," Matsu answered. "By then, the prospect of seeing her again frightened him. He was ashamed of his weakness. It was easier to speak through me."

I paused a moment before I said, "There's no reason why Sachi shouldn't come back now."

Matsu sat heavily down on his stool. "She has had to live through one disgrace in her lifetime, and because I have been a foolish old man, she will have to live through another."

"I could talk to her."

"It wouldn't do any good," Matsu simply said.

"I could try."

Matsu suddenly leaned forward across the table. His strong, rough hand gripped my shoulder, and he said firmly, "I will not have Sachi hurt any more."

WINTER

DECEMBER 5, 1937

I 've tried to paint again, but with little success. My thoughts have mostly been on Sachi's abrupt return to Yamaguchi. Matsu has spent most of his time alone in the garden since the argument with Kenzo. The garden has once again become his refuge, the only place he seems to feel any comfort. It's there that Matsu becomes the artist; adding and mixing colors. Yet, even as the garden regains its former appearance, something is missing. Sachi's presence, which had held us and the garden captive is gone, leaving an emptiness that can't be filled.

This morning I made up my mind to visit Sachi, despite Matsu's wishes. I struggled with whether I should tell him or not, but in the end decided to keep it a secret. I was afraid Matsu wouldn't let me go, or worse, would want to go along with me. I needed to see Sachi alone.

For the first time since I arrived in Tarumi, I was up before Matsu. The house creaked in the stillness. I could hear the sounds of Matsu's restless sleep come from his small room as I stepped quietly into the kitchen. I grew warm writing the note in which I lied that I couldn't sleep and was out for a walk. Then I signed it quickly, and left it on the wooden table.

Outside, the sun had just risen, lighting up the sky a pale gray. Matsu would be up shortly. I closed the bamboo gate behind me and quickly walked down the dirt road that led to Yamaguchi.

The cold morning air stung my lips and fingers. My legs felt weak with anxiousness. It was the first time I'd made the journey to Yamaguchi without Matsu. What if Sachi didn't want to see me? Should I turn away quietly, or should I force her to listen to what I had to say? What was it that I wanted to say? These thoughts ran through my mind as I began the gradual climb up the mountain.

By the time I reached Yamaguchi, I was short of breath and had warmed into a sweat. Since the storm, I'd done nothing more vigorous than help to clean up Matsu's garden. I stopped for a moment to catch my breath. Every time my lungs ached, it was a reminder that I was also hidden away. Most of the time these thoughts clutched at me right before I fell asleep, in the semidarkness of my room, watching the shadows of the pine trees dance against the *shoji* windows.

When my breathing calmed again, I walked through Yamaguchi to Sachi's house. The sun shone weakly as the village stirred out of sleep. There was a pungent smell of boiling herbs which reminded me of Ching's bitter teas. I could hear voices and see shadows within the houses as I hurried along. When Sachi's small house came into sight, I decided to tell her that I'd become concerned when I heard she could no longer come down to visit us. It was a flimsy excuse, but one I hoped Sachi wouldn't question.

I climbed the steps of her house and knocked lightly on the door. When there was no answer, I knocked again and waited. It never occurred to me that Sachi wouldn't be at home. Then I heard a muffled noise from within the house and the front door opened a small crack.

"Who is there?" Sachi's voice asked, meekly.

"It's Stephen-*san*," I answered.

The door opened wide, and Sachi pulled her scarf closer to her face and bowed toward me. *"Ohayōgozaimasu,* Stephen-*san,* I am very happy to see you," she said, obviously surprised.

"Ohayōgozaimasu." I bowed.

"Is Matsu-*san* with you?" Sachi asked. She stepped forward and looked past me.

"No, I came alone. He told me you weren't coming down to the house for a while, and I was wondering if you might be ill, or if there was anything I could do."

Sachi looked away. She stepped back and opened the door wider. "Come in, Stephen-*san,"* she said.

When I stepped into the warmth of her house, the sweet smell of *congee* filled my head.

"Please sit," Sachi said, pointing to the cushions by the low black lacquer table. Then she disappeared into the kitchen, only to reappear a few moments later carrying two cups of tea. "You must be cold and thirsty after your long walk."

I took the small clay cup from her and sipped from it. The warm, slightly bitter tea soothed my dry throat. I smiled, looked up, and asked, "Is everything all right?"

"Has Matsu-*san* led you to believe otherwise?" she asked.

"He said very little."

Sachi laughed softly and sipped her tea. "It is just like Matsu," she said, shaking her head. She sat down at the table across from me. "Matsu didn't want to tell you that I could no longer go down to Tarumi. My presence there has brought great dishonor to all of you."

"What do you mean?" I asked.

"I was seen by Kenzo-*san* on the morning you were gone."

"What difference does that make?"

"I have disgraced you and Matsu, as well as myself."

"You have disgraced no one," I said.

Sachi lowered her eyes. "I should never have gone back down to Tarumi. I should have known better than to think the past had quietly gone away. Kenzo was so angry when he saw me with Matsu. He thought that we had purposely deceived him for all these years."

"But you and Matsu might never have become friends if it weren't—"

"There is no excuse," Sachi interjected, her voice trembling.

I put down my teacup and looked hard at what I could see of Sachi's pale, tired face, partially hidden under the dark scarf. Something in her voice made me want to reach across the table and take her hand. Without thinking I leaned toward her, and in the next instant my hand moved up and slipped under her scarf, resting on the white, puckered scars. They felt smoother than I expected, like the exposed veins on an arm. Sachi sat frozen at first, not really acknowledging what was happening. Her eyes reacted first, opening wide with realization as she let out a small cry and quickly turned away from me.

She rose from the table and backed away from me. "You must go now, Stephen-*san*."

"I came here to tell you you don't have to hide from us. The scars make no difference to me, and I know they never did to Matsu," I said frantically.

Sachi continued to back away. "I will not dishonor you any more than I have," she repeated. "Please, you must go now."

I stood up, my heart beating faster. I knew I couldn't leave without convincing Sachi that she could never disgrace anyone. I didn't want to upset her, and I had no idea what possessed me to touch her scars.

"I just want to talk," I pleaded. "I'm sorry if I embarrassed you."

Sachi shook her head slowly. "There is nothing to talk about."

"There's a great deal to talk about. Matsu needs you!" I said at last.

Sachi stopped. She seemed startled. She stood perfectly still for a moment, then, without saying a word, pulled the scarf down and away from her face. She turned the damaged side of her face to me, as her left eye strained to open wider. The scars appeared like a matted white web, stretched from her chin to her eye. Part of her nose was eaten away and there was a small depression near her mouth, which made her lower lip sag downward. I was more astounded to see her entire face uncovered than I was by the distorting scars. Her hair was pulled tightly back into a chignon, and in her good eye I could still see her youthful beauty. If Sachi was trying to shock me then she was in for a surprise. I had known from the moment I met her that she was very attractive. But it wasn't until I came to know Sachi that I began to see how beautiful she really was.

"Does Matsu need this?" she whispered, the dark scarf gathered around her shoulders.

I never took my eyes away from her scarred face.

"Yes," I answered.

Sachi bowed her head and said nothing.

I thought Sachi would lead me to the front door for a brief and final good-bye. Instead, she simply bowed and gestured for me to follow her. I stood up and waited, as she slid open the *shoji* panel which led out to her garden and we stepped outside.

The sunlight hurt my eyes as they adjusted to the bright light, and to the spare clarity of the garden. The strong smell of wet pine added to the sense of peace and quiet she had created.

Sachi immediately went to work as if I weren't there. She took hold of a claw-tooth rake and stepped out into the sea of gray stones. Then, with quick, easy strokes, she began to recreate the wavy patterns in the stones in front of her. Her scarf was still draped around her shoulders and she no longer made any attempt to cover her face. The crackling sounds of the stones hitting against one another reminded me of the tiles in my mother's mah-jongg games.

At that moment I hoped my mother was feeling all right. When I first received the letter from her about my father, I couldn't believe what I was reading, followed by my own selfish thoughts of having my already disrupted life disturbed again. Until this moment, I had blocked out what my father's indiscretion really meant to my mother, the hurt she must feel. I knew that as soon as I got back to the house, I would write my mother a long letter.

I stood aside and watched Sachi gain strength and momentum as she worked. She moved backward, covering her tracks with each new stroke as she worked her way to where she had begun. Suddenly, Sachi stopped and turned to me.

"Would you like to help?" she asked.

"I don't want to ruin the pattern," I answered, as I stepped back and shrugged my shoulders.

Sachi raised her right hand up to cover her laugh. "How can you ruin stones, Stephen-*san*? You can only rearrange them, and who knows if it won't be for the better."

She handed me the rake and stepped out of my way. Very slowly, I began to move it through the stones in front of me, careful not to disrupt the smooth, wavy lines the stones formed. It was a strange feeling, much different from working with the fluidity of brush and paint, or water and earth. The weight of the stones pulled against each stroke and left a distinct feeling of strength and permanence.

"I often change the patterns in the stones," Sachi said. "When I first began the garden, I would sometimes change the pattern several times a day."

"What did Matsu say?" I stopped and asked.

"Matsu said nothing. He knew it was the only way I could keep my sanity."

I remained silent, not knowing what to say.

Then Sachi's voice filled the air again. "Who could know that Matsu would save my life. I always thought it would be Kenzo, until that fateful day that Tomoko took her life."

"Tomoko?"

"Matsu's *imōto-san*," Sachi paused. "His younger sister. She was my best friend and very *kirei*. It was as if she received all the beauty in the family."

"She took her own life?"

"Because of this," Sachi said, pointing to her scarred face.

"I'm sorry."

Sachi shook her head. "Tomoko was one of the first in Tarumi to realize that something was wrong. She found a rash on her arm that wouldn't go away. At the time, we thought it was nothing. When it began to spread, Tomoko didn't know what to do. She became quiet and wouldn't leave her house, even when I begged her to walk with me. As girls, we often walked down to the beach and back, laughing and drawing attention to ourselves. It was as if we owned the whole village."

"Did you know Matsu then?"

"Only as Tomoko's *o-nii-san:* the always silent brother working in the garden." Sachi paused. "Why Tomoko was one of the first chosen, no one will ever know. Perhaps because the two of us were too vain, too frivolous."

I picked up the rake and moved toward Sachi. "You don't have to say any more," I said to her.

"I have kept silent for so long, I've lost the reason why," Sachi answered. "Perhaps it is the right time for me to remember the past. You see, the morning it had spread to her face, Tomoko went mad. It was Matsu who came to get me, hoping I could somehow calm her. But Tomoko refused to let anyone see her. Nobody knew what was going on. She'd always been the most beautiful girl in Tarumi, and she carried the temperament of one who often gets her own way. Even her father's anger didn't make any difference. It wasn't until several months later that others in the village began to come down with the disease. And it was a whole year after that before I found the first signs of it on my arm," Sachi said, touching her scarred skin.

"Was Tomoko still alive then?"

Sachi shook her head slowly. "She was the first, and all alone then. No matter what she did; drink strong teas, spread herbs on her face, pray to the gods, nothing worked. The disease remained, only to worsen as each day passed. Tomoko wouldn't see anyone. I was only able to speak with her through her *shoji* door. Most of the time she would answer my pleading with a flat, 'Go away.' It was less than a month later that Tomoko took her life. Matsu was the one who found her, lying face down in her own blood. Tomoko had committed *seppuku*. She had sliced herself open with her father's fishing knife."

"I'm so sorry." I leaned heavily on the rake. The cold wind blew as we stood among the sea of gray stones.

Sachi let out a small sigh, then took the rake from my hands. "Even though Matsu was Tomoko's brother, and one of Kenzo's best friends, I had paid very little attention to him. He was always so quiet. Even Tomoko joked about his silence. 'Matsu is like a mountain,' she would say, 'nothing will ever move him.' How he and Kenzo became such good friends none of us ever understood. Yet, there was something magical between them. Kenzo began to spend more time with him in the garden or fishing, trying to break down the wall Matsu had built around himself. Kenzo was always outgoing. He was nice-looking and full of jokes and ideas. Everyone liked him, or wanted to be around him at his *o-tōsan*'s teahouse. I was so honored when Kenzo chose to be with me. Even Tomoko was happy for me. She always had plans to move to Tokyo and work for some large company. Tarumi had always been too small for her. She always seemed to be looking for something more."

"And you never wanted more?" I asked.

"I was never as brave with my dreams."

"So after Tomoko's death, you began to know Matsu better?" I continued.

Sachi smiled. "Matsu was the only one who wasn't afraid to speak to me about Tomoko. From the beginning, he faced her death with a certain respect and understanding. He knew that beauty was everything to her. Without it, Tomoko's only choice was death. I was devastated, and Matsu was the only one who gave me any peace. Kenzo tried to console me, but for some reason I couldn't face him. In a strange way, he reminded me more of Tomoko than Matsu did." Sachi abruptly stopped, then touched my arm. "It's getting very cold, Stephen-*san*. We should go back inside."

I glanced at the lines I'd created in the stones. They weren't as even as Sachi's, but the waves were apparent, and I had felt the simple power of moving them. I followed Sachi into the warmth of her house. She went into the kitchen and came out with a pot of tea and some rice crackers.

"How was Matsu as a young man?" I asked, sitting down on the low cushion by the table.

"Much as he is now. He never had the same ways as the others. He kept to himself. But I do know that Tomoko was wrong about Matsu never going away. He did have dreams of leaving Tarumi."

"So why . . ." I stopped, realizing the answer sat across from me.

"I believe that Matsu has always had an inner strength, even as a young boy. Some are born that way, perhaps. Certainly Matsu was," Sachi answered.

"So you came to be his friend after Tomoko's death?"

Sachi nodded. "Yes, after her death. He came to my house the morning after Tomoko was buried to give me her lucky stone." Sachi pointed to the two shiny black stones that sat on the table in her front room. "We found them when we were young girls and always associated them with good luck and all the other dreams of youth. I remember Matsu handed it to me saying, 'From Tomoko.' Nothing more. Then he bowed, turned around, and began to walk away. I was the one to stop him. After all the years of ignoring him, I needed to hear his voice."

"What did he say?"

"He told me Tomoko was at peace, and that I should go on with my life." Sachi stopped and smiled to herself. "Somehow, I believed him."

"Matsu's words do have a certainty to them," I said.

"Stephen-*san*, does Matsu know you're here?" Sachi suddenly asked.

I picked up my teacup and sipped from it, avoiding her eyes. "I left him a note saying I went for a walk."

Sachi stood up. "I think you should go back now. Matsu will be worried."

I looked up at her. The scarf no longer hid her lovely face. Something in the urgent tone of her voice let me know that our conversation was over.

"Can I see you again?" I stood up and asked.

"I would be honored to have your company, Stephen-*san*." Sachi bowed. "As long as Matsu knows."

"I won't deceive either one of you again," I said.

She simply smiled.

When I left, Sachi stood at the door. She leaned slightly against its wooden frame, her dark scarf once again pulled up to cover her face.

December 6, 1937

I left Yamaguchi, my head filled with Sachi's rich insight and careful words, that slowly began to give me the pieces of her story with Matsu. I couldn't forget the oddly smooth feel of her scarred face, and how she finally trusted me to see and touch it. Even if I had had to lie to Matsu about going to Yamaguchi, I realized how much I needed to know that Sachi was protected again, safe from Kenzo's cruel words.

As I entered through the bamboo gate, Matsu was in the garden, kneeling by the pond and sprinkling food into the murky water. I could tell by the quick turn of his head that he was anxious.

"I went to Yamaguchi," I quickly confessed, my eyes avoiding his.

"Is Sachi all right?" he asked.

"She's fine. I just needed to see for myself."

"And did you?"

"Yes."

Matsu nodded his head and let out a grunt of satisfaction. Then he slowly stood up and pointed toward the house. "Your *o-tōsan* is waiting for you," he said.

"My father's here?"

"He arrived about an hour ago," Matsu said.

I felt a sinking feeling in my stomach. I hadn't expected to see my father until I had had time to think about what I wanted to say to him. A hundred thoughts went through my head as I walked slowly toward the house. As I removed my shoes in the *genken* and stepped into the hall, I decided it was best to let him do most of the talking.

I found my father waiting for me in my grandfather's study. He sat comfortably on a low cushion, sipping tea. Amidst the confusion of all my painting supplies, he sat impeccably dressed in a dark-gray suit, with a matching fedora on the floor beside him. Paints and canvases lay scattered upon the floor and on top of the cloth-covered black lacquer desk, which I had pushed aside to accommodate my easel. Matsu no longer paid attention to how I used the room. When it became clear that my painting would have to share the small house with us, we reached an unspoken understanding. While Matsu's kitchen and garden were his domain, my territory consisted of my room and my grandfather's study. We always approached each other's area with a certain amount of care and respect.

I entered the study, with its sharp, strong smell of paint and turpentine.

I bowed instinctively. "Ba-ba, I didn't know you were coming. I'm sorry you had to wait. I went to visit a friend."

His eyes looked worried and unusually tired as he reached up and touched my arm. "You look well, Stephen. I'm happy to see that you are strong enough to be up and around. Mah-mee and I were very worried about you. I know you wrote her to say you were recuperating, but at the last minute I decided it might be better if I came to see for myself."

I straightened up and stood before him. "I'm fine."

My father smiled, then looked at the easel where the painting of the garden sat. "You've become quite accomplished."

I know I blushed, I could feel the warmth move through me. After so many years, I was still embarrassed and apologetic when it came to explaining my painting to my father. "I'm just getting started again. I'm sorry for all the mess," I said shyly, as I moved a white canvas out of the way. "You really didn't need to come all this way."

My father motioned for me to sit down on the cushion across from him. "I not only wanted to see if you were well," he hesitated, "but I also needed to speak to you about another matter."

I wanted to turn around and leave the room while I still had the chance. Instead, I sat down heavily on the stiff cushion, my legs weak from nervousness and the long walk. I swallowed my anxiety, then calmly said, "I received a letter from Mah-mee."

My father cleared his throat, as his tired eyes avoided mine. Then in a strained voice, he said, "Mah-mee told me she had written to you. At first, I was very angry that she would tell you of our personal matters, especially while you are still recuperating. A Japanese woman would never do such a thing."

I looked away from him, trying hard to mask my anger. "Maybe Japanese women aren't so aware of what their husbands are doing," I snapped. I leaned over and poured myself a cup of tea, hoping I could restrain myself from saying anything else that I might later regret.

I could feel my father stare hard at me. At first I thought he would be angry at my lack of respect, but he simply took off his wire-rimmed glasses and began to wipe them with his handkerchief. He seemed to be deep in thought. When he finally put his glasses back on again, he looked at me and said, "Your mother was never to have known."

"How could you have deceived Mah-mee like that?" I asked, my voice shaking.

"I never wished to hurt her. You must believe me, Stephen. The money had been put aside from my business dealings. I know it was foolish of me not to have kept it in another account, but there has always been enough money to cover all the household expenses, including Mah-mee's spending." My father stopped and shook his head slowly before he continued. "But business has been slow with this war escalating, while your Mah-mee's spending has increased."

I thought of how lonely my mother must sometimes be, always

losing herself in charities, her constant shopping sprees for the latest styles from Europe, and the long lunches and mah-jongg games that often ended in losses.

"How long have you been seeing this woman?" I wanted to know.

My father paused. "For more than twelve years," he finally answered.

I was stunned. My father had been with this other woman since Pie was born. It would have been easier to forgive him if it had been a casual, quick affair—one born out of male need and satisfaction, rather than one that had the strength of time and, most likely, love.

My father sipped his tea and spoke calmly, "It isn't what you might think. Yoshiko works at a department store near my office and is a very good woman. She has devoted her life to me, and I wanted to make sure she would be comfortable through this insane war."

"What about your own family?" I asked. My cold stare moved from the empty teacup I was cradling to his concerned, attentive gaze.

My father never flinched. "I have never compromised my devotion either to you children or to your mother. It was because I loved you all that I could never leave one for the other. Yoshiko has always lived quietly with the fact that my family came first."

"And you think that makes everything all right?"

There was a sudden noise from outside that made us stop. We both watched as Matsu shuffled by the front window carrying his gardening tools. My father waited for him to pass before he answered.

"I'm not here to apologize to you, Stephen. This has never been a simple matter for me. I have spent my life doing what I thought was the right thing to do. I've never tried to hurt anyone, not in my business dealings and certainly not with my own family. I've always followed my judgment in everything, weighing one decision against the other. But in this matter, I didn't have any choice but to follow my heart. We are all here to live out our own fates. I just hope you can try to understand what has happened. The most important thing is that you know I love you all very much."

I watched my father as he calmly continued to explain himself. He spoke slowly and precisely as if well rehearsed. I don't know why I should have thought anything would suddenly have changed in his appearance. Still, I looked closely for it in his tired, dark eyes, and in his graying hair that was always neatly combed back with an oil smelling of roses. I was old enough to understand everything he said, but as his mouth softly formed the words, I knew the sense of integrity I had long admired in him had died, and that I was already grieving for its loss.

"So now what?" I asked, after an uncomfortable silence between us.

"We go on living," he answered.

"Are you and Mah-mee going to divorce?"

My father leaned forward and grasped my arm. "Nothing will change, Stephen. Nothing."

DECEMBER 7, 1937

My father and I spent the rest of the evening speaking about the ongoing war. I listened politely, wishing I could be back alone in my room. It felt like I was sitting across from a stranger, as I searched for words to fill up the thick silence. Even the subtle signs of familiarity—my father combing his fingers through his gray hair, or constantly adjusting the knot of his tie—couldn't bring me ease. I watched him nod his head sadly, confirming my fears about the fierce Japanese drive that continued toward Canton. At the rate they moved through China, Canton would be overtaken within months. The carnage of death and destruction left my father speechless. I couldn't even begin to imagine Sachi and Matsu as my enemy, yet it felt strange to think that as I sat comfortably within their midst, Japan continued to ravage our homeland. I always knew my father loved Japan second only to China, and it now appeared he would have to show his loyalty to one or the other. I had no doubts his loyalty lay with China, the land of his ancestors, but it wouldn't be without pain. I felt the heaviness of his thoughts, and couldn't help but wonder if it meant I would soon have to return to Hong Kong to be with my mother and Pie. The words moved slowly to my lips, but I couldn't bring myself to ask.

Matsu made us miso soup, deep-fried bean curd, thin-sliced marinated beef and rice for our evening meal, then disappeared for the rest of the night. For a while, I could hear Bach playing low from Matsu's radio in the kitchen, and then: silence. When we had exhausted our strained conversation, my father asked if I would like to spend the holidays in Kobe with him. After I gave him a noncommittal response, he stood up, excused himself, and went out for a walk. By the time I heard him return, I was already in my darkened room, pretending to be asleep.

I woke up to find my father had taken an early train back to Kobe. There was a dampness in the air, and I was relieved that I wouldn't have to see him again. I suppose he felt the same. All I know is that a numbness had settled in me, and I barely felt a thing.

There was a stale taste in my mouth all morning. My father had returned to his other life in Kobe, and I knew I'd failed both of my parents. I wasn't able to accept my father's mistress, yet I couldn't make her disappear from our lives as my mother wanted.

"Your *o-tōsan* left very early this morning," Matsu said, waking me from my thoughts.

We sat and ate our usual breakfast of rice and pickled vegetables at the kitchen table. I had hardly said a word all morning. Usually, I would be the one to talk and ask Matsu questions, but his interruption only irritated me. Matsu had disappeared for the entire evening, and now he wanted to know what had happened. I simply nodded my head, without answering.

Matsu didn't say anything more. When he finished his food, he stood up and went about his business in the kitchen. I couldn't help but sulk. I ate solemnly, forcing the rice into my mouth until I had eaten most of it.

"It was good," I said, as I handed him the bowl and bowed, hoping to make up for my rudeness.

Matsu nodded, then began to wash the bowl. When I was almost back in my room, I heard him raise his voice to ask, "What are you doing today?"

I couldn't stay cooped up in the house, even though I knew I had to write a letter to my mother. "I don't know," I answered. "Maybe I'll go for a walk later."

Matsu came to the kitchen doorway, wiping his hands on a towel. "I'm going to Tama later. You might like to see it."

"What's there?" I asked.

Matsu smiled. "It's a Shinto shrine. Didn't your *go-ryōshin* ever tell you about the one at Tama?"

"No," I said, shaking my head.

My parents had never placed a great emphasis on religion. What I learned during my childhood was through attending St. Matthew's, a Catholic primary school in Hong Kong. The classes were taught by nuns, who swept down the halls in mysterious dark skirts and veils. Each morning before class, we recited "The Lord's Prayer," which would hum through my head for the rest of the day. As a little boy, I had taken it all in; the pageantry of mass, the colorful robes of the priests and bright stained glass windows, the secret knowledge that I had been saved. When I moved on to a private English middle school, I felt I had lost a childhood friend who had known all my secrets. Yet it seemed to gradually fade from my mind as life went on.

"It's not far from Tarumi," Matsu continued. "We can leave in a few hours."

"You never struck me as the religious type," I said, beginning to feel better.

Matsu swung the towel over his shoulder as he turned back into the kitchen. "There's still a lot you don't know about me," he said.

I began a letter to my mother, making sure to keep it focused on my father's visit and the upcoming holidays. I had once hoped to be with my family at Christmas, but as it approached with no word from Hong Kong, I relaxed at the thought that I would be spending it in Tarumi. The letter felt as if it took hours to write. I had no idea how much my mother knew of the situation between this woman Yoshiko and my father. Instead, I wrote my mother of my father's unexpected visit, our brief discussion of the money he had withdrawn to help this friend in her business, and how worried he had been about my accident. My words felt clumsy and scattered, but I had to tell her something. I changed the subject to the ongoing war. I didn't want to alarm my mother, but I wanted to know if she needed me to return to Hong Kong. Then I asked about Pie, whom I hadn't heard from in a long time. Was she all right? How was she doing in school? I smiled just to think of her, realizing how much I wanted to have her curious questions and quick mind here to dispel all the sadness I felt.

I ended the letter trying to reassure my mother of my father's decision to help his friend. "It's a business arrangement more than anything," I wrote, though I knew she would never really believe it. All I could hope was it might give her the excuse she needed to pretend that all was well again. I hated lying to my mother, I hated my father for making me have to.

I was happy to be out of the house and in the fresh air. We walked down the beach road and through the main street of the village to the Tama Shrine. It felt as if the entire village were asleep. Not one dog came to sniff or snap at our heels as we sauntered down the road.

Matsu carried a bundle wrapped in a dark blue and white cotton *furoshiki.* "It's our lunch," he said, with a smile.

But as we approached Kenzo's teahouse, Matsu suddenly became quiet. I could see the muscles in his neck tense. I wondered what would happen if Matsu and Kenzo should meet on the street. Would they pass by each other in silence? Or would they continue the angry words started at the house? I strained to see inside the darkened teahouse, but there was no movement.

From the village we continued on a dirt road that led up into the mountains. It wasn't long before we came to a clearing, and in the center of it: the Tama Shrine, posed serenely on a rise above the village of Tarumi. The first thing that caught my eye was the three identical faded red gateways, which you walked through in succession to the entrance to the shrine. Each one was simply made of two upright wooden posts, with a lintel across the top which extended past the upright posts and was carved into the slight curve of a smile. Just below it was another horizontal beam that connected the posts without extending beyond them. They each resembled a large bird perch. I had seen similar gateways in Kobe, but with elaborate carvings and designs, constructed in iron or stone.

"The *torii* gates," Matsu said. "It is said when you pass under them, the worshipper will be purified in heart and mind before reaching the shrine."

We continued up a path lined with odd-shaped, flat stones, and through the remaining two *torii* gates. The shrine itself was housed in a simple, square, wooden building, which looked like any house in the village. Matsu stopped at a stone trough by the entrance. There was a wooden ladle hanging by its side which he picked up and dipped into the water. I watched him drink from it, but instead of swallowing the water, he rinsed it around in his mouth, then spit it out into the dirt. He dipped the ladle into the water again and rinsed each of his hands. When he had thoroughly cleansed himself, he handed the ladle to me and gestured for me to do the same thing.

"To purify yourself before entering the shrine," Matsu whispered, as if he didn't want to disturb the gods.

I tried to copy his movements, surprised at how cool the water tasted. I was tempted to swallow it, to quench my thirst after our long walk, but I could feel Matsu's eyes watching me, so I simply repeated what he had done. Only then did he turn and remove his sandals, leading me into the wooden building which held the shrine.

Inside, there was a strong smell of burning incense and sweet rice wine. We stepped up onto a wooden platform where the shrine itself was no more than a stone table with an intricately carved wooden box. It housed what Matsu told me was the fox deity; the *kami,* Inari. In front of the shrine were thin sticks of burning incense and an empty blue-glazed rice bowl. To the right of it, a wall was covered with what seemed to be hundreds of small white slips of paper. Matsu whispered that they contained prayers and offerings from the villagers. I carefully watched as he stepped up to the altar and clapped three times, then reached up to pull gently on a thick, braided rope attached to a wooden clapper in the ceiling. The quick, slapping sound echoed through the small building. Then as Matsu closed his eyes and bowed, I stood quietly out of the way and waited.

When Matsu straightened up again, he reached down into the *furoshiki* he carried and brought out some sticky rice to place in the glazed bowl before the shrine.

"You?" he asked. Matsu stepped out of the way and urged me forward.

I shrugged my shoulders and hesitated. I felt embarrassed doing something so foreign, but Matsu pushed me toward the shrine, then placed my hands out in front so I could clap as he had done. "You must let the gods know you are here," Matsu whispered.

I quickly clapped three times and pulled on the rope. I stared hard at the enclosed shrine and the bowl of rice. The burning incense stung my eyes. I bowed low and tried to concentrate on some kind of prayer. My mind was confused. Who or what should I pray for? There were too many thoughts cluttering my head to choose only one. I wanted to pray for my parents' marriage, or Sachi and Matsu's happiness, or for the war to end in China. I could feel Matsu standing behind me, waiting. So I simply closed my eyes tight and prayed for all of us.

On a slope covered with pine needles overlooking Tarumi, we sat down to eat the lunch Matsu had brought along. He unwrapped the *furoshiki* to reveal a three-tiered, black lacquer food box and a thermos of green tea. Each layer of the box was filled with assorted sushi and fish cakes. I was impressed that he had prepared everything in such a short time. Matsu lifted off the top layer of the box and handed it to me. With my fingers I picked up a fist-shaped sushi of rice wrapped in marinated tofu, and took a bite out of it.

"Do you visit the shrine often?" I asked.

Matsu put an entire sushi into his mouth. He chewed thoughtfully and swallowed before he answered, "Only when I feel it's necessary."

"Why did you feel it was necessary to come this morning?" I asked.

"I thought it might be necessary for you to come here," he answered.

"For me?" I asked, surprised.

"Because of your *o-tōsan*'s visit," he answered, picking up another sushi.

I suddenly felt Matsu knew everything. I grew angry at the thought that he might even be a conspirator in what my father had been doing. The half-eaten piece of sushi I held slipped from my fingers onto the ground.

"Did you know my father had a mistress?" I asked, accusingly.

Matsu stopped eating as his eyes grew wide at my question. The smile on his face disappeared. "I don't concern myself with your *o-tōsan*'s private matters," he answered.

"Is that why you've remained our servant for so long, so you can keep my father's secrets?" I snapped. I regretted my words even as I said them. I knew it was wrong to take my anger out on Matsu, but it was too late. My shame seem to echo through the cool air.

"I have found great honor working for your *ojī-san* and your *o-tōsan*," Matsu answered.

I quickly stood up, dusted my trousers of pine needles, and bowed very low toward Matsu. "I'm sorry, I had no right to say that to you, Matsu-*san*."

Matsu took his time before he finally looked up at me, his stare softening. "It was the anger speaking, not the man," he said. He patted the ground beside him for me to sit down again. "You must realize, Stephen-*san*, that it changes nothing about the way your *o-tōsan* feels about you, but only what you now feel for him. It is sad to think that sometimes one person's happiness must come at the expense of others."

I nodded my head and remained silent. I thought about my father, and how he had always worked hard for his family. My illness had grieved him deeply, and it was his idea that I come to Tarumi to recuperate. I glanced over at Matsu, embarrassed by my behavior. He sat deep in his own thoughts. Only then did I remember how he too must be thinking of Sachi and suffering from the loss of his friendship with Kenzo.

"At first," I paused, "I thought you might have come here to pray for Kenzo-*san*."

Matsu turned toward me. "It is useless to pray for someone else. I come here to pray for myself."

"But you've known him since you were young. He's your best friend!"

"Then we will have to leave it to the strength of our history together," he said.

I lay back onto the ground and pillowed my head with my hands, absorbing all Matsu's words. I wondered if it might be like that for my parents. Would their history together be enough to hold them in marriage? Could I somehow change the events between my mother and father? It made me feel a little better to think of such possibilities. I closed my eyes and listened as the wind softly whispered through the trees.

DECEMBER 21, 1937

A letter arrived from my mother today. I'd been waiting to hear from her, yet I hesitated to open it at first, frightened of what her words might tell me. Since my visit to the Tama Shrine, I tried not to think of my parents' marriage. It felt like just another casualty that seem to be slipping from my life.

> *Dear Stephen,*
> *I have not been well lately. I received your letter and I'm grateful you were able to speak to your Ba-ba. He told me, too, that the money was used in a business venture. And for me not to worry. Under the circumstances, it seems I have no choice but to believe him. After all, I am just a woman with four children to raise but with no education in making a living. Your Ba-ba and I married when I was only fifteen. A perfect match. His Auntie Chin saw me walking with my sisters down in Central. She rushed to tell her nephew, your father. You've heard this story many times, forgive me. I'm old now. Almost forty. I wouldn't know what to do out there in the world.*
> *I know I shouldn't tell you of these thoughts, Stephen. I want you to know I'm not complaining. I have had a better life than most. If it must change somewhat to suit your Ba-ba's needs, so be it. Perhaps our marriage is at the point he and I must go our separate ways. I can accept this fact—I must—*

provided the family stays together in every other respect. Your Ba-ba has agreed to this.

Our main concern is that you feel better. I hoped to be with you during the holidays. I know you'll understand my health keeps me here now. I've already sent your Christmas presents. Your Ba-ba would like you to go up to Kobe to be with him. I think the trip will do you good.

Until then, my Stephen, know that I love you. My main concern is for your health and happiness in the coming year.

Ching reminds me to tell you to keep warm and dry.

> *Much love,*
> *Mah-mee*

I put down the letter and immediately felt melancholy for the life I once knew in Hong Kong. The sound of my mother's voice through her letter sent a dull ache to my heart. In the past few years, my parents had ceased to be the same two people I had known and grown up with. I remembered holding their hands as a little boy, never feeling more secure as I walked between them down Lee Yuen East Street. In my mind I heard again the frantic bargaining of street vendors and customers, and the grinding halt of the streetcars in Central. In the evenings back then, before my father's business began to take him away, we'd sit and eat Ching's minced duck and salted chicken around our big black lacquer table, my parents trying to make conversation as we children teased and tumbled over ourselves. Now the thought that they would stay together in marriage as a business arrangement filled me with heaviness. I had to admit that things had begun to change shortly after Pie was born. My father went more often to Japan, for longer periods of time, until he lived there more than with us in Hong Kong. The Ba-ba I knew as a small boy was no longer the same. Whenever he came home on brief visits, bringing gifts and quick hugs, I began to feel that somehow even the air we breathed was different.

I walked to the village this afternoon to wire my father that I would be staying in Tarumi for the holidays.

93

DECEMBER 25, 1937

I woke up this morning to my first Christmas in Tarumi. Matsu slid open my door and said in a light, easy voice, "Come along. There's something I want you to see."

I quickly got up and slipped on my clothes. Matsu stood in the *genken,* impatiently waiting for me.

"What is it?" I asked, rubbing the sleep from my eyes.

Matsu moved out of the way as I approached, pointing to the garden. "I thought you might like a Christmas tree," he said. There in the far corner, Matsu had decorated one of his pine trees with colorful pieces of origami cranes and fishes.

I stood silent, and didn't know what to say. I had just been in bed with thoughts of what I would be missing back home in Hong Kong. Every year when we were young, my mother insisted on having a live Christmas tree with ornaments in our house. We would get up to the warm aroma of pine, only to be quietly pushed into the dining room for breakfast by Ching, while we waited for my parents to get up so we could open our presents. The two or three hours of waiting were excruciating for Pie and Henry. Pie barely ate, while Henry ate everything in sight, as they both stared back and forth from the clock to the tree. I was old enough to know that my parents were sleeping off the effects of the Christmas Eve party they had attended the night before and wouldn't be up for hours.

For years, our Christmas dinners were held at The Hong Kong Hotel. There, we sat down for a five-course continental dinner, including goose, potatoes, and bread pudding. Along with dinner came my mother's yearly lecture on how to use the numerous pieces of silverware lined up beside our plates. "Always move from the outside in," her voice sailed across the table at us. The first year of this tradition, Ching was also asked to come along, but refused to eat a thing when she saw the complicated set of utensils. If she couldn't use chopsticks, she wouldn't eat. After that, Ching remained in the safe confines of her kitchen, and my mother took on the responsibility for us at Christmas dinner.

* * *

"It's the nicest Christmas tree I've ever had," I finally said.

Matsu nodded happily without saying a word. He stayed for a moment longer and stared at the tree. Then I saw him smile to himself, satisfied with what he had created. He turned around and began to walk to the kitchen. "How would you like your eggs cooked?" he asked.

JANUARY 1, 1938

I'd always heard how *Ganjitsu,* New Year's Day, was a national festival for the Japanese. Having grown up in Hong Kong with the firecrackers and vibrant-colored celebrations of Chinese New Year, I find there's something more spiritual in Japan on this day of renewal. There's the giving of simple gifts, visits to the temples and shrines, and debts that are repaid from the previous year. All the bad and hurt are erased, and everyone is granted a fresh start for the coming year. So I couldn't have been happier when it was decided that we would be going to Yamaguchi to celebrate the New Year with Sachi.

After an early breakfast this morning, Matsu and I wrapped up the food he had prepared in a *furoshiki* to take with us to Yamaguchi. For days leading up to the New Year, Matsu had been busy preparing sushi, herring roe, and red bean cakes. The sweet aroma of boiling beans filled the house. Over the doorway Matsu had hung a *kado-matsu,* a type of wreath he made out of pine, plum, and bamboo boughs. I also noticed that there were two more of these wreaths leaning against the wall in the *genken.*

Earlier in the week I had gone into the village and bought Sachi a miniature pine tree, no more than a foot tall, set gracefully in a clay planter. This morning I gave Matsu a good-luck *daruma* doll, which stares blindly with no eyes painted in. The custom is to paint in an eye and make a wish. If the wish comes true, then the other eye can be painted in. Matsu stared at the eyeless face for a few moments, then bowed toward me before he placed it gently on a kitchen shelf. He quickly disappeared into his room, and returned a moment later with a book of Japanese poetry for me.

On our way out of the house, Matsu stopped to pick up one of the wreaths he had made for Sachi, while I waited for him, cradling the miniature pine in my hands.

"What does the wreath symbolize?" I asked, when Matsu returned with a second wreath and we started down the road.

Matsu swung the *furoshiki* he carried and glanced down at the wreath he held in his other hand. "Each tree is symbolic of prosperity, purity, longevity, and loyalty."

"Who is the other one for?"

Matsu turned around as if someone might be there. "For Kenzo-*san*," he finally said.

By the time we arrived in Yamaguchi, the entire village was alive with celebration. Men and women wore bright, colorful kimonos. The small houses seemed to have come alive with ferns, wreaths, and oranges adorning their doorways. We couldn't move a few feet without being offered dried chestnuts and *toso*, a sweet *sake*. Matsu happily declined all offers, intent on our seeing Sachi first.

Unlike the festive atmosphere of the village, Sachi's house appeared quiet and unassuming. The only sign of the New Year was what Matsu called a *shime-nawa*, a rope of twisted straw festooned with strips of paper hanging across her entranceway. It was supposed to bar all evil spirits from entering the house.

Sachi opened the door even before we reached it. She bowed low several times, then led us excitedly into the house. Instead of the subdued colors she usually wore, Sachi had on a red and yellow kimono. They were the first bright colors I'd ever seen on her. Before anything else, she insisted we each have a bowl of *zoni*, a broth containing *mochi*. She looked beautiful as she moved around nervously packing the *mochi* and black beans she had prepared for the celebration. Afterward, we would join the rest of the village in celebrating the New Year.

Later, as I sipped *toso* along with Matsu, Sachi, and the rest of the villagers of Yamaguchi, I realized how this was *Hajime*—a first ceremony for me. If the New Year represented a new start in doing everything, from taking a first bath to planting a new flower, this day would be a new start for all of us. I wondered what Keiko was doing as I watched Matsu and Sachi happy again, hoping this could mean a new start for the two of them. I tried to imagine Kenzo thinking the same thing down in Tarumi, as he looked at the pine and bamboo wreaths hanging on the doors of the village houses, remembering his two oldest friends.

JANUARY 15, 1938

In the past week I've received a new watch, a cashmere sweater, two shirts, and some books in the mail from my parents and Pie. It felt like the holidays haven't ended. Then yesterday I received a letter from King. It was postmarked from Hong Kong, which meant that he had returned home from Canton for the holidays and I hope had received my card.

I immediately realized how much I missed him. His easy words brought back to me my old life at Lingnan University, the manicured grounds and stately brick buildings, the long hours of studying, and the late night rush for bowls of *jook* to fill our hollow stomachs. It was only toward the end of his letter that the magic disappeared, and I was left stunned by his words.

> *"I'm sure you've heard some version of the Nanking massacre. It's been reported that thousands of innocent Chinese men, women, and children have been killed and raped needlessly by the Japanese bastards. I would fight right now if I thought it would do any good, if I thought we had any chance against them. But as they move closer to Canton, I know that many Lingnan students are too afraid to return after the holidays. I've persuaded my family to let me go back. But only after my solemn promise that I would return to Hong Kong if the Japanese devils get too close. I only wish you were taking the boat back to Canton with me."*

I suddenly felt as if the walls were closing in on me as I folded King's letter, stuffing it back into the thin envelope. There had been nothing on Matsu's radio about the massacre, only another victory speech of how the Imperial Army had bravely captured Nanking and Tsingtao with little resistance. There was part of me that wanted to be back in the thick of things with King, that grieved for all those helplessly slaughtered in Nanking, even while another part of me couldn't imagine having to leave Matsu, Sachi,

97

and Keiko. I tried to sit down to write King a letter, but couldn't seem to get beyond the first line: "I received your letter and wish I could be with you . . ."

FEBRUARY 4, 1938

Setsubun, The First Rites of Spring, has arrived even with the winter cold still with us. Matsu told me last night to get a good night's sleep so I would be ready to go with him to the Tama Shrine.

"What for?" I had asked.

"You'll see soon enough tomorrow," he answered.

I rose early and dressed warm, thinking we would get an early start, but we didn't leave till late, and it was after noon by the time we reached Tarumi. Many of the villagers were also making their way up the mountain to the shrine. I could see that through the *torii* gates and near the shrine, a crowd had already gathered. I looked around at what were now familiar faces, looking for Keiko and her family. Matsu also seem to be looking around for someone, whom I could only guess to be Kenzo. I'd hoped the silence between them would disappear with the New Year, but it remained. They had not spoken since the incident at the house, and though Matsu was quiet about what he felt, I could often feel his sadness.

But neither Keiko nor Kenzo was among the crowd. Our attention was soon drawn to a clanging noise and the two Shinto priests who stepped up onto the wooden platform. They were dressed in red and gold samurai-like robes, and each carried a large bowl filled with what appeared to be beans.

"What are they doing?" I whispered to Matsu.

"It is called *mame-maki,* bean throwing. Every year, winter and its demons of cold and pestilence are thrown out with the beans. They are also symbolic of the earth being impregnated with the seeds of life."

Matsu's voice was soon drowned out by the growing excitement of the crowd. They raised their hands and began to push forward as the priests dug deep into their bowls and threw out handfuls of beans at us. As the beans rained down, the crowd began to chant in unison: *"Fuku wa uchi, oni wa soto,"* which I understood to mean, "In with good luck, out with the devils."

*   *   *

By the time we started back to Tarumi, it was late afternoon and I felt tired. I hesitated asking Matsu to stop, since the only place I knew of to rest was Kenzo's teahouse. The festivities of the past few months and the walk to the shrine had been more than I was used to. I had gained strength from all my exercise, but when we at last walked back into Tarumi, my body felt a sticky weariness.

The village seemed to come alive as villagers slowly filled the streets again. There were people running everywhere, and my heart began to race as I looked hard again for any sign of Keiko. As we approached Kenzo's teahouse, I saw a large crowd gathered in front. Matsu made a grunting sound, but said nothing. He stopped for a moment, hesitated, then walked over to the teahouse.

"What is it?" he asked, as we came nearer the crowd.

Several excited faces turned our way, eager to tell us what they knew. But when they saw that it was Matsu, they stopped abruptly and held their tongues. Whispers drifted through the crowd, and it was evident many had heard that the two friends were at odds. Whether they knew the cause or not didn't seem to matter to the growing gossip. It felt like an eternity before an older woman, dressed in a heavy, dark kimono, stepped toward Matsu and said quietly, "It's Kenzo-*san*."

Matsu pushed roughly through the crowd and hurried into the dark teahouse. I followed him without thinking. It took a moment for our eyes to adjust to the darkness, and when I began to make out the shadows, the first thing I heard was a moan erupt from deep down in Matsu's throat. I rubbed my eyes and followed his frozen stare upward to the wooden rafters. Above the counter, not more than three feet away from us, hung Kenzo's limp body.

Matsu lowered Kenzo's body from the wooden beam. He wouldn't allow anyone else to touch his friend. I could hear the low thud of Kenzo's body as it fell to the counter. Stunned, I stepped closer to see his blank, bulging eyes and the bluish skin of his face which looked waxy and unreal. I turned toward Matsu, who stared hard at his friend and didn't move for a long while.

99

Then he bent down toward Kenzo, whispered some inaudible words into his ear, and carefully closed his eyes. Without saying another word, Matsu turned around and walked slowly out of the teahouse, through the waiting crowd, and down the road to home.

FEBRUARY 5, 1938

I'm not clear how I made it back to the house yesterday after Kenzo's death, but my legs were weak and heavy and I was short of breath and coughing by the time I stepped through the bamboo gate into the garden. All I remember is I felt as if I couldn't breathe, drowning in the sweet, nauseating smells that came from the garden. I felt sick to my stomach, and before I could reach the house I had thrown up by the steps of the *genken.* After that, time felt like a dream. I don't know where Matsu suddenly came from, but he helped me into the house, cleaned me up, and put me to bed. I remember his face, tired and pale. I wanted to say something about how sorry and embarrassed I felt, but I closed my eyes and fell into a deep sleep.

I stayed in bed most of the day recuperating. Other than my legs feeling weak and wobbly, my lungs felt fine again, but Matsu insisted I rest. I didn't have the energy to resist. He checked on me constantly, bringing me rice crackers and a clear seaweed broth to drink. I could see how tired he still looked, his eyes bloodshot from lack of sleep, helped along by the whiskey which lingered on his breath. Neither one of us said a word about Kenzo, though I couldn't close my eyes without seeing the frozen image of his bluish skin, and his glaring, dead stare.

All morning I could hear Matsu's radio play from the kitchen. The classical music lulled me in and out of sleep, until a Mozart concerto was abruptly interrupted by the grating sound of a woman's high-pitched voice. I shook myself awake to listen: "The Imperial Japanese Army in China continues its brave, victorious march south. It is futile for the Chinese to resist any longer. They should simply surrender to the kindness of the Japanese Army and all will be well."

For some reason, Matsu made no attempt to turn the radio down, or to switch stations as he usually did when the news came on. Instead, it was as if he purposely let the piercing, self-righteous voice grow louder.

"It is the will of our most Imperial Majesty that Japan find its proper place in the world. It won't be long before the Japanese Army holds Canton within their grasp."

I listened with a thirst to know what was going on in China, and how it might soon affect me. After the Japanese army reached Canton, there would be little to stop them from continuing on to Hong Kong. The British colony had always been a business center, not a military stronghold. I lay in bed and began to worry about whether I should return to Hong Kong to be with my mother and Pie. I wondered what my father planned to do, and if I should instead join him in Kobe. My heart began to beat faster with each thought.

After lunch, Matsu checked to see if I needed anything. When he saw that I had eaten and was feeling much better, he seemed to relax as he picked up my empty dishes and carried them back into the kitchen. I must have fallen asleep, only to awaken a few hours later to find the house completely quiet. I lay in bed and listened for any sounds of Matsu moving around the kitchen: the scraping of a stool against the wooden floor, or the dull clink of metal as he sharpened his knives. When I heard nothing, I felt strangely alone and afraid. Then when the wind suddenly blew, the *shoji* windows shook as if the whole house was moving.

I rose from the futon, my back sore from lying down so long. I went to the kitchen for a glass of water, and then out into the garden. There was no sign of Matsu anywhere. I wondered where he had gone as I stood alone, amidst the black pines and the blooming Japanese quince. I breathed in slowly to settle my nerves. Unlike yesterday, the sweet, intoxicating smells of the garden embraced me, surrounding me with a deep sense of comfort.

Matsu didn't return until almost evening. I was in my room, trying to read a book when I heard his heavy steps in the *genken*. A few moments later he slid open my *shoji* door, and bowed quickly to let me know he had returned.

"How are you?" he asked abruptly.

"I'm feeling better," I answered. I felt silly now for having been afraid when he was gone.

Matsu stared down at me for a moment, then rubbed his cheek and gave a soft grunt of approval. He appeared more at ease, his face softer in the evening light. I wanted to ask him where he'd been, or tell him how I'd been worrying both about him, and about this insane war that was quickly approaching my family and friends. I sat up on my futon hoping to continue our conversation, but Matsu had already turned away, hurrying to the kitchen to begin our evening meal.

February 6, 1938

"Kenzo will be buried tomorrow morning," Matsu said quietly, as we sat across from one another in the kitchen eating our morning meal of rice and pickled vegetables. I felt tired, but much stronger.

His voice startled me. It was the most Matsu had said to me since he found me sick in the garden and put me to bed. Kenzo's suicide had nearly silenced him. I still wondered if he had gone to see Sachi, or back to the Tama Shrine to pray for his great loss, but I refrained from asking. In fact, I was afraid to mention Kenzo's name. The quieter Matsu became, the closer I watched him. I guess there was part of me that was afraid he might do something crazy. Since I'd arrived in Tarumi, Matsu had been the anchor and I was the one afloat. I wasn't ready to switch places.

"Where?" I asked, suddenly wide awake. "At the Tama Shrine?"

Matsu shook his head. "It will be a Buddhist ceremony."

"Would it be all right if I went to the burial with you?"

Matsu looked up at me and his face softened. "If you wish," he answered.

"I know I didn't know Kenzo-*san* very well, but I'd like to pay my respects."

"I think he would be honored," Matsu said.

I took the opportunity to keep him talking. "What about Sachi?" I asked. "Does she know?"

Matsu paused a long time and stared at his food. "I went to see her yesterday," he said at last.

I stopped eating and looked anxiously up at him. "How is she?" I asked. I could almost feel the white, puckered scars which ravaged the side of her face.

Matsu leaned back heavily against the wall. "Sachi knew the minute I entered her house that something was wrong. She stood by the door and watched me, as if she understood everything just by the way I walked. Then she simply asked, 'Is it Kenzo-*san?*' I couldn't look her in the eye, so I just nodded."

Matsu paused and swallowed before he could continue. "Sachi raised her hand to cover her mouth. She couldn't talk. She gestured for me to sit down while she disappeared into the kitchen. When she finally came back, she brought tea. She sat down and said one word: 'When?' I told her Kenzo had been found yesterday, that he had hung himself."

I lowered my head, remembering the heavy thud of Kenzo's body on the counter as he was taken down.

Matsu waited for me to look up again. His face seemed to relax as he continued to speak. "At first, Sachi was speechless. She just sat there, as if I had slapped her with the words. It felt as if we would sit there in silence forever. At last, she looked up at me and began to speak strangely of the past.

" 'Do you remember that year of the *Tama Matsuri?*' she asked me, 'the festival so many years ago when Kenzo was one of the *mikoshi* bearers and the entire village was drunk with celebration?'

" 'Yes,' I answered, surprised she would bring something up from so long ago. It was the summer she and Tomoko were fifteen, the two most beautiful girls in the village. Kenzo had been one of the young men chosen to carry the shrine, which was a great honor. It had been a good year of fishing for Tarumi and everyone was celebrating their good fortune. Even my father came away from his gardening and joined in the festivities.

" 'When the crowd became so excited,' Sachi went on, 'I was

sure I would be trampled. It was you who helped me up, wasn't it?' she asked me.

"I shrugged and hesitated. 'That was so long ago, why bring it up now?' I asked her. Sachi smiled sadly and touched my hand. The moment had been buried in me for so many years, it no longer seemed to belong to me. You see, that day when the shrine was carried out, the crowd began to run toward it in a wild frenzy, urged on by the beating drums and clanging bells. I was behind them, when I saw Sachi and Tomoko running, pushed frantically along with the crowd. The next thing I knew, Sachi had stumbled, while the crowd kept pushing forward. Even Tomoko kept moving, unaware of what had happened to Sachi. I had just a moment to grab Sachi from behind and lift her to her feet. She was so light, it took so little effort. By the time she turned around, I had disappeared into the crowd."

"Why didn't you let her know it was you?" I asked.

Matsu cleared his throat. "It all happened so quickly. I didn't want to embarrass her. Later, when the festival was over, Tomoko spread the rumor that it was Kenzo who had saved Sachi, even though he had been carrying the shrine all the time."

"Didn't Sachi or Kenzo say anything?"

"Sachi never mentioned it, until now. It's sometimes easier to believe what everyone else believes. Besides, they were sweet on one another, and what could be more romantic?"

"And now that she knows the truth?" I asked.

"Sachi only said, 'Sometimes you can't see what is right in front of you. I'm sorry, Matsu-*san*.'

" 'Those years are like another lifetime,' I told her.

"After a while, Sachi said, 'In many ways, Kenzo-*san* and Tomoko were much more alike, so full of life. I can't help but think he might have found a better life if he had just moved away from Tarumi.'

"I kept silent. Only I knew Kenzo would never have left Tarumi without her. He couldn't bring himself to accept Sachi the way she was after the disease, but he could never leave the memory of her. I was honored to be his friend and hold his secrets. I never meant to betray him. In the end, it was he and I who were so much alike: faithful to the same woman for all these years."

104

"You and Kenzo never saw anyone else?" I asked.

Matsu laughed. "Who would want me?" he asked, pointing to his face. "I used to think Kenzo's *kami* must be smiling down on him. If success was measured by the number of friends you had, then Kenzo was a successful man, but no one could ever take the place of Sachi." Matsu looked down in thought.

I wondered if he considered his own life unsuccessful.

"Will Sachi come down for Kenzo-*san's* burial?" I asked.

"No," Matsu answered.

"Would it be all right for me to visit her soon?"

Matsu looked past me as if I weren't there. "In time," he said, troubled.

I could tell something else bothered him. He rubbed the edge of his bowl, a pensive expression on his face. "I had hoped to give Sachi some peace of mind when I left," Matsu continued, "I didn't want to leave her so alone. But I made the mistake of telling her Kenzo hadn't suffered much. Sachi just looked at me in disbelief, then in a voice full of defeat, she whispered, 'But haven't we all been suffering for years?' "

Matsu stopped. I picked up my bowl and began to eat again in silence. I knew any more questions would simply be an intrusion.

After breakfast Matsu went out to his garden, while I sat down at my grandfather's desk to write a letter to my mother. My head spun from all the events of the past few days. I wanted to visit Sachi, but I didn't know what to say to her. Though Kenzo's death was filling my mind, I did not mention it to my mother. I assumed she knew him, and I didn't want her to worry about anything else. Instead, I wrote hoping that she felt better, stressing how much I liked the presents she had sent, though I'd missed being back in Hong Kong with her. Then I spent the rest of the letter recounting how nice my holidays were here, and how well taken care of I was by Matsu. All the while I was also careful to stay away from the subject of my father.

I sealed the letter into a thin blue envelope and searched for Matsu to tell him I was going to mail it. He was still in the garden, balanced on his knees as he planted a new pine tree.

"I'm going to the village to mail this letter to my mother," I said.

Matsu glanced up at me. "Are you feeling all right?" he asked.

I knew my being sick yesterday had to do with all the physical exertion I'd been doing, rather than with my illness. I immediately thought of Ching's and my mother's concern if they knew what I'd been doing. "Go slowly, go slowly," I heard their voices ring out.

"I'm fine," I said reassuringly. "Do you need me to get anything while I'm there?"

Matsu slowly stood up from the ground. He looked closely at me for any signs of fever or fatigue, and when he was finally satisfied that I was fine, he asked, "Can you pick up the mail? It will save me the walk."

"Of course," I answered.

Matsu smiled at my eagerness, his skin wrinkling into small creases across his forehead and around his eyes. It was the first time since the day I arrived in Tarumi that I began to realize Matsu was no longer young. For the past few months, he had proven that he was anything but old. I watched him dig deep into his trousers and pull out a small metal key.

"Your *ojī-san*'s name is still on the box," he said, as he handed me the key.

"I'll be back soon," I said, slipping the key into my pocket.

At the bamboo gate, I turned back to see Matsu carefully lower himself onto his knees. The sky was dark and gray overhead, and I felt my eyes strain against tears. I wanted to tell Matsu everything would be all right, that Kenzo's death was his own choice, just as Tomoko's had been. It would be so simple for Matsu and Sachi to be happy now, to let go of the past. But, even as these thoughts came to the tip of my tongue, I swallowed them, and began to walk down the white, sand-dusted road to the village.

The village felt cold and dark by the time I'd posted my letter, collected the mail, and stepped back out of the post office. I looked quickly through the stack of envelopes, but found nothing addressed to me. I glanced across the street at Kenzo's darkened teahouse, where pieces of black cloth covered the *shoji* windows.

On the door, draped in black, was a photograph of Kenzo. I stood there quietly, staring at all the black cloth, still unable to accept that Kenzo was really gone.

The leisurely pace of the village went on as usual, though the old men who sat outside of storefronts discussing fishing, their families, and the war spoke in low, respectful voices. They neither stared nor stopped their conversation when I walked by. It was the first time I felt my presence in Tarumi was no longer a novelty. Women carried baskets or babies on their backs as they moved to and fro doing their daily shopping. I felt someone tap on my arm, and turned to see Keiko standing behind me.

"*Konnichiwa,* Stephen-*san.*" Keiko bowed as she took a step back. She wore a dark kimono and carried a brown basket filled with deep orange persimmons.

I smiled, surprised. It seemed the only time I had come into the village without instinctively glancing down the dusty street looking for her.

"Keiko-*san, konnichiwa.*" I returned her bow.

"It is very sad about Kenzo-*san,*" she said. She glanced over at the teahouse. "The entire village is in mourning. Why would Kenzo-*san* want to end his life?"

I shook my head slowly, careful not to say too much. "It's very sad."

Keiko shifted the basket she carried. "I know that he and Matsu-*san* were close friends."

"Yes, they were," I said. Then I offered, "Let me carry that for you."

Keiko hesitated, then relinquished the basket and bowed several times in gratitude. She smelled lovely, like jasmine.

"Where are you going?" I asked.

"I was on my way home."

"Well, I'm finished with everything here. May I carry this home for you?"

Keiko took another step back and quickly answered, "It isn't far, Stephen-*san.* Please, I must go." She reached out and took the handle of the basket, as her hand brushed against mine. We stood there, neither one of us letting go of the basket.

"Are you afraid Mika might see us?"

Keiko shook her head. With one unexpected pull, she jerked

the basket back into her own hands, scattering persimmons all over the ground. I quickly bent down and picked them up for her, then cradled them in my hands as her eyes watched my every move.

"I will see you again soon," she said, reaching out for the fallen persimmons.

I purposely held them back. "What are you so afraid of? I just want to help you carry the basket home," I said, exasperated.

Keiko's eyes moved away from the persimmons and looked pleadingly into mine. "Please, they are for my father's meal. He's very old-fashioned, and I'm already late."

"Are you afraid your father won't like me?"

"Please, Stephen-*san*."

I paused, but seeing her anxiousness I placed the persimmons back into the basket without another word. Keiko bowed, then looked up gratefully at me before she hurried away. Seeing Keiko's fear, I couldn't help but wonder whether her father was so old-fashioned that he had forbidden her to be alone with a young man. Or if it had to do with the fact that I was a Chinese young man. I stood there and didn't move, long after Keiko had vanished around the corner.

FEBRUARY 7, 1938

Kenzo's burial brought out the entire village. Gathered together was an assortment of old men, women, and children. Until Keiko had mentioned her older brother, I took it for granted that most of the young men from Tarumi had gone to seek their fortunes in larger cities. Now, I couldn't help but realize that most of them had joined the Japanese Army. When I questioned Matsu about the lack of healthy young men in Tarumi, he simply shook his head and said, "They've gone off to fulfill the dreams of dreamers."

The first month after I arrived at the beach house, I had somehow convinced myself that being in Tarumi kept me far away from what was happening in China. But the realization again hit me right in the face as I walked beside Matsu: I was the only young man in the crowd. While the villagers had grown used to my presence, I felt obvious and uncomfortable.

I tugged hard to tighten the *obi* sash of the black cotton kimono I had borrowed from Matsu. Just this morning, I realized I had nothing dark to wear. Unlike certain Chinese burials where white is worn, a Buddhist ceremony required dark colors. Matsu laughed and handed me the too-large black kimono, which could be wrapped twice around me. It was the only thing I could wear on such short notice, so with it hanging loosely from my body, I tripped clumsily after Matsu in a pair of wooden sandals.

The sweet smell of burning incense filled the air as the procession made its way to the Buddhist temple just outside the village. Matsu had told me that, unlike the Tama Shrine where births and marriages were celebrated, burials were always Buddhist ceremonies. In the Buddhist faith, it was believed that through a life of right living and thinking, one could achieve Nirvana.

The temple was a large, wooden structure. It was by far the most ornate building I'd seen in Tarumi, strangely reminiscent of Hong Kong, with its red and gold walls and curved roof tiles. It stood within walking distance of the village so that the many ancestors of the villagers buried or cremated there would not be lonely.

The crowd moved in a dark wave down the dirt road, slowly entering the temple. Matsu was silent throughout the entire procession, simply bowing his head to those who showed their sympathy at the loss of his good friend. If the villagers knew anything else, they kept it to themselves, giving Matsu the respect of their silence.

Inside, the large room was hot and filled with the thick smell of burning incense. There was a simple wooden altar up front, but no sign of Kenzo's body. Monks in flowing orange robes began the ceremony with low chants which hummed throughout the room. The chants were consistantly accompanied by the steady clanging of gongs and cymbals. We bowed several times and repeated the chants, praying that the soul of Kenzo would find supreme happiness. During the ceremony, I glanced around and saw Keiko a few aisles away, dressed in a dark kimono and veil. I recognized her by the small pearl ring she wore on her right hand. Next to her stood Mika, and then an older man and woman who must have been their parents. While I couldn't see her mother's face clearly, I saw that her father was thickset and balding, with more the air and appearance of a businessman than a fisherman.

When the ceremony was over, I decided to approach Keiko and her family. Still, I couldn't forget the day before in the village when Keiko tried so hard to get away. In my mind, I again saw those same dark eyes imploring me to let her go, and I stopped cold when I saw her family standing nearby. But it was too late, for Keiko turned just in time to see me. She quickly took hold of Mika's arm and began to pull her away, but not before her father turned toward me. He stood there solid and unmoving. His unsmiling glare cut right through me, sizing me up. I stood frozen, not sure what I should do, yet too close to ignore him. Then he leaned over and whispered something to Keiko's mother. I could see her mother nodding submissively. When her father turned back to me, it was with a look so full of hate I simply bowed my head and walked quickly away.

Outside the temple, I looked around for Keiko's family, and was relieved to find them already gone. At least I knew why Keiko was always anxious to get away from me. Her father's dislike of me for whatever reasons was obvious. I had never felt such hatred, and shivered just to think of it.

Voices rang out in the distance as scattered groups of people moved back along the dirt road which led to the village. I stood aside waiting for Matsu, when out of the corner of my eye I saw her. Dressed in a black kimono and veil, her slight, graceful figure hovered among the trees. From the moment my eyes fell upon her, I knew it was not an illusion: Sachi had come after all. She lifted her veil and her eyes caught mine for just a moment as she bowed low in my direction. I looked around to make sure no one was watching, then returned her bow, but when I looked up again, Sachi was already gone.

MARCH 7, 1938

Everything seems to move in slow motion, or not at all. The radio and the week-old newspapers sent to me by my father from Kobe prove only that the war in China moves with a quick brutality, leaving a sour, anxious taste in my mouth. Every day I wait for a letter from my mother, or a message from my father telling me to return to Kobe, where at least I'd be closer to the current news, but a troubling silence remains.

I've felt afraid since I saw Sachi and Keiko at the Buddhist temple. They've both disappeared from my life, vanished from sight. While I know Sachi is safely hidden away in Yamaguchi, I go down to the beach every day, hoping for a glimpse of Keiko. Her father's cold stare of hatred seems far away now, but like a nightmare, it comes back in full force at the most unexpected moments. I can't help wondering if I were Japanese, would I still be feeling such hostility from him? Or could it be some past grievance between our families that makes him hate the sight of me? It's the only time that I feel I'm amidst some kind of enemy here in Tarumi. Yet, all I know is that I want to see Keiko again, and I only hope she feels the same. But each day has brought only the endless sea and an empty white beach.

After Matsu stayed close to the house for weeks, he disappeared this morning and I couldn't find him anywhere. I had secretly hoped he would go to Yamaguchi, even if it was without me. The thought of Sachi alone after Kenzo's burial worried me, though I didn't dare approach Matsu with it. Ever since Kenzo's death, it was as if the new life I'd discovered in Tarumi had stopped. I'd fallen back into being an invalid, sleeping late and doing as little as possible. Day after day, Matsu worked silently in his garden, keeping his grief to himself. My promise to Sachi stopped me from sneaking away to visit her. In my mind, I could see her thin, black-veiled figure hovering among the trees, and sometimes I wondered if it had all been just an illusion. Still, I'd kept her appearance at the temple a secret, not knowing if she wanted Matsu to know. It seemed as though he were purposely staying away from Sachi, as if Kenzo's death had made them strangers. At times, I wanted to shake Matsu and wake him from this deception. But I realized he needed time, so I've kept out of his way, and quietly waited.

MARCH 14, 1938

I felt restless this morning and decided to do some sketching in the garden. Matsu had gone into the village and I'd just sat down by his favorite silk tree, when I heard the dull clapping of wooden sandals, and saw a shadow behind the bamboo fence move slowly toward the front gate. I stood up and waited, my heart beating faster. The shadow stopped just short of the gate and didn't move for the longest time, when all of a sudden there was a faint knock. I knew immediately it was Keiko. At once I swung open the gate to see her standing a few feet away, dressed in a pale blue kimono.

"*Ohayōgozaimasu,* Keiko-*san.*" I hoped she wouldn't run away.

Keiko bowed low and quietly returned my greeting. But instead of looking me full in the face, her gaze remained directed down to the ground.

"Is everything all right?" I asked.

Keiko wouldn't look up at me. "I have come to apologize for my *o-tōsan,*" she finally said.

"You don't have to." I followed Keiko's gaze down to the dirt. "Your brother and the war . . ." I managed to get out before my voice stopped. I wondered if they had even heard anything from her brother, or if Keiko knew much about the Nanking massacre.

"It was Toshiro's own decision to go fight for our Imperial Emperor. There is no excuse for my *o-tōsan* to have been rude to you," she whispered. "He has brought shame to our family."

At that moment I wanted to touch Keiko's face, to raise her lips to mine so that I could kiss her, but I knew it would only scare her away. Instead, I stepped back and bowed again. "Keiko-*san,* would you do me the honor of sitting with me in the garden for a moment?"

Keiko glanced over her shoulder. "I must return, Stephen-*san.*"

"Then let me walk with you. For just part of the way," I said quickly. I stepped away from her and toward the gate before she could say anything more.

Instead of taking the main road, we walked down the length of the beach, the warm sand soothing against my bare feet. I looked up at the dune, fearful that we might see Mika, only to relax when I saw that Keiko and I were alone.

"I was hoping to see you again," I spoke first.

Keiko walked slowly beside me. She still avoided my eyes. I couldn't tell if she was shy, or still embarrassed by her father's rudeness. "It has been very difficult to get away," she said. "Mika is constantly by my side and my *o-tōsan* is very strict. I told them I was going to go pray for Toshiro at the Tama Shrine, knowing Mika would prefer to stay at home."

"I wasn't even sure if you wanted to see me again."

Keiko suddenly stopped walking. "I did," she said softly, kicking some sand away with her wooden sandal. "I hoped you would accept my apology."

I took a step closer to her, and could feel Keiko's body tense against mine, but she didn't move away. I touched the smooth white skin of Keiko's cheek, then lifted her chin so that her eyes met mine before I leaned slowly forward and kissed her. I would have kissed her again, if she hadn't pulled away.

"I must go now, Stephen-*san,*" she said, her face flushed.

I didn't want her to leave so soon, still feeling the warm rush of desire. But I stood there, my feet pressing deep imprints into the sand. "When will I see you again?" I called out to her.

Keiko stopped for a moment, then turned back toward me. "I will come to you," she said. Her voice drifted off into the air even as I tried hard to hold onto it. Then she began to run to the sand dune, lifting her arms just enough so that her kimono sleeves flapped gracefully through the air like wings.

SPRING

MARCH 28, 1938

*I*t has been much warmer the past few weeks. Since the day I saw Keiko, I've felt much lighter. It's as if the darkness of winter has lifted. Every day I can see spring arriving in the smallest ways, mostly in the form of the double cherry blossoms sprouting from Matsu's weeping *Higan,* and the clear, light scent I smell every time I step into the garden.

When I returned from my swim today, Matsu followed me into my room from the garden. "There's a letter for you," he said, putting the thin blue envelope down on the table.

"You've been to the village already?" I asked, surprised.

"I needed to get some rice," he answered, "and I thought I would save you a trip getting the mail."

I looked away from him, down at the large, even writing on the envelope, and knew instantly it belonged to Pie. "It's from my *imōto,*" I said, happily.

Matsu smiled in a knowing way. "I'll be in the garden," he said.

After he left, I quickly grabbed the letter and read it, anxious to know how Pie was. I could see her large, dark eyes and hear her high, clever voice as I read her words.

"Dear Big Brother," she wrote, *"You must be angry at me for not writing, but when I explain why it has been so long, I know you will forgive me."* I couldn't help but feel a lump in my throat at her explanation. *"For the past month, I have been going after school to the Red Cross refugee center in Wan Chai. I do everything, from rolling bandages to sorting donated clothes and filling care packages. Mah-mee doesn't know what I'm doing, so please don't say anything. She thinks I'm at the Queen's Theatre watching the latest Errol Flynn movie, or shopping in Central. She wouldn't understand the way I know you will. Mah-mee is afraid of all these poor and starving refugees pouring into Hong Kong from China, and prefers that we stay at a safe distance. It doesn't matter that the Japa-*

117

*nese devils have raped and slaughtered their families and friends,
leaving them homeless and running for their lives! Mah-mee believes she does more than her share by donating to her charities. She
would rather live her own life of mah-jongg games, while pretending all those starving in the streets are invisible. Besides, I don't
know why, but Mah-mee has been in a bad mood lately, going out,
or hiding in her room. Ching won't let me make a sound when I'm
at home, so I might as well be out.*

*"When you return, you won't recognize the Hong Kong you left.
In the past few months, the mountains near Wan Chai have become
home to thousands of refugees. They live in makeshift houses made
of whatever they can find, like wood scraps or cardboard. Entire
families are crowded into filthy, dark boxes. They're like ants on a
hill. It doesn't take long before these families are sick with a hack-
ing cough or diarrhea. When it rains heavily, most of the shacks
slide down the mountain sides like paper houses. Many families
have been buried in mud and debris. No sooner is one shantytown
gone, than another goes up in its place. It isn't enough to try and
give them money, I had to do something."*

Pie's words had gone straight to my heart. At twelve years old,
she already had more courage than any of us. The only thing that
had dampened my happiness was the slight, innocent remark at
the end of Pie's letter. "I heard Mah-mee tell Ching she would
like you to come home soon, because it might no longer be safe
for you in Japan. I can't wait to see you again!"

I could almost hear my mother's voice ring out in the still air. I
put down the letter, wishing I could tell her how safe I felt here
with Matsu and Sachi, and how I was just getting to know Keiko.

APRIL 15, 1938

I made up my mind to see Sachi again this morning. I'd waited
long enough for Matsu to grieve. But I got out of bed only to discover the house empty. I checked every room for Matsu, but he
had apparently slipped away sometime while I was still asleep.

While I waited for him, I clicked on his radio and heard some
unexpected good news: "The battle of Taierchwang was merely a
temporary setback. The Imperial Army will continue to push for-

ward against Chinese resistance. Those lives lost in the name of our Imperial Majesty have obtained great honor."

Then I kept busy by completing another sketch of the garden I'd begun earlier. I decided to start another painting in my grandfather's study, when I heard Matsu finally walk in from the garden. He paused a moment at the *shoji* door and coughed before he entered the room.

"I heard on the radio there were big losses at the battle of Taierchwang," I said.

Matsu simply grunted in response.

I continued to mix the paints, halfheartedly trying to begin work. I was looking for any distraction to continue the happiness I'd felt since I heard of the Chinese victory at Taierchwang. I finished squeezing out some yellow paint onto the wooden tray.

But instead of quickly leaving the room as he usually did, Matsu stood by the desk watching me. He reached out and touched the white canvas propped up on the easel. "Good," he said, "another painting."

"I hope I can begin something," I answered.

"You will," he said, knowingly.

I wished I could be as certain as Matsu, who never seemed to have a second thought about anything. He was always as definite as stone. I looked away from the empty canvas.

"I'll leave you to your painting," Matsu said. "I have to start lunch."

"It's still early," I mumbled. I only half heard him as I continued to mix colors.

"I thought we would visit Sachi afterward."

I nodded absentmindedly. Suddenly, what Matsu had said sunk in. I looked up with a quick jerk of my head. I wanted to tell him how happy I was about going to see Sachi, but he was already out of my grandfather's study and back in his kitchen. I could hear him pour water into the old, battered pot he loved and set it with a dull clank on the fire to boil.

The walk to Yamaguchi was filled with anticipation. We left shortly after a simple lunch of noodles and fish cake. Matsu carried a small package that I guessed might be a gift for Sachi, but neither of us said anything. We walked up the mountain road in silence, each occupied with our own thoughts.

Besides seeing Keiko, and receiving Pie's letter, I was finally going to visit Sachi. As happy as I felt, I couldn't get rid of the bitter taste that I might have to return to Hong Kong soon, and that this could be my last visit to Yamaguchi.

As we came closer to Yamaguchi, Matsu slowed down and turned around, as if he suddenly remembered I was there behind him.

"Do you smell something burning?" he asked.

I stopped, and for the first time really paid attention to the trees and brush around me. There was a slight breeze which blew hot air our way. I instantly realized how quiet it was. There were no birds singing, and it seemed like I could even hear the slight intake of Matsu's breathing, and then it hit me: the faint smell of smoke that tinged the air. I looked up to the otherwise clear sky and saw a dark cloud of smoke rise above the trees between us and Yamaguchi.

"Look!" I said.

"Go back!" Matsu turned and began to run up the path.

I paused for a moment not knowing what to do. Matsu had already left a veil of dust behind him. Without thinking, I followed him up the road, moving as fast as my legs and lungs would allow me.

Matsu quickly created a distance between us, steadily running up the last half-mile to Yamaguchi. The heat and smoke grew stronger the farther I climbed. My heart was beating hard, but I refused to let my burning lungs slow me down. I paused once and looked up to see Matsu disappear into the smoky clearing. I took several deep breaths and continued up the path, following Matsu into the center of the small village, blinded by the stinging smoke as I used my hands to shield my mouth and eyes. I couldn't help but think of Pie's letter, and how the refugees who lived on the mountains were swept away by the rain. Yamaguchi had survived for years on this mountain; it would take more than rain to bring her down, but no one ever said anything about fire.

From what I could see, the houses on the edge of the clearing were still untouched by the flames. Whatever was burning came from the other side of the village, closer to where Sachi lived. My heart felt as if it would jump out of my chest. The deeper I ran into the village, the thicker and darker the smoke became. I coughed, and felt a stinging dryness in my throat as I searched my pocket for a handkerchief to cover my mouth. I forced myself to keep going and began to hear muffled voices rising above the hissing and crackling of burning wood. Before I knew what was going on, I was clipped from behind by someone who ran past me. I was knocked forward, but managed to right myself before I fell.

"*Mizu!*" the man shouted. "*Mizu!*"

I followed him. The large wooden buckets of water he carried splashed from side to side and onto the ground as he hurried toward the fire.

"Let me help you," I shouted, as I caught up to him. Whether he understood me or not, he relinquished one of the buckets, the rough rope scraping against my palm. With two hands, I was able to balance it without losing so much water.

Farther on, I could feel the intense heat and see the orange-red flames engulf a wooden shack, then jump up to the sky. The flames seem to swallow it within minutes as the hazy shapes of men and women rushed forward with buckets of water to put out the roaring flames. Other men climbed trees, cutting down the overhanging branches before they caught fire. I glanced quickly around but couldn't find Sachi. From out of nowhere, I heard Matsu's voice yell out directions to contain the fire before it reached any more of the houses. Behind me I heard a woman's voice scream and begin to sob. I swung my bucket of water as hard as I could, watching the water fly up to the roaring flames, doing very little to extinguish them.

Someone touched my shoulder and I turned around to see the man who'd given me the bucket. He gestured for me to follow him. He was small, yet powerfully built, but when we came to a large water barrel, I noticed the fingers on his hands were almost all eaten away. The thick, coarse ropes from the buckets of water he carried had burned long, red strips across his forearms. With the stumps of his arms he moved with remarkable speed, lowering a bucket into the barrel and pulling it up again filled with water. I dunked my handkerchief and tied it over my mouth and nose, then filled my empty bucket, too. It was plain to see that the barrel would never hold enough water to put out the driving flames. Still, we filled our buckets and repeated our struggle over and over again.

It felt like hours before the last flames were finally put out, and the smoke cleared enough for us to see that the fire had only consumed two or three houses. Using dirt from a fire break Matsu dug around the houses, the fire had been smothered before it could travel any further. We all stood dazed, covered in black ash and dirt. In the distance, I could see Sachi's house untouched. Huddled on her steps, she consoled another woman whose house had been lost.

I pulled my handkerchief off and wiped my face. When Matsu realized I had been one of the firefighters, he came over and gripped my shoulder. "Your *o-tōsan* would be very proud of you."

"How did it begin?" I asked.

Matsu rubbed the smoke from his eyes, red from the burning heat. "Nobody's certain yet," he answered. Then, in a voice filled with concern, he asked, "Are you all right? How are you feeling?"

I smiled. Even though my lungs still burned, and the desire to cough pulled at my throat, I didn't want to worry Matsu and simply said, "I've never felt better."

Matsu and I looked at the smoldering fire, as the villagers gathered around it, throwing water onto the blackened debris which hissed and smoked. I watched, and swallowed the smoky air. Most of the villager's dark veils and cloth bandages had fallen away during their desperate fight with the fire. But none of the terrible scars, the missing noses, fingers, and limbs stopped any man or woman from fighting bravely to save Yamaguchi. They stood around, and wiped the black ash from their faces, already making plans to rebuild.

"It's a good thing you decided to visit," I said.

Matsu laughed. "The *kami-sama* of the village must have been with Yamaguchi today."

"They're lucky to have you," I added.

Matsu looked away. "It's a good thing we stopped it. If the fire

122

had burned out of control, they would have lost everything."

"Is this the first time they've had a fire?"

"This is the biggest one that I know of," Matsu said. "They have been very careful. You must be, to live so far away and survive without any real mishaps." Matsu shook his head. "I guess it will only become harder as we all grow older."

I thought of how difficult it must be, to be so far from help in case of any emergencies. There was no Red Cross to turn to, no volunteers like Pie to help out, no family. It seemed so unfair that they would always have to fight alone to keep what little they had.

"Dōmo arigatō, gozaimasu," we suddenly heard a voice from behind us.

When we turned around, Sachi was kneeling on the ground, bowing so low her forehead touched the dirt.

Sachi poured out green tea into her familiar clay cups as we sat at her low table. The smell of smoke seem embedded in every crevice, from our clothes to the *tatami* mats.

"I told Tanaka-*san* not to save so many magazines. They were just sitting there ready to catch a spark," Sachi said, shaking her head. "Now they have lost everything they had."

"It can be replaced," Matsu said.

Sachi shook her head sadly. "They should not have to rebuild their lives twice."

"As long as they are alive to do so, that's what is important," Matsu said, as he drank his tea, then pushed the cup toward Sachi to be refilled.

"I've never seen such bravery," I added.

Sachi looked up and smiled. "It is not an act of bravery to try to save your own village. It is an instinct to protect what you possess. Bravery is when you step in to help when you have nothing to lose. Matsu-*san* and you, Stephen-*san,* are the brave ones."

"We had more to lose than you could know," Matsu said. I watched Sachi look down and blush.

I quickly drank the rest of my tea and stood up. "I think I'll go out and see what's going on," I said, glancing down at the two of them.

"Be careful, Stephen-*san*," I heard Sachi call out as I closed the door behind me.

When the smoke had finally cleared, the oil lamps glowed a hazy yellow in the darkness. The thick smell of smoke and scorched trees would linger much longer. The villagers, whom I guessed numbered near a hundred, gathered close by the burned area to pray and offer their many thanks to the *kami-sama* of the village at a makeshift altar.

We decided to spend the night at Yamaguchi. It made no sense to walk all the way back to Tarumi, only to return the next day to help clean up. Those who had lost their homes moved in with others in the village, their crowded shacks a welcome shelter. Matsu and I stayed at the home of a male villager, Hiro-*san*. He and I had already become fast friends carrying buckets of water from the water barrel to the fire. As soon as he heard that Matsu and I were staying, he was the first to volunteer to put us up for the night.

"We've had tougher times than this," Hiro-*san* later told me. "No one can tell Mother Nature what to do. We are powerless in her hands." He swung his deformed arms in front of me and smiled a toothless grin. We were sitting on the floor of his small two-room house. It was clean and spare, devoid of even the simplest luxuries and possessions. "Years ago, back in 1923, we had an earthquake which didn't leave a house standing."

"Was anybody killed?"

"We buried some," he answered, pointing out the window toward another clearing. "Over there, behind those trees. It might have been worse if we had stronger housing. Fortunately, our lightweight materials took fewer lives when they collapsed." Hiro knocked lightly on his thin walls, which were mainly pieces of *shoji* and wood scraps nailed together.

"How did you get the materials up here?" I asked. It was the first time I realized that everything had to be carried up to Yamaguchi.

Hiro pointed to his other small room where Matsu was preparing our bedding. "Mainly Matsu-*san*," he said, in a loud clear voice. "In the beginning, we could not have survived without his help. He is the true *kami* of Yamaguchi, which is what must have brought him here today."

I nodded my head proudly. "He never ceases to surprise me."

Hiro shifted his legs under his *zabuton,* then lowered his voice. "I've known Matsu-*san* for more years than I can remember, and he has never been a man you could take at face value."

"I guess you could say that about everyone here in Yamaguchi," I added.

Hiro laughed. "And what about you, Stephen-*san?* What does your perfect face tell us?"

"That I have a lot to learn," I answered, leaning over and filling his cup with tea.

I woke up earlier than Hiro or Matsu, my muscles tight and sore from fighting the fire. I slowly got up from the futon, pushing through the dull ache in my arms and legs, then quietly dressed and slipped out the front door before they awoke. The sun had just risen, with most of Yamaguchi still asleep. I took a deep breath, my throat dry and sore. The heavy smell of smoke lingered in the air, while the black, burnt scar left by yesterday's fire looked naked and raw in the gray morning light. I could faintly hear the dull stirrings of someone already awake inside one of the fragile shacks. I began to walk slowly toward Sachi's house, though I knew it was too early to bother her. Still, I had the strange urge to see her rock garden again, to sit amidst its quiet and think about how I was going to face all the noise of Hong Kong again.

I walked around to the side of the house toward the sleeve gate, just as we had done the day Matsu and I came to visit. The gate made a soft, creaking sound as I swung it open and gently closed it. When I turned around, the bright light of the morning sun had just filled the garden. It left the rushing stream of rocks aglow. I stood watching the way the light played off the rocks, knowing that in a few moments the sun would shift its position, and again the garden would appear different.

"Ohayōgozaimasu, Stephen-*san."*

I jumped when I heard Sachi's soft, unexpected voice. When I

125

turned around, she had just stepped out of the house in a blue cotton kimono and slid the *shoji* door closed behind her. Sachi appeared so thin and small, but her presence immediately filled the garden with a life of its own. It was as if she had suddenly lifted the garden from stillness and given it a soul. Then she came closer to me and bowed, rising slowly and completely removing the dark veil which covered her head and hid her scars. She smiled and said, "I thought I heard someone out here. You are up very early, Stephen-*san.*"

"*Ohayōgozaimasu,*" I bowed. "I couldn't sleep anymore." When I stood straight again, Sachi's hand was raised, shielding her eyes against the bright morning light.

"I find I don't sleep very much anyway," she smiled. "I become too anxious lying there. It makes much more sense to get up and begin doing something."

I breathed in the warm, smoke-tinged air, feeling both happy and sad in the quiet garden with Sachi. The same nagging thoughts of having to leave Tarumi came back to me. Each day as the war escalated in China, the faceless voice on the radio called on more Japanese young men "to fulfill the wishes of His Imperial Majesty," or to "dispel all the anxieties of your Emperor." Pie's letter and the large number of refugees who flooded into Hong Kong let me know it was only a matter of time before I'd have to leave Matsu and Sachi. But I tried to hold back these disturbing thoughts, so I wouldn't lose one precious moment of our morning together.

"And Matsu-*san?*" Sachi asked.

"He's still asleep."

Sachi nodded. "He must be exhausted. I often wonder where he gets all his energy." She glanced around her immaculate garden, then touched my arm lightly. "Come, Stephen-*san,* I would like to show you something."

I followed her to the back of the garden, where larger rocks naturally formed a small mountainside. I could see where Matsu had lent his special touch, filling crevices with a cascading stream of rocks, lined with patches of green moss along the edge. Sachi walked up a narrow path, quick and steady. Halfway up she stopped and turned to make sure I was still behind her. Sachi then kneeled and looked down among the rocks. I followed her smiling gaze to see what she had discovered. There, between two large rocks, grew a neat cluster of blooming flowers, startlingly beautiful, a splash of blue-purple rising out of a green patch of leaves, somehow thriving among the muted, gray stones.

"How are they able to grow here?" I asked, amazed that anything so delicate could grow among rocks.

Sachi smiled. "One of the small miracles of life," she said. "As Matsu would say, you cannot change the will of the gods once it is set."

The bubble-shaped buds sprouted up on tall, thin stems like sticks of incense.

"They're beautiful," I said.

"And persistent," Sachi laughed. She held a bud gently between her fingers. "They're called balloon flowers. You see how the buds are shaped like small balloons?"

I nodded happily, then leaned back against a rock and watched Sachi carefully tend to the sprouting buds. I could see in her face, what I had seen a hundred times in Matsu's when he worked in his garden: a perfect calm. I also began to wonder if the balloon flowers were really a miracle, or had Matsu secretly planted the seeds, knowing that Sachi would soon discover their beauty?

Then, as if she knew my thoughts, Sachi stopped, looked up at me, and said, "Time does change some things. I remember when I couldn't stand the sight or scent of a flower. They brought me nothing, neither beauty nor calm." Sachi pointed down to her garden. "I wouldn't allow Matsu to plant any flowers in this garden, because it was too difficult. They reminded me of the past, of Tomoko, and everything that came into my life only to leave after a short, beautiful burst."

"And now?" I asked.

Sachi brushed her hands together, and still kneeling, sat back against her legs. "And now, Stephen-*san,* I am thankful for any kind of beauty that may find its way to Yamaguchi. I never dreamed that after all these years I would have the good fortune to find a new friend such as you."

I paused in thought and ran my fingers through my hair. "I'm not sure how much longer I'll be staying in Tarumi. The war seems to be dictating my future."

Sachi nodded her head sadly. "You see, Stephen-*san,* even in

Yamaguchi we can't hide from it, we are all touched by the madness of it."

I didn't know what to say. It was hard to imagine our countries were at war, and that Sachi and I should be enemies. I felt Sachi's gaze upon me. "No matter what happens, I know we'll always be friends," I simply said.

Sachi smiled. "I would never think otherwise, Stephen-*san*."

I suddenly remembered Kenzo, something I'd almost forgotten about in all the excitement of the fire. "I'm sorry about the loss of your old friend, Kenzo-*san*."

Sachi looked down at her balloon flowers, then back at me with a pained expression. "I had always hoped we could find a way to live the rest of our lives in some kind of peace. I prayed to the gods for it, but it wasn't to be."

"I thought I was dreaming when I saw you at Kenzo-*san*'s burial," I said. I had no idea what Sachi's response might be and didn't want to embarrass her.

Without hesitation, Sachi answered, "I wanted to make sure Kenzo's spirit would be at peace. I knew it was important for me to say good-bye. I didn't decide to go until the very last moment, so Matsu had no idea I was there. He would have only worried needlessly."

"I never told Matsu I saw you," I quickly added, grateful now I had kept her presence a secret.

Sachi bowed low toward me.

We sat back in the silence as if it were a warm hand closed around us, protecting us. It didn't last for long. The day was beginning, and the distinct sounds of an awakening village could be heard in scattered voices and heavy pots of water put on the heated stones to boil for tea or rice.

I wanted to ask Sachi so many questions, the distant voices giving courage to mine. "You never wanted to live with the others in the village?" I asked.

Sachi took a deep breath, taking her time to answer. "I don't remember ever having made the choice. It was Matsu who built this house for me away from the village. At the time, he knew I couldn't face being so close to the others. He was the one who carted every piece of wood and stone up the mountain, when no one else would come within sight of us. In many ways, it was Matsu who built Yamaguchi. Many of us would have simply perished without him."

"That's what Hiro-*san* said."

"Ah yes, Hiro-*san* has been in Yamaguchi since the very beginning."

"What about Kenzo-*san?*" I dared to ask.

This time Sachi looked away for an even longer time. I waited patiently until she finally continued, "It all seems such a long time ago. I sometimes think I have lived two separate lives; one as a foolish young girl, and the other as a wiser woman who came to learn too late in life what was really important. All I remember is, when the disease chose me, Matsu was the only one I could stand to see."

"But why Matsu? You hardly knew him."

"Perhaps that's why. That, and his being the only one who could help me understand Tomoko's death when it seemed so senseless. Then, when I became afflicted with the disease, I panicked, and there was no one else I could turn to."

"Not even Kenzo?"

"Especially not Kenzo. How can I explain this, Stephen-*san?* He was someone very dear to me, someone I loved very much, but I always knew there was something lacking between us. When you're young, you can excuse many things, hoping they will strengthen with time. Kenzo was a good man, but he never had the inner strength to deal with such a tragedy. As long as things went smoothly, all was well. When the disease spread to me, I knew that he would never really understand how something so dishonorable could happen to us."

"But there's no excuse, it could have been treated, kept under control!"

Sachi shook her head. "Back then we had no idea what to do. All I knew was it would eventually turn me into a monster, and it had to do with some weakness within me."

"So you went to Matsu?"

Sachi stared blankly past me, then almost whispered. "It was Matsu who found me in my deepest shame."

I remained silent, hoping Sachi would put all the pieces together for me. But when she didn't continue, I asked, "I don't understand. How did Matsu find you?"

"It is a long story, Stephen-*san*," Sachi answered. She leaned over and touched her flowers tenderly.

"Please, if you're up to telling me, I would be honored to hear it."

"Sometimes it is better to let go of the past," Sachi faltered.

"Sometimes you can't let go of the past without facing it again," I added.

"You are as persistent as these flowers, Stephen-*san*," she smiled. "I can see you won't be leaving this house without taking some part of my past along with you."

"Only if you should honor me with it."

Sachi watched me closely for a moment, then touched the white scars that lined the left side of her face. She took another deep breath and let it out slowly. "You must be hungry, Stephen-*san*, let us go inside. The rice should be just about ready."

Without another word, Sachi stood up and dusted off her kimono as she made her way back down the path. I slowly rose and followed, taking it to mean she had said enough. But when Sachi reached the bottom of the path, she turned to me and said, "I would not want you to listen to my story on an empty stomach."

I sat down at Sachi's familiar, low black lacquer table as she disappeared into the kitchen. She returned with a tray of tea, pickled vegetables, and two bowls of steaming rice, then she kneeled at the table and placed them in front of me. It was hot and delicious. I'd forgotten how parched my throat felt when I woke up this morning. I had left Hiro's without drinking or eating a thing, so Sachi's rice and vegetables were a gift. When I had finished, she pushed her bowl toward me without saying a word and gestured for me to eat some more. Grateful, I watched Sachi sip from her cup of tea. I could tell by the way she looked blankly past me that she was already deep in remembering. I remained silent, waiting. Then in a soft, clear voice Sachi began to tell me her story.

* * *

"If I had been brave like some of the others, I would be in the other world now. I still remember the salty ocean water, stained red with blood that morning so many years ago. And I often recall my father's voice telling me how the samurai maintained their honor by committing *seppuku*. The hardest part was the first thrust of the knife. After it ripped through your body, all worldly pain would be put to rest.

"I still dream sometimes that I have the chance to do it all over again, only this time I swim into that ocean of red. At least then, there would be no memories. I know it was a child's wish to think I could forget, but the memories haven't faded with time as I hoped. By seventeen, I had shamed my family twice; first, when the disease chose me, and then when I was too weak to honor them with my death.

"My father had hoped that by my ending my life, he could retain the honor of our family. And in the end, I didn't even allow him to have that. It would have simply been doing *'ko,'* submitting to his wishes. It was an obligation, the supreme duty of a child to adhere to one's parents, but I failed my father.

"Only now, as I move toward the end of my life can I begin to understand the enormous task that was asked of me, and to forgive myself for not completing it. And like a child, Stephen-*san,* I have reached the age where I may be unhampered by shame, finally free to tell you my story, which even now feels as if it were still just *kino* and filled with so many dreams.

"I remember the first time I met Matsu. I was twelve or thirteen and had gone to visit Tomoko. Before then I had only seen her brother in passing or from a distance. Matsu was three years older than I, and already more muscular than most of the men in the village. He resembled his father, both of them thick and silent as they worked together in the garden of their house. Tomoko, with her mother's fragile beauty, seemed unrelated to the two men I met that morning. They awkwardly greeted me with quick bows, and while his father went to look for Tomoko, Matsu turned back to his work, gently smoothing dirt around a new planting. I stood there on my wooden sandals, rocking back and forth against the flat, uneven stones that lined the path to their house, wondering if I should try to make polite conversation.

" 'Sumimasen, Matsu-san,' I said timidly. 'What is it that you're planting?'

"Matsu took a moment before he looked up, as if he wasn't sure I had really spoken to him. 'Chrysanthemums,' he finally mumbled.

"I was about to continue our conversation when I heard Tomoko calling for me. When I turned back to Matsu, he was already at work digging another hole as if I had never been there.

"Afterward, Tomoko and I often saw Matsu walking from town to your *ojī-san*'s beach house. He would mutter something and bow as we passed on the road, and there were times when Tomoko, in a playful mood, would tease her brother for being so sullen. 'Matsu, you're too much like an old man, come with us down to the beach!' she would say, laughing. He would only shrug his shoulders and walk quickly away from us. Sometimes, when I turned back, I could see that Matsu had stopped and was staring after us as we continued to laugh and make our way down the road.

" 'What's the matter with Matsu?' I asked Tomoko one of those afternoons.

" 'He's all right,' Tomoko answered, serious for a change. 'Matsu's like my father. They get along better with silk trees and chrysanthemums than with people.'

"At the time I didn't think to ask anything else. After all, Matsu was only Tomoko's older brother. I dismissed his remoteness as something that would never affect me.

"Yet my friendship with Tomoko flourished. We did everything together, growing strong like stalks of bamboo. While we might sometimes bend one way or the other, it would take a great deal to break us. Even now, after so many years, I have to smile when I recall that the one thing about me which constantly annoyed Tomoko was that I was slightly taller. And like most things having to do with appearance, she was greatly conscious of it, holding her shoulders straight back with her head lifted regally to give her more height. In turn, I humored her by slouching a bit.

"Tomoko had a spark which seemed to ignite everything she touched. You couldn't help but be drawn to her beauty and enthusiasm. And she did everything quickly, from her school work to her household duties. Perhaps too quickly, now that I speak of it. Sometimes a body can simply burn out too soon. But how I waited for Tomoko each day, knowing that once she was finished with her work, she would come to my house to get me. And no matter how much work I had to do, Tomoko could always persuade me to follow her. We would usually take a walk down to the beach, wearing the American-style cotton dresses Tomoko's mother had sewn for us at her daughter's pleading. Tomoko always wanted to be the first to do things differently from the other girls, and I was always her willing accomplice.

"It was right after my fourteenth birthday that Kenzo began to pay more attention to us. Sometimes he and his friends would be down at the beach or grouped at his father's teahouse where Kenzo helped after school. At first I thought he was interested in Tomoko, but he slowly began to speak more to me. Tomoko would tease me, saying, 'You see, Sachi, Kenzo-*san* doesn't even see me when you are around. I might as well be invisible!'

"But Tomoko was far from invisible. She was too beautiful not to be noticed. And though she was pursued by many of the young boys in Tarumi, she never had any real interest in them. Tomoko always spoke of going to Tokyo after middle school, and of finding work there in a large office, or perhaps a department store where they carried all the latest fashions. No village boy was going to ruin her plans. Even as a young girl, she always seemed to be aware of how far she could go with her beauty. I sometimes still wonder if she had valued other things as well, would she be with us now? While it wouldn't have stopped the disease from touching her, it might have allowed her to live with it. But that seems to be another story, Stephen-*san*.

"I didn't know at first what good friends Kenzo and Matsu were. I more or less stumbled on the fact one day when I saw them together at the teahouse. It was the first time I had seen Matsu as a real person, laughing and talking comfortably. But as soon as I made my presence known, Matsu stood up, bowed politely, and returned to being Tomoko's silent brother.

" 'How do you know Matsu-*san?*' I asked Kenzo. He simply

smiled and answered, 'It isn't as if Tarumi's a large city. Matsu's always been a friend of mine.'

" 'But I thought he didn't like people?' I said, naively.

Kenzo laughed. 'Only some people,' he answered.

"Afterwards, I made a few weak attempts to speak to Matsu when I was visiting Tomoko, but his abrupt replies led me to believe that perhaps I was one of those people he chose not to like.

"I was too blinded by my youth, along with what I knew was a life blessed with good fortune to notice anything else. Kenzo and I continued to grow closer, and by my fifteenth birthday we were betrothed by our parents. I prepared to become his wife by learning from my mother to cook the foods he liked, such as pickled cabbage and *tonkatsu,* and to keep a neat home. During those months of preparation, everyone and everything else simply hovered in the shadows. You see, Stephen-*san*, I'm ashamed to say that it wasn't until Tomoko's tragedy, and then my own, that I really began to know Matsu.

"And so it was almost a year after Tomoko died that the whitish rash appeared on my left forearm. It was no larger than a yen coin. At first, I thought nothing of it, until I started to feel feverish and dizzy and the rash wouldn't go away. Then I had to admit that it might be a sign of the disease. I panicked, remembering it was a rash that first appeared on Tomoko's face. I hid it from my family under the sleeve of my kimono and after a while, the rash began to fade away, only to return a few months later. By then a favored day for the marriage between Kenzo and me had been chosen by our families. I was so young, and until then I had thanked the gods for my lucky match with a young man whom I loved. But every time I dared to look at the blotchy rash, it was like a nightmare. I didn't know where to turn, and then I thought of Matsu. He had been so kind and understanding when Tomoko had taken her life. He was the only one who wasn't afraid to speak to me of her death, who told me Tomoko would want me to go on with my own life. I felt I could trust him to help me face whatever it was.

"One afternoon when I knew Matsu would be working at your family's house, I stopped by to talk to him. I remember being very scared. I didn't really know what I was going to say. I just somehow prayed he would know what to do to make the rash go away.

" 'Konnichiwa, Matsu-san,' I said. He was so surprised to see me, he almost stumbled in his hurry to rise from where he was planting round islands of green moss. Even now I feel bad, because I hadn't really spoken to him in months, even though he had been so kind to me about Tomoko. Nevertheless, that day in your *ojī-san*'s garden, Matsu bowed low and said, 'I am honored to see you again, Sachi-*san*.'

"I didn't know what to say, so I simply held out my left arm. At first, Matsu stood back, as if I might strike him if he came closer. 'What is this?' I asked, pointing to the pale, blotchy patch. At once he moved closer to me, taking my hand in his and letting his fingers lightly brush over the rash. Matsu never seemed to be afraid of the disease, nor any of us here in Yamaguchi, even after we became monsters to the rest of Tarumi.

" 'Is it the same thing Tomoko had?' I asked.

"Matsu was silent for a long time, before he said, 'I can't be sure. Have you seen the *isha?*'

"At the time there was a young doctor vacationing in the village. I told him I hadn't shown anyone. I didn't want my family or Kenzo to find out. Matsu bowed and told me to wait for him, he would take care of everything. In the next moment, he was gone. It seemed an eternity until he returned, but when he did, he brought with him the reddest plums I've ever seen. 'Eat them,' he told me, 'they will give you strength. I've asked the young doctor to meet us here.' Then he brought me some cool water and while we waited for the doctor to come I ate and drank. I would have done whatever Matsu told me at that point, but I don't think I said more than two words while we waited. Then later, after the doctor came, I said even less while he examined my arm and confirmed my worst fears. 'I'm sorry,' the young doctor said, shaking his head. 'Every day there are new treatments that may help to keep it under control,' he went on, but all I remember hearing was a terrible scream that filled my head, drowning all the rest of his words. When I calmed down again, all I could hear was Matsu's voice talking quietly to the doctor, thanking him for his time. The next thing I knew the doctor was gone with a basket of plums and Matsu was silently leading me back home.

"I hid the rash for as long as I could. Matsu tried to convince

135

me to tell my family, but I was too ashamed. I knew it would be a great dishonor for my father to bear, and I couldn't even imagine telling Kenzo. Then, several months after it first appeared on my arm, the rash began to spread up my neck toward my face. I knew I could no longer hide the truth. It would only be a matter of time before everyone would notice.

"The night I told Kenzo, he thought it was all a big joke. 'But you look beautiful,' he laughed. 'Who put you up to this?' Then I showed him. I will never forget the look in his eyes when he realized it wasn't a joke—a look of both fear and betrayal. He quickly dropped my hand and without a word, backed away from me and walked out. I never saw Kenzo again until that day at your *ojī-san*'s house. And even after so many years, I saw the same betrayed look in his eyes.

"I don't want you to be angry with the dead, Stephen-*san*. Kenzo didn't know what else to do. I know now that it was too much for him. He believed life should be simple and uniform, filled with a sense of order and honor. In the end, he did stay with me in his own way, the only way he knew how.

"At first my father would also not accept it. He dragged me to the Tama Shrine to pray and be purified by a curing priest. When everything else proved fruitless, he resorted to trying the *moxa* treatment, which was igniting a little cone of powder directly on my skin to burn away the rash. Aside from the agonizing pain and the smell of scorched flesh which I'll never forget, the darkened rash soon reappeared and spread to another spot. My father would no longer look at me and my mother simply cried. By then, four other villagers had found signs of the disease. It must have been incubating for years before it showed its face to those of us most susceptible to it. My father was afraid it might spread to my younger brother, and the villagers also grew frightened. They wanted the afflicted ones sent away from them. There had been rumors of a place for our kind in the mountains, but no one really believed these mountain people existed. We had nowhere to go, no way to know what would become of us. It seemed easier simply to end our lives.

"There was nothing left for me to do. I cried until I had no more tears left. Then I prayed for a day and night so the gods would give me strength. The next morning those of us cursed with the disease sought to end our misery and restore honor to our families. While the village still slept, the five of us walked silently to the edge of the sea.

"Even now I can feel the cold waves pushing and pulling against my legs as I stood knee-deep in the ocean that morning. There was a flock of birds flying overhead, as if they had come to watch, their squawking voices leading us on. As the water lapped around me, I saw one man, the father of a school friend, walk straight into the ocean. He never turned back, nor hesitated. One moment he was there, and in the next he had been swallowed by the sea. It was a nightmare.

"One older woman took a knife from the sleeve of her kimono, raised her hands, and slashed her wrists. I remember how the blood streamed down her arms, staining the water around her. She turned toward me, and with a strange, calm smile, bowed low before handing me her knife. It felt so light and cold in my hand, I wondered how it could possibly end a life. I looked down at the sharp blade, and saw my hand covered with the woman's blood. I wanted to scream, but it seemed I had suddenly lost my voice. Just as quickly, the knife slipped from my hand into the water.

" 'Don't be frightened, child,' the old woman mumbled, 'Find the knife and end your misery. Return honor to your family.'

"But at that moment I knew I didn't have the courage of Tomoko, nor of this woman dying before me. When she reached out toward me, I pushed her back, and she fell to her knees, still crying out for me to end my life, as a wave washed over her.

"I turned away from her and just began running. I ran and ran, away from the beach and all the death and dying. Even now, I don't remember what I was thinking. The greatest honor I could have given my family was that of my death, and I ran from it. I was frightened at not fulfilling my obligation, not giving *ko* to my parents. Yet, there was a voice inside of me that kept telling me to escape. I ran away from Tarumi, as if it were the diseased one. At nightfall I hid among the trees along the stretch of road that now leads to Yamaguchi.

"It was so cold that first night alone, and I was so hungry. I began to think that maybe death was a better way, after all. I had never before felt that black void of abandonment, but I knew no one would be looking for me. As far as my family and the village were concerned, I had drowned with the others that morning. Everything had been planned without anyone's knowledge. We had each left notes for our families, hoping we would honor them better in the other world. I had said good night to my family for the last time, knowing that the moment I stepped out of the house that morning, I would no longer be a burden on them. The only way I could still honor them was to allow them to think I was dead.

"But the following morning in the woods, I was awakened by the sounds of footsteps. I was so cold I had covered myself with a pile of leaves. If I moved, I would surely draw attention to where I was, so I lay silent and still, hoping whoever or whatever it was would move on. I remember staring up through the leaves to the very blue sky. It appeared so sharp and clear it seemed unreal. When I heard the steps growing closer, I closed my eyes and began praying to the gods. When I opened my eyes again, I could hear breathing and almost feel the warmth of another body, it was so close to me. Then, I heard his voice call out, low and soothing: 'Sachi! Sachi, it's me Matsu, let me help you.'

"I thought I had died and gone into the other world. How had he ever found me?

" 'Matsu?' I whispered, springing up from the pile of leaves like a wounded animal. I forgot everything, even the shame of allowing him to see me in such a state.

"Matsu took one look at me and began to laugh. 'Is that you?' he asked, 'or is it the fox god, Inari?' It was the first time Matsu had ever joked with me. He had always been so quiet.

"But it wasn't the time for laughter. I was so tired and hungry. If I had been the god Inari, I might have made some food and water appear. But it was my good fortune that Matsu found me. Smiling kindly, he bowed low and helped me brush away the leaves.

" 'I have been looking all night for you,' he said.

" 'Are there others?' I asked, my throat so dry and sore I could barely get the words out.

" 'They think you have gone into a better world,' he answered.

" 'How did you find me?'

"Matsu just smiled. He opened the *furoshiki* he carried and took out a bottle of green tea. Even though the tea tasted cold and bitter, I have never been more grateful for anything else in my life. He also brought along some rice cakes and a package of dry seaweed which I ate hungrily.

"When I had finished, I bowed to Matsu and asked again, 'How did you know I was here?'

" 'Tomoko,' " he whispered.

" 'What about Tomoko?' " I asked, swallowing the last of the bitter tea.

"Matsu gathered up what little was left of the food and wrapped it back up in the *furoshiki*. 'I followed you and the others down to the beach yesterday morning. I wondered if you might try to find your way to peace as she did.'

" 'I couldn't,' I began to cry, turning away in shame. Then Matsu leaned over close to my ear. He smelled of sweat and the earth as he whispered, 'It takes greater courage to live.'

"I am a lucky one. I know now that there are rare people who will help you carry your burdens through this life. I remember my mother telling me it was because these people were doing penance for a wrong they had done in a past life. It is my belief that perhaps I had wronged someone and was serving my own sentence. But what of Matsu? Had he been so cruel in another life? In Tarumi he had always made his way as quietly as possible, never creating any disturbances. But look what he has become to me, my bearer of burdens, the last one I would ever have dreamed of being my savior.

"After that, amidst the silence of those trees Matsu told me of others who had chosen not to end their lives. Instead, they had begun a village in the mountains, a village called 'Yamaguchi,' where they were trying to live out their lives the best they could.

" 'How do you know so much?' I asked him.

" 'It is where I had hoped to take Tomoko,' he answered."

I leaned back heavily, and the *shoji* wall rattled as if there were an earthquake. A shiver ran through my body. I couldn't take my eyes off Sachi, I could only draw in a deep breath of sweet air and let it out again. I had no voice for words. Then as if Sachi understood exactly what I was feeling, she placed her withered hand on mine, giving me her warmth.

"We began our journey up the mountain that morning. I felt comforted having Matsu there, like a warm protecting blanket. Matsu had seen all my *haji,* the shame which burned inside of me, yet he did not abandon me. For a moment, I had even forgotten the ordeal of the day before. It was like a bad dream with only one saving grace: my family thought I was dead. I suddenly felt lighter, relieved of the burden that had been placed on me as a living person. Yet, there was still someone who knew that I existed, which made me feel like a real person again, not a ghost roaming the earth.

"But the nightmare returned all too soon. When we reached the clearing, I saw with my own eyes that Yamaguchi was only the beginning of my horrors. At the time, the village was no more than a few broken-down shacks occupied by lepers with much more advanced symptoms than mine. Matsu told me that many of them had come from other parts of Japan. I tried to be polite, but I had to cover my mouth and nose with my hand against the nauseating smell of rotting flesh which preceded several of the mutilated villagers. They seemed to know Matsu already. Most of them were dirty and unkempt, their soiled bandages half falling off, and the stench grew stronger the closer we came to the center of the clearing. When I saw the raw, open wounds, the flesh eaten away where noses and mouths had once been, the fingers and toes that had dropped off, I felt sick to my stomach. They were all monsters. I remember thinking that if Yamaguchi were to be my fate, then death would be kinder. I looked at Matsu and suddenly saw him as my enemy for bringing me to such a place. Without a word, I turned around and began running. I had no idea where I was going, but I started back down the mountain path. The sun was hot and heavy overhead and the bright light hurt my eyes.

" 'Sachi! Sachi, where are you going?' I could hear Matsu calling after me. I became more frightened when I heard his dull footsteps closing in on me. I tried to run faster, the throbbing in my head growing stronger until I tripped over something and fell headfirst onto the ground. I don't remember what happened next, but when I awoke, it was dark. When my eyes adjusted to the shadows, I saw that I was lying in one of the makeshift shacks, the outline of a woman by the door, asleep. I thought about running away again, but just sitting up made me dizzy. I was dressed only in my undergarments and I couldn't find my kimono. I was so scared and tired, and there was nowhere else for me to go. I closed my eyes again and the next thing I knew it was morning and I could hear the woman quietly moving around the small, bare room.

"At first, I pretended to be asleep, opening my eyes just enough to watch the blurry figure dressed in black pour water from a wooden bucket into a basin. But before I had a chance to decide what to do, the slight old woman turned around and was at the side of my futon looking down at me. I don't know if she knew I was awake or not, but then she knelt down beside me and gently wiped my face with a wet towel before laying it on my forehead. I don't think I've ever felt anything more soothing. It was only then that I opened my eyes to take my first good look at Michiko, the *obā-san* of Yamaguchi.

"Even now, when I think of her kindness, there is pain in my heart remembering my first reaction to her. When I fully opened my eyes and saw the noseless face and the distorted features eaten away by the disease, I let out a scream that brought the entire village to the door of the shack. The next thing I knew, Matsu was standing beside Michiko reassuring her. She nodded her head, bowed, and moved out of the way. I would only calm down when Michiko had left the room and I was alone with Matsu.

" 'Why did you bring me here? Why couldn't you just let me die in the woods?' I screamed at him.

"Matsu stood there silent. After a long time watching me, he simply said, 'Go then.'

"Then it was my turn to be silent. I didn't know what to do or where to go. I quickly slipped on my soiled kimono which lay on the ground next to me, then started to get up from the futon, not caring if Matsu was there or not. He never moved to stop me, though I heard him shuffling his feet against the dirt floor before he turned around and left the shack. After a few moments it was

Michiko who returned, this time her face covered by a dark veil. She bowed low and said, 'Forgive me for frightening you.'

"I stood there ashamed, but couldn't bring myself to look at her. The kindness in her voice filled me with *haji*. Then I felt her deformed hand lifting my chin, so that I had no choice but to look up at her veiled face. And through the dark cloth I could see the outlines of her lips form a smile.

" 'I'm sorry,' I whispered.

" 'What is there to be sorry about?' she said, 'I would be frightened by this face if it were the first thing I saw in the morning. I often forget what effect it has on those who first come here. Especially a young girl as *kirei* as you, Sachi-*san*.'

" 'I can't stay here,' I said.

"Michiko didn't answer me right away. She ladled some water into a pot and placed it on the heated stone to boil. 'There aren't many choices for us,' she finally said.

" 'I'll end my life rather than stay here!' I threatened, taking a step toward the door, only to stop and wait for Michiko to say something. Instead, she turned away from me, remaining as silent as the earth. I watched her reach up to the makeshift shelf, take down a jar filled with green tea and sprinkle some leaves into a clay pot. When the water boiled, Michiko poured it into the pot of green leaves and we both waited in the thick silence. I felt strangely calmed by this simple ritual I had seen my mother do many hundred times before. It was all that seemed to make sense in this place and I held on to it as if I were drowning. I should have been halfway back down the mountain, but I couldn't let go of the sweet, warm smell, the last thin thread to my childhood.

"I have stayed in Yamaguchi from that day on. Matsu began to live between the two worlds, returning to Tarumi to work, sleep, and buy the much-needed supplies and building materials for Yamaguchi. To this day, I don't know what he must have told his family about his disappearance all those months he spent taking care of me. Fortunately, Matsu was always one to go his own way, even as a young boy.

"But you must remember, Stephen-*san,* I was barely seventeen and had never been away from my family. It did not all occur with

142

the ease of my words. I was hysterical for months, and wouldn't talk or trust anyone except for Matsu and, little by little, Michiko. I don't know if I was more frightened by the fact that I was living among monsters, or the thought that I would soon turn into one of them. You see, I was very selfish then, thinking the world revolved around me. Tomoko and I had always been treated like princesses when we were young, and I never knew what it meant to go out of my way for others. And though it shocked me to realize that Tomoko's brother was creating a new life for me, I was totally dependent on him.

"Even now after so many years have passed, I still don't know how Matsu and Michiko were able to stand me. When I first realized what my life had become, I couldn't help but throw my anger at them. Yet, they put up with my hours of crying and my refusal even to get up and bathe. They surely must have thought that I was the monster, and not all those who were courageously trying to build Yamaguchi. But never once did either of them raise a voice to me.

"There were so many nights I lay on a thin futon on the hard ground of Michiko's shack, unable to sleep. I felt as if I would suffocate as I listened to Michiko's labored breathing, my eyes burning with tears. I cried out of a deep loneliness for my past life, and because it was all I had left. How many times did I wonder what Kenzo was doing? Or, if my mother had stored away my wedding kimono along with my other childhood treasures in her black lacquer chest? Sometimes I felt like I would go insane not having the answers to such simple questions. Of course, it was always hardest during the night, when the darkness stole away any signs of hope. Sometimes I would strike my forehead with my fist until my face was bruised and my fingernails had dug bloody pockets in my palm.

"Only slowly did I begin to heal. Every so often I was overwhelmed by a phantom pain that cut through me like a knife. I was certain that if I looked down I would find blood all over, like the knife I once held in my hands, but it was all in my mind. Over the months I learned to keep these thoughts to myself. So when Matsu thought I was well enough that I would no longer hurt myself, he gradually began to leave me with Michiko for longer periods of time. Then, one morning Matsu just didn't come. We thought nothing of it since he would often skip a day, but when he didn't return for several more days, I began to worry, pacing the small shack I shared with Michiko. What if something had happened to him? He was the only connection I had left to my former life. The thought of losing the one person in Tarumi who knew I existed was too difficult to bear. Michiko tried to soothe me by saying, 'Matsu-*san* will be here soon, there's no need to worry.' But the fear inside of me just grew stronger. For the first time since I'd arrived in Yamaguchi, I walked out of the small shack by myself and began to wander around the village, anxiously looking out for Matsu. And while there was no sign of him, three old lepers began hobbling after me, trying to talk. 'Where are you going, Sachi-*san?* Let us help you,' they said. I know they didn't mean any harm, but I was young and still frightened by their deformities and strange smells. When one of them reached out and tried to take my arm, I began screaming. It wasn't until Michiko came running that I calmed down. I remember that in her hurry she had forgotten to wear her veil. But when I saw her dark eyes and heard the soothing words she whispered, I let myself relax in her arms, feeling safe at last.

"Sweet Michiko-*san*. Even now after so many years I can still see her, and I sometimes dream of her walking through the door with her quiet words. I came to welcome her monstrous face, which had once terrified me. I can't forget the ragged hole where her nose was and the crusted sores where her eyebrows used to be. The leprosy had nearly consumed her entire face. She must have already been in the last stages when I came to Yamaguchi. She disguised the smell of her decaying flesh by rubbing crushed eucalyptus leaves all over her body. What was left of her hair she kept shiny by washing with a seaweed mixture. She would tell me many such secrets during our few years together. By the time I knew her, she was shrunken and old, and I tried not to imagine the woman she was before the disease.

"But even better than the advice she shared as I adjusted to my new life were the stories Michiko told me. I thirsted for every word as if my life somehow grew with them. And so it was that

Michiko nurtured my body those early days, and kept my mind alive with her many stories.

"On the third night of Matsu's absence, I was so terrified that he would never return, I lay huddled in my bed. I wouldn't eat a thing, only sipped the pungent green tea Michiko brought to me. I had just closed my eyes and begun to cry again when I felt her beside my futon and heard her soft voice fill the room. 'When I was young, Sachi-*san,* my mother told me stories when I wasn't feeling well. One story which I treasure most I would like to tell you now.'

"I didn't say a word, just lay there nodding my head in the flickering light of the candle, waiting.

" 'There was once a girl named Sumiko,' Michiko began, 'who was born in the Mie Prefecture, near the city of Toba on the Shima Peninsula. Ever since she was a little girl she had dreamed of becoming an *ama-san,* a pearl diver, like her mother. Sumiko thought they were the most beautiful women alive, dressed in their white cotton clothing from head to toe. Even as a small child she watched her mother dive into the sea over and over again, bringing up with her the rough, sea-shaped oyster and abalone shells until she filled a large wooden bucket. Sumiko's father watched from shore, as the village men had for hundreds of years. Only women dived for the shiny pearls. It was believed that women were better able to stand the cold. Some of the *ama-sans* stayed underwater for so long Sumiko was afraid their lungs would burst and their lifeless bodies would float to the surface like seaweed. But her father always reassured Sumiko that her mother could hold her breath longer than anyone. To Sumiko, the *ama-sans* were like a school of white dolphins flipping gracefully through the water. And every evening Sumiko would lift the rough shells from the bucket, prying open their closed mouths to find the translucent pearls hiding under their tongues.'

"Worried as I was about Matsu's disappearance that evening, Michiko had my attention. I lay there listening, trying to imagine those women pearl divers, gleaming white on the glassy surface of the sea. Michiko's voice filled the small room like magic.

" 'Sumiko was married at fourteen to a village boy named Akio, whom she had known all of her life. Their families were happy and so were they, especially when Sumiko became an *ama-san*. The water was so cold that day, but the moment she dived deep into the water and pulled up her first shell, she felt as if the sea were part of her. She dived again and again, filling not one bucket, but three. Akio had to threaten to jump in and pull her out before she would stop. Sumiko thought she couldn't have been happier—until the day she discovered she was expecting her first child. When she told Akio, they both laughed with joy.

" 'But as with all life, things don't often turn out as planned. As Sumiko grew bigger and bigger with child, Akio began to worry and asked her to stop diving. "When our baby is big and strong, you can dive again," he said. Sumiko knew it was a reasonable request and reluctantly agreed.

" 'But, being an *ama-san* was in her blood. After a week of not diving, Sumiko became ill. She grew so weak she could barely get out of bed. The village doctor was summoned, but he couldn't find anything wrong. Sumiko seemed perfectly healthy and the baby was doing fine. Yet, Sumiko grew weaker each day that she didn't dive. Akio's heart grew heavy. If he didn't do something soon, he would lose both Sumiko and the baby.

" 'One night Sumiko grew faint and cold. Akio was barely able to detect her heartbeat. Out of sheer desperation, he carried his frail wife down to the sea. As he braved the cold waters, Akio feared this would be their last chance. He lowered Sumiko into the cold water, holding her up in his arms. Like a miracle a great warmth surged through her body, warming the water around them. Very slowly Sumiko's eyes opened wide and she regained her strength. Akio called out her name with happiness, but Sumiko only looked at him with blank eyes, then turned away and dived into the sea. Akio tried to stop her, but in a moment Sumiko had disappeared. He watched for hours, hoping she would return, but the calm, dark water held no sign of her.

" 'For three months Akio mourned his loss. Then one night as he was preparing for bed, he heard a strange voice singing. Rushing outside, he was delighted to see Sumiko standing beside their house. She was completely dressed in the white clothes of an *ama-san,* and she was thin again. "Where have you been?" asked Akio, but before he could embrace her, she lifted toward him something wrapped in a white blanket: Their baby! Akio was filled with joy as he held his little daughter, but when Sumiko turned back to the sea, he cried out for her to stop. At the water's edge of the sea, she called out to him, "I must return to the sea now. My life as I knew it is over now. See that our child lives well." And with that, Sumiko vanished forever.

" 'Though he never knew where she had gone, Akio seemed to know that some mysterious blessing had allowed his wife to bring his daughter back to him. He raised his little Kuniko to be a fine young woman, who looked so much like her mother his heart often ached looking at her. And when she expressed a wish to be a pearl diver like her mother, Akio never said one word to stop her, knowing that somewhere in the dark depths of the sea, Sumiko would always be there to protect her.'

"When Michiko finished telling me this story, I felt I'd been awakened from a dream. All night long I lay in bed thinking of Sumiko the pearl diver, and how she had managed to give her daughter life, knowing that she couldn't stay and watch her grow. What bargain had she struck with the sea that allowed Sumiko to return her daughter to her husband? These thoughts turned around and around in my head until I fell into a deep sleep.

"When Matsu finally returned the following day, he appeared pale and thinner. I learned that he had been very ill and wasn't able to make the journey up the mountain. I felt every bit the fool I was. I never stopped to think how much effort and energy it took him to travel back and forth to Tarumi. He had always seemed indestructible.

" 'Are you feeling better?' I bowed.

Matsu nodded his head. 'Much better.'

" 'I was worried that something might have happened,' I said, timidly.

"Matsu smiled. 'Were you all right here with Michiko?'

" 'She helped me through a difficult time,' I admitted.

" 'What happened?' Matsu asked, concerned.

147

" 'It's not important now,' I answered, getting up and putting on some water to boil.

"I could feel Matsu's eyes watching me intently. I was becoming very uncomfortable under his gaze when he said softly, 'You've changed.' Then he quickly asked, 'What did you talk about with Michiko? Did she tell you she was once a pearl diver?'

"I stopped short, surprised, then asked Matsu, 'Do you know if she had a little girl?'

"At first Matsu was quiet, his forehead creased in remembering. 'Yes,' he finally said. 'She did have a daughter.'

"You see, Stephen-*san,* that day I learned that there were greater losses than mine. Every man and woman in Yamaguchi had a life before coming here. From then on I could never look at any of them without asking myself: 'Whom did they leave behind? How much did they give up? What bargains did they try to make?' If I hadn't learned humility before then, from that day on I knew what the word meant. Here in Yamaguchi I learned that beauty exists where you least expect to find it.

"Very slowly, Matsu and Michiko taught me how to live with the others. And with myself. Gradually the thought of ending my life left my mind. As if I were a child learning to walk again, Matsu enticed me to take one step at a time: Bringing me first to Yamaguchi, then building me a house, and finally, creating this garden for me to tend.

"During those first years the village grew slowly, taking on a strange life of its own. We planted vegetable gardens which soon grew lush in orderly rows as clean and straight as the flight of a heron—so different from the gardeners' spreading scars, ragged and splotched. The terrible rotting smell was made bearable with fresh bandages and eucalyptus leaves. More shelters were built to house the displaced who found their way to Yamaguchi. The kindness of these villagers soon made me see how wrong I was in thinking they were monsters. They brought me rice and what little they could spare to help me feel more comfortable. In turn, I began to work in the vegetable garden, gather wood for the fire, and carry water up from the stream.

"But the fourth year brought me more grief. Michiko grew increasingly weak. The smallest thing would tire her, so that even the simplest cooking and cleaning became my responsibility. We had switched places and I was the one nursing Michiko. I remember those days so vividly. By then her body was a mass of rotting flesh. She could only lie down in excruciating pain, her nerves invaded by the disease. Near the end she became completely blind and unable to move. I could only pray to the gods to let her go quickly, freeing her from her suffering. But never once did Michiko curse the life she had been given.

"On the morning of her death, after she had had a terrible night of pain, I was awakened by Michiko calling out the name 'Kuniko' in one labored breath. By the time I reached her side, she was already gone. I stroked her ravaged, almost featureless face, feeling a great relief that she had at last found peace. I will never forget the calm dignity with which she always lived and that she carried into death.

"In the stillness of the early morning, I bathed her wasted body one last time. I needed to be alone with Michiko for just a little longer before I let the others know of her death. I ached inside at the thought of never hearing another story from her. I wanted her voice to fill the silence. I keenly hoped that in the split second before her death, Michiko really did believe she had found her daughter Kuniko again. That thought gave me comfort, along with knowing that she was once again happy, diving into the cool sea, bringing up handfuls of pearls.

"After Michiko-*san* passed away, another part of my life in Yamaguchi began. Matsu started building me this house so I would have a place of my own away from the others, yet close enough to the village in case I needed help. Whenever he stayed in Yamaguchi, Matsu was at work on the house before I rose each morning. I helped him as much as I could. And it was in the simple act of driving a nail into wood or putting a *shoji* screen into place that I'd end each day too tired to feel sorry for myself. I think it was also a way for Matsu to communicate with me. He has always felt more comfortable working with his hands. And I have never seen him so relaxed as he described each step of building the house. 'Sachi,' he told me, 'the windows should be placed here so that the warmth of the sun will stay into the evening. We could plant a silk tree there later if it becomes too much.' It was only natural that Matsu would want to plan for a garden.

" 'Please, Matsu-*san,*' I told him, not long after the house was completed. 'I don't wish to have any flowers.'

"Never once did he question me. I needed my life to be simple, without any beauty to remind me of all I had lost. And though I had not told him that, Matsu must have seen it in my eyes. 'Don't worry, Sachi,' he said, 'there will be no flowers.'

"He left early the next morning after the house was completed, saying he would be back sometime in the afternoon. I slowly tried to adapt to my new home in Yamaguchi, yet I kept to myself. With Michiko gone, the thought of being alone still frightened me. I couldn't yet bring myself to be with anyone else. Even the thought of my own family seemed distant, belonging to another life.

"And you have seen what kind of garden Matsu made for me. He returned that afternoon carting two bags of gray, palm-sized, flat stones. The next weeks were spent clearing the land and planning what would be placed where. I have never seen Matsu so excited as the day we began to lay the stones down carefully side by side, until we had formed a rippling pattern. 'It will be a garden created from your imagination,' he said, urging me to rearrange the stones any way I wanted them to be.

"Stephen-*san,* I spent hours rearranging those stones, as if they held some strange, mesmerizing power that brought me calm. Day after day Matsu carried bags of pebbles and stones of different shapes and sizes up here with the help of a borrowed mule and cart. I anxiously awaited them as if I were trying to fit each piece together into a complicated puzzle I needed to finish. I felt as if I had fallen into a trance which I couldn't come out of until the garden was completed. With Matsu's help and patience, I had created something from the most common elements, and when the garden was finally finished, I realized for the first time in my life that I had accomplished something. What I had thought would be barren and distant was instead filled with quiet beauty. I remember I turned to Matsu as we stood looking at the rock garden and asked, 'Did you know it would be so simple and beautiful?'

" 'I knew its beauty would appear if we worked hard enough,' he answered.

" 'But I never expected it to be like this.'

"Matsu smiled. 'Beauty can be found in most places.'

"I turned to face him, really looking for the first time at his thick, strong features. They were so different from Tomoko's, I thought again that they couldn't really be related. After a moment I said, 'I thought I no longer had any desire for beauty. I've had it all my life and look what it's done for me!'

"Matsu then shook his head, looking out toward the garden. 'Sachi-*san,* you've only known the ordinary kind of beauty which appears on the outside. Perhaps you now desire something deeper.'

"I wanted to say something back to him, and I knew deep down that he was right, though I didn't have the words yet. Until that disease chose me, I had lived a charmed life of grace and ease, while Matsu had always to work hard for what he desired. He has always known where beauty comes from. Later on, when the disease spread over the left side of my face, I tried to accept the burden placed on me, to tell myself that real beauty comes from deep within. But I'm afraid sometimes I reverted back to my spoiled ways. But, Stephen-*san,* can you imagine what it was like to watch your own face slowly transformed into a monster? Have you ever awakened in the morning from a series of nightmares, fearing what you might have turned into during the night? I will not lie to you and tell you that it was easy. There were times when I thought I could actually feel my skin shrinking, pulling against my bones and muscles, slowly suffocating me. Matsu comforted me as much as he could by having me work on the house, or in the garden, but no matter how much pleasure I found in them, they were still cold and inanimate. I longed for my past life. Matsu always knew that the peace of mind I needed could only be found within myself.

"About the same time, Kenzo suspected something was going on because of the supplies Matsu constantly needed. He began to send food and messages to me. Yet, tins of pickled cabbage or a chicken couldn't replace the fact that Kenzo would never be able to face me again.

"I was in my early twenties by the time the garden was completed. I remember it being the end of summer and Matsu had to return to Tarumi for several days to help his father. I missed him terribly and found myself unable to sleep. We had become so close. I began pacing the floor like a caged animal. Each day I grew increasingly filled with anger and rage at this disease which was consuming my life. How could I stand the loneliness of Yamaguchi? How could I continue to live as an outcast? Dark thoughts of ending my life again entered my mind.

"Then something strange occurred. A strong wind began rattling the house, and I was suddenly compelled to go out into the garden, the wind calling me. I opened the *shoji* screen and stepped out into its embrace, soothed by the still, gray rocks. I remember how I stood there in my bare feet, the dull sensation of the stones pushing and crackling beneath my feet. It was like a dream to think I had worked for months to create it, only to finally realize what was in front of me. In that moment, it all came to life. Suddenly, I could hear the water flowing and see the soft ripples on its surface. But most of all, I could now relish the fact that its beauty was one that no disease or person could ever take away from me. I stood there for a long time until I felt like I was no longer myself at all, but part of the garden."

Then Sachi's voice stopped. She turned her head away from me toward the garden, listening. A few seconds later I heard the soft sound of footsteps, realizing what she had already known, that someone was entering the gate to the garden.

APRIL 22, 1938

I can't forget Matsu's face when he found me at Sachi's house last week. It wasn't a look of surprise, but one of happy satisfaction, as if he had already placed me sitting at the table with her and his intuition had been confirmed. I remember being annoyed at first by his interruption. I wanted to hear more of Sachi's story, but I knew the minute Matsu entered the house, her lulling voice as I had known it would have to stop.

Matsu had come to tell me that we would have to return to Tarumi. He had much-needed supplies to buy to rebuild the two burned houses, and wanted to return to Yamaguchi with them as soon as possible. He exchanged a few words with Sachi, too quick and low for me to understand, but whatever he said, she seemed pleased and bowed low several times to him.

We left Sachi's house so quickly I felt cheated by the fact that I hadn't thanked her properly, hadn't told her how grateful I was that she trusted our friendship. Instead, I only thanked her for the rice and vegetables, simply saying, *"Sayōnara,"* as she stood by the door watching us go.

We walked back down the mountain saying very little. I imagined that Matsu was keeping a mental list of everything he needed to buy and bring back to Yamaguchi—nails, boards, blankets, the most essential things. My own thoughts drifted back to Sachi's flawless childhood, which had been irrevocably set apart by the suffering she endured as a young woman. I couldn't imagine how terrible it must have been for her; dead in the eyes of her family and then having to live a life with lepers, knowing that it would soon become her own fate. It must have been worse than looking in a mirror, to see your own destiny in the faces of those walking right in front of you. All of a sudden I remembered something that Mah-mee had once told Pie when she had complained of not winning a drawing contest she'd entered. "It's better this way. If you have too much good luck when you are young," Mah-mee said, "there won't be any luck left for when you are old."

Just then I heard Matsu cough and clear his throat. I looked up to see that he was stopped ahead on the dirt path, waiting for me to catch up to him. I had lagged behind quite a bit, slowed by my own daydreaming and my sore muscles, which made themselves felt as the path grew steeper down the mountain. As I approached him, I took a good look at his thickset body and his strong, powerful arms and legs, wondering what it might have been like to know him as a young man. He hadn't physically changed so much over the years. Even as a young boy I remembered Matsu's same strong features as he worked around my grandfather's garden. There was always a mystery about him, the way he flew in and out so quickly, as if he were always racing to be somewhere else. I wonder now if he had been on his way to see Sachi. But as the distance closed between us, I could also see that the years had softened him, his body heavier, his short hair completely gray.

"I'm sorry," I said, "I'm moving rather slowly today."

"There's no need to hurry," Matsu said, squinting at the sun. "I was just going to ask how you are feeling?"

"I'm all right," I answered, though I'd been feeling a tightness in my chest which I knew would go away once I had a chance to rest. There was no reason for Matsu to have to worry about one more thing.

"You can lie down when we get back," he said, as if he knew my thoughts. Perhaps that's how it was when two people live in the same house for a long enough time. You begin to read each other's minds.

Matsu was quiet, slowing his pace to mine as we walked down the path. "You were up early this morning?" he suddenly asked.

"I couldn't sleep."

"Neither could Sachi?" he asked.

"No," I answered, amused that he was, in his subtle way, trying to find out what we'd been talking about. "I just wanted to see her garden. I wasn't certain she would be up, but she was."

"She didn't used to be an early riser," Matsu said. Then suddenly embarrassed by how he might know, added, "When they were girls, she and Tomoko would have slept until noon, if they had been allowed."

"Were you very close to Tomoko?" I asked. Even though it it was obvious from Sachi's story how different they were, I was still curious as to how Matsu felt.

He seemed surprised at first, but then he cleared his throat again and answered. "Tomoko and I were very different; like fire and rain. I think I only began to know her better just before she took her life."

"What do you mean?"

"That she became more alive to me during those difficult times," he said, picking up his pace as his words spilled out. "Before then, she was a silly young girl who didn't care for anything except herself. But in the days before she took her life, she began to see the nonsense of it all, even if it was too late. I won't forget the night she came to ask for my help. Until then, she had locked herself in her room for days after the whitish rash was discovered on the side of her face.

" 'Ani,' Tomoko whispered, bringing me out of a deep sleep. I thought I was still dreaming. But when I felt her cold hand on my cheek, I sat right up. At first I thought it was my mother kneeling beside me, but the small, smooth hand and the dark, thin outline told me it was Tomoko.

" 'Is everything all right?' I asked, thinking something had happened to our parents.

" 'I need your help,' she said.

"I leaned over and tried to light the oil lamp, but Tomoko stopped me. 'Leave it dark,' she whispered.

" 'What is it?' I asked.

" 'I need you to help me do something.'

" 'What is it?' I repeated, annoyed to have been awakened by her. I thought it was just another one of her foolish ideas.

"Tomoko hesitated. She was quiet for what seemed a long time. Even as a baby she was noisy and outgoing, very different from any of us. I waited. I could feel her shifting her weight from one knee to the other.

"She finally bent close to my ear and whispered, 'Can you get me father's fishing knife?' Ever since she was little, she was forbidden to go near it.

" 'What for?'

"This time she did not hesitate answering. 'I don't want to live like this.'

" 'Like what?' I asked.

"I waited for Tomoko's answer. Through the *shoji* walls the light from the moon allowed me to see her clearly. She looked like a different girl from the one I'd always known, pale and serious. Her eyes stared blankly at me.

" 'With this disease.'

"At the time, we were still hoping it wasn't leprosy. No one else in the village had come down with any signs of it. But Tomoko grew frantic when it spread to her face. She went into hiding. 'It will get better,' I remember trying to reassure her.

" 'No,' she shook her head. 'I know it won't.'

" 'You know you aren't to touch father's knife,' I whispered. I was still not fully awake, and this solemn young girl didn't seem anything like the Tomoko I'd always known.

" 'Then you won't get it for me?' Her eyes suddenly flashed alive.

" 'No,' I answered.

"Tomoko stood up and walked out of my room, her hand covering the side of her face. Each day after, I tried to talk to her. I wanted to tell her about Yamaguchi, but she remained closed up in her room. 'I won't live like this,' she repeated over and over again in a chant. It was as if she already knew what would become of her. Three days later when I went to check on Tomoko, my sixteen-year-old sister had found my father's fishing knife and ended her life."

When we arrived back at my grandfather's house, I felt as though we'd been gone for weeks, not just one day. The cherry blossoms had bloomed overnight. Even the smallest tree's branches were fully dressed with pink blossoms. Everything in the garden smelled sweetly remote, and felt so distant, I thought I would have to reacquaint myself with it all over again. I longed to be back in Yamaguchi instead, sitting warmly in Sachi's house listening to her story.

After he spoke of Tomoko, Matsu had become quiet again, returning to his garden. He did insist I stay put and rest, especially if I expected to return to Yamaguchi again to help him rebuild.

MAY 15, 1938

We've made several trips back to Yamaguchi carting supplies. Matsu hopes to begin building tomorrow. This morning he went into the village for the last of the supplies, while I stayed home to rest. I tried to lie down, only to get up and move restlessly through the house. The empty white canvas sitting in my grandfather's study stared at me blankly. The hardened dollops of paint on the wooden tray reminded me of my last attempt at painting. Down the hall, the kitchen felt scrubbed and faded with use. I wandered freely into Matsu's small, back bedroom. It was spare and devoid of any luxuries, except for the stack of magazines he received from his older sister in Tokyo and the radio beside his bed. I clicked on Matsu's radio and the static hum of the real world entered my life again. The voice was high and scratchy as it announced proudly that Hsuchowfu, an important railway junction between Nanking and Peking, had been taken by the Japanese. I

156

felt my blood suddenly rise. The Japanese had succeeded in paralyzing much of the northern and southern parts of China. Now there was nothing left to stop them from taking Canton, and it was evident that they would leave little untouched along the way. I choked at the sudden realization that Hong Kong might be next.

I quickly returned to my grandfather's study, sat down, and began to write two letters, one to my mother and another to Pie while I still had the strength. Every time I thought about having to leave Matsu and Sachi I felt a dull ache. I told Mah-mee that I continued to grow stronger, and considering how aggressively the Japanese were moving through China, it might be wise if I returned to Hong Kong as soon as possible. I essentially told Pie the same, only I began to tell her again about Yamaguchi and how proud I was of her and her work with the Red Cross.

When Matsu returned from the village, I sealed the letters, then went to tell him of my decision to return to Hong Kong. But before I was able to say anything, Matsu slipped off his shoes in the *genken,* then handed me a blue envelope addressed to me from my mother.

> *Dear Stephen,*
>
> *I received your last letter. Don't worry, I am feeling better. My health is slowly returning. Ching has been brewing me soups made of Chinese yam roots, astragalus roots, and the fruit from the matrimony vine. "It strengthens the blood," she says. I do feel warmer now. For a while, I felt as if a cold wind blew through my body.*
>
> *Do you remember Uncle Sing? He is the friend of your Ba-ba's from his Canton days. We met one day down in Central and he has joined in on several of our mah-jongg games. As a young man, Uncle Sing was also sickly. He reassures me you will grow out of it. It lightens my heart.*
>
> *As for you, it would be better if you stay in Tarumi a bit longer. To get stronger. At least through the summer. Hong Kong is already suffocating. You must have fresh air to recover fully. You will be close to your Ba-ba there, and he will let you know if things become more difficult. Even if the Japanese devils should capture Canton (which they may not), don't forget that we in Hong Kong are under British sovereignty.*

I think it is better if Penelope and I do not come to Tarumi as planned this summer. Not while your father and I are still sorting everything out. I hope you understand. We might go to Macao to visit Anne and Henry. Or perhaps—No matter, I don't have the strength to think of such things now.

Ching reminds you to rest. I will write again soon.

Love,
Mah-mee

I crumpled my mother's letter in my hands and again felt unsettled. It was true, after almost a year in Tarumi I had adapted to the Japanese way of life, from the quiet gardens to the mountain village of Yamaguchi, but unlike my father, I was still pulled home by the scents and sounds of my other life. I picked up the letters I'd just written and laid them in the bottom drawer of my grandfather's desk. My heart felt heavy knowing I wouldn't be able to see my mother or Pie any time soon. And hard as I tried, I couldn't remember any Uncle Sing.

A sudden, high scraping noise coming from the garden startled me from my thoughts. I jumped up and hurried outside to see what it was. There in the far end of the garden was Matsu, sharpening something on a spinning grindstone.

"What are you doing?" I asked.

Matsu waited until the last turn of the wheel slowed, then came to a complete stop. He held up the knife so I could clearly see its ivory handle and honed blade. "It was my father's fishing knife," he said.

MAY 30, 1938

I haven't written in weeks. Matsu and I have spent most of our time in Yamaguchi rebuilding the two houses lost in the fire. It felt like we were far away from the real world. I barely saw Sachi during those days since she and the other women were busy pounding *mochi*, getting ready for the celebration in honor of the newly built houses. It was their way of thanking us for all our help, but just to see the burst of energy that the village had taken on was thanks enough. While the women prepared for the celebration,

Hiro-*san* and most of the men who no longer had the fingers and hands to help build happily gave advice, bringing us water and food at regular intervals.

As I watched Matsu work, I began to see what Sachi meant when she said that he was most at home working with his hands. He thrived fitting and nailing in every piece of wood, maintaining the same concentration he had working in his garden. Matsu worked with skill and confidence, as he first visualized, then created walls and rooms until both of the houses were completed.

The celebration was one of the best nights of my life. The center of the village was surrounded by yellow lanterns, forming a perfect circle of light. Matsu and I sat in the middle as honored guests, drinking *sake* and eating sushi, or *mochi* dipped in soy sauce and sugar. Sachi never looked happier as she talked and laughed, and Hiro-*san* sang and told stories. It seemed as if our laughter could be heard miles away, perhaps even drift down into Tarumi—ghost voices carried by the wind.

By the end of the evening I fell into a *sake*-induced sleep that had me dreaming of Yamaguchi. Only instead of being in Japan, the village was in the midst of a bustling Hong Kong, the cars and crowds going about their daily business. And in the center of it all, I could see Pie passing out warm clothes and wrapping white bandages around Sachi and Hiro's eaten-away limbs.

SUMMER

JUNE 6, 1938

The warmer, brighter days of summer seem to get me up and out earlier. I walked into Tarumi with Matsu this morning. I hadn't been to the village since Kenzo's burial two months ago, though it feels longer. Kenzo's teahouse remains closed, the black mourning material taken down, the doorway still boarded. The bad spirits of his suicide seem to linger. When we passed by the teahouse on the way to the post office, Matsu glanced over to it as if he still expected Kenzo to walk out and greet him. But when there was nothing more than the sound of our own dull footsteps along the dirt road, he turned quickly away and stared straight ahead.

I went to the village to mail two letters I'd written to Mah-mee and Pie. A few days earlier, my father had wired me that he would be coming to visit the following weekend. I wanted to write to my mother again before I saw him. The letters essentially said I was fine, but because of my mother's letter, I no longer mentioned my return to Hong Kong. While I felt more at ease to know I would be staying in Tarumi, I also knew it would just be a matter of time.

As we were leaving the post office, I saw Keiko across the road coming in our direction. Unlike our previous meeting in the village, Keiko didn't shy away at all. Instead she moved directly toward Matsu and me, and bowed low in a friendly greeting.

"*Ohayōgozaimasu,* I am honored to see you here this morning," she said.

I could see Matsu try to suppress a smile, as he bowed back, then quickly found an excuse to leave us alone.

I really missed seeing Keiko. With all the work we'd been doing in Yamaguchi, there was little time for anything else. But seeing her again right in front of me, with her dark eyes and strong scent of jasmine, brought back the rush of desire I'd felt at our last meeting.

"How have you been?" I asked.

"Very well," she answered, timid again.

"I've been very busy. I haven't had much time to come into the village."

At first Keiko remained quiet, then all in a rush, she said, "I thought perhaps you might have left Tarumi and gone back to Hong Kong."

"No, what would make you think that?"

Keiko glanced down at my feet. "I managed to walk by your house once, but no one was there."

"I was helping Matsu do some work elsewhere," I quickly answered.

"I see." Keiko stood silent for a moment, then looked up at me and asked, "Can you meet me tomorrow afternoon around three o'clock at the Tama Shrine?"

"Of course," I said.

I could see she wanted to smile, but held it back. She looked around to make sure no one was watching, then reached out and touched me lightly on the hand before she bowed and turned to leave.

While we walked home, Matsu respected my silence as I remained quiet with thoughts of Keiko. By the time we returned to the house and stepped through the gate into the garden, neither one of us was prepared to find Sachi there waiting, dressed in a dark kimono and veil.

"What's wrong?" Matsu said, even before he bowed.

"It's Hiro-*san*," Sachi answered. "He passed away in his sleep last night."

Matsu wouldn't allow me to return to Yamaguchi with them. I knew he was right to think the uphill walk would be too tiring so soon after our return from Tarumi. I didn't argue with him. As always, Sachi was kind and wise. "Stay here, Stephen-*san*. Hold on to your last memory of Hiro-*san*, the night of the celebration when he was happiest and most alive."

After they left, I sat in the garden for the longest time. I tried to comprehend what it meant to die, to move on to an eternal sleep and never wake up again. Ever since I had come to Tarumi, I'd seen more deaths than in all of my life in Hong Kong. Everything before me was changing. I knew I would never be able to step back into my comfortable past. Ahead of me lurked the violent prospect of war, perhaps bringing the deaths of people I knew and loved, along with the end of my parent's marriage. These were terrors I'd somehow escaped until now. And as I sat among the white deutzia blossoms, I felt a strange sensation of growing pains surge through my body, the dull ache of being pulled in other directions.

JUNE 7, 1938

Matsu didn't return from Yamaguchi last night. I stayed up late, then couldn't sleep. I waited all day until I had to meet Keiko at the Tama Shrine, but there was still no sign of him. I left Matsu a note on the table, and when I finally began the walk to Tarumi and the shrine, I was late and already exhausted.

Keiko was pacing back and forth in front of the first *torii* gate when I arrived. She wore a plum-colored cotton kimono and carried a beige parasol. When she saw me, she stopped as if suddenly paralyzed. By then I was hot and sweaty from the uphill climb, my shirt sticking to my back, my face hot and flushed. I couldn't help but wish we had met somewhere closer.

"*Konnichiwa.*" Keiko bowed.

I waited until I was close enough to reach out and touch her before I stopped, bowed, and returned her greeting. "*Konnichiwa,* Keiko-san, I hope you haven't been waiting long."

"Not long at all, Stephen-san," she answered.

We both stood awkwardly for a moment before Keiko turned away. "I must not forget," she said. I watched her go toward the shade of some trees, and from behind them retrieve a *furoshiki* and return to me. "I thought you might be thirsty after the long walk."

"I am," I smiled.

We walked away from the shrine, to a slope covered with tall, thick pines. I could almost taste the rich perfume of pine resin, mixed with Keiko's jasmine scent. She stopped in a small clearing and sat down, then carefully untied the *furoshiki* and spread out its contents. It felt as if we were in a small, cool room surrounded by a wall of trees. I sat beside Keiko and quickly drank down the sweet, cold tea she handed me. Then she gave me bean cakes and rice crackers which I ate heartily, though she did not taste a thing. I leaned back on a bed of pine needles and allowed myself to relax, closing my eyes.

It's just then that the scent of jasmine grows stronger. I open my eyes to find Keiko watching me, her face so close to mine we must be breathing one another's air. I want to say something, but instead I raise my face up to kiss her. She doesn't pull away. Instead, she lets the weight of her body fall against mine, a warmth I welcome at once. I place my hands around her waist and hold her tightly against me, kissing her harder. And still she doesn't pull away, except to loosen her hair, letting it fall down her soft, pale shoulders. I've never felt skin so soft. It's only then that I untie her sash, my mouth finding her breasts, her hands reaching down to what has already become hard and lost, seeking somewhere soft to hide.

It was the simple rustling of wind through the trees that woke me. For a moment I was dazed trying to climb out of the dream. When I fully opened my eyes, I saw Keiko sitting across from me, smiling. I'm not sure how long I was asleep, but I remained silent with embarrassment as I lifted myself up and sat against a tree.

"Do you feel better, Stephen-*san?*" Keiko asked.

"I'm sorry, I wasn't able to sleep very well last night," I answered.

She leaned over and handed me a cup of tea. "You must be very tired."

I nodded my head. "How long have I been asleep?"

"Less than an hour," she answered, wrapping her arms around herself. In the shade of the trees, the temperature had dropped considerably.

"I'm so sorry," I said again.

"I'm only sorry to have disturbed you."

"I wish you had earlier."

"No," she said, "you should never pull someone away from his dreams."

"How do you know I was dreaming?" I asked.

"How could you lie in a place like this and not dream?" she asked me back.

Then Keiko sat up on her knees and politely changed the subject as she packed up the *furoshiki*. She told me she loved the quiet of Tarumi, and dreaded the hordes of summer visitors who would descend upon the village by the end of the next month. "While they're here, I only want to leave," she said. Her greatest wish was to go to a university to study architecture. Even as a little girl, design had always fascinated her. As I listened to Keiko's soft, melodious voice, I longed to possess her certainty, and to hold her slender fingers in mine as we began our slow descent toward Tarumi.

By the time I arrived home, it was late afternoon. Matsu had finally returned from Yamaguchi looking pale and tired. He sat on the steps of the *genken,* barely raising his head when I came through the gate.

"We buried Hiro-*san* this morning," he said, as I approached him.

"I'm sorry."

"His heart gave out. He went peacefully in his sleep," Matsu said, rubbing the top of his cropped head with the palm of his hand. "He deserves to be in a better world now."

"I'm sure he is," I said, awkwardly.

"Hiro was in Yamaguchi from the beginning. He was originally from the north, somewhere near Hokkaido. How he ever came so far, I'll never know now. He always said he would tell me one day."

I stood there silent, and looked down at the top of Matsu's gray head. I tried to imagine the terrible pain he must feel, to have lost both Kenzo and Hiro in such a short time. And as I watched him, I could suddenly see small cracks in his armor, grief in the curve of his back and shoulders. For so long, he had been the strength of both worlds, the unlikely hero. And as if he knew my thoughts, Matsu looked up at me trying to calculate why death had subtracted another person from his life. I saw something in his eyes that made me think he wanted to speak, so I waited patiently. But he only breathed deeply and sent the palm of his hand over the top of his head again. In the end, Matsu said nothing more. He stood up slowly. When I looked into his eyes all I could see was how they were dulled, glazed by tiredness. He went in and began dinner.

JUNE 15, 1938

My father has come and gone again. Every time I see him, it's with new eyes. This time he seemed to have aged, but otherwise he was as immaculate and handsome as always. I didn't mention the letter from my mother and he didn't volunteer any information. He tried to pretend everything was the same, and perhaps it was in his mind. After all, there would be little, if any, change to his life in Kobe.

At first I easily adopted my father's tranquil mood, and we spent most of the two days he visited in a state of calm. Neither of us wanted to disrupt this tranquility, so we stayed away from any subject that might be the least bit antagonistic. Thus, my mother was rarely mentioned. Mostly we focused on what a mild winter it was, and what a wonderful warm spring we had enjoyed. Because of it, my father believed that we might have a wet summer season. And when we had finally exhausted all safe topics, we talked of more important issues, such as the war and whether it would affect my stay in Tarumi.

"Has the war changed anything in Kobe?" I asked him.

We had walked down to the beach after lunch on his second day back. My father dressed in white slacks and a pale blue shirt. For the first time, he took off his loafers and walked in the sand barefoot.

"There is a kind of excitement in the air," he answered. "They are advancing toward Canton every day, you know. There are few obstacles left in their way which they won't just destroy."

I noticed how my father always referred to the Japanese as "they," as if it made them farther removed from him. But as I watched him walking slowly beside me, I realized that in many ways he was more Japanese than Chinese now. He had so easily adapted to the restraint and simplicity of Japan, and had always hated the crowds and noise of Hong Kong.

"I've been thinking, Ba-ba. Maybe I should return to Hong Kong sometime soon," I said.

My father looked toward me, shading his eyes with his open hand. "Perhaps you should stay here through the summer, then return in the fall," he said. "I don't foresee any problems."

"What about Mah-mee and Pie?" I asked. It was one of the few times I had mentioned them during his visit.

"We have already spoken and have agreed that you should stay a while longer," he answered blandly. "There is no immediate danger of any fighting reaching Hong Kong."

I kept walking. It was evident that he and Mah-mee had found some time in between their problems to discuss my staying in Tarumi. Their joint decision somehow still surprised me, even after Mah-mee's calm letter. Everything was more dignified and logical than I thought. There was a distinct finality to it that caught me off balance. I felt a heaviness in my chest that had nothing to do with my illness, and everything to do with the regret I felt. Even if it meant leaving the life I had in Tarumi, I couldn't help but hope my father had changed his mind, that he had really come to get me and we would soon return to Hong Kong.

"If you think it's for the best," I finally managed to say.

I could see my father relax. "Stephen, perhaps you would like to come to Kobe for the *O-bon* Festival? It would be a nice change for you."

I shrugged my shoulders. "I think Matsu mentioned a celebration here in the village," I lied. I didn't want him to see how I felt. I looked down and began to unbutton my shirt. "I think I'll go for a swim. Do you want to come?"

My father smiled. "No, you run along, I'll watch you from here."

JUNE 29, 1938

My father was right. The weather has changed dramatically in the past two weeks since his visit. We've had what Matsu calls "The

Baiu" or "Plum Rains" which are said to last exactly six weeks. While sometimes there are downpours, more often there are sunny days mixed in with days of misty drizzle that hang on, leaving everything damp and mildewy. In Hong Kong, I'm used to summers where I could actually see tears trickling down the walls from the humidity. The plum rains are an almost refreshing change from the endless blue skies we've had.

This morning when I went out to the garden, a cloud of mist had descended upon it. I don't think I've ever seen anything more beautiful. I didn't notice Matsu already at work at the far end of the garden until he suddenly stood up and began walking out of the mist in my direction. "What's wrong?" he said, "you look like you've just seen a ghost."

I've tried to capture this ghostly beauty on canvas, but like anything too beautiful, it becomes hard to recreate its reality. There's something about being too perfect, that evenness which at times appears stiff, almost boring. I finally gave up after several tries.

July 5, 1938

I've spent a great deal of time down at the beach, which has been relatively empty because of the unexpected rains. I swim in the warm mist, and sometimes I stay submerged under the water when it begins to rain, watching the drops dance on the surface like fingers touching skin.

I saw Keiko once in the village when I went in with Matsu. She was with Mika and only glanced quickly in my direction, bowing just enough to give respect. Mika did the same before she pulled her sister off in another direction. But, unlike our other chance meetings, I could see that there was something in Keiko's eyes that had changed. She stood in the thick mist, her hair damp against her forehead with some secret knowledge as to who I was. She had watched me sleep, maybe even understood the fact that I was dreaming of being with her. There was something intimate between us now. I could feel it pull us closer, away from all the others even as I watched her turn and walk away from me.

170

JULY 9, 1938

This morning Matsu told me the story of a small village in the mountains where the plum rains never cease. Year-round the heavy mist lies over this village, never lifting for a moment to allow the villagers time to see the blue sky, or breathe in fresh, dry air. When I asked him why they would stay in a village that never saw the sun, Matsu raised his head and smiled. "Because they are honored the plum rains have chosen their village to stay with," he answered. "They feel bad luck will befall them if the mist should rise. Bad spirits will find their way to the village."

I walked outside to find the garden still covered in thick mist. I found myself startled by strange sounds coming from nowhere, shadows moving without faces, spirits trying to find their way. But after so many weeks of it, I'm beginning to feel suffocated by the rains, by the thought that it will never lift and I'll never feel the sun again.

JULY 16, 1938

The plum rains have suddenly stopped. I woke up to find the sky a soft, pale blue, which also means that the summer season in Tarumi has officially begun. By early morning there were voices and footsteps of children and their parents making their way down the road to the beach. What was once my sanctuary has become a place I purposely avoid. Families lie side by side under colorful umbrellas on the beach, trying to keep out of one another's way. It's almost comical. Occasionally I see a girl who reminds me of Pie, and I can't help but watch her frolic on the beach from a distance. Then almost in the same instant, I realize that Pie must have grown a head in the past year, that perhaps she has changed more considerably than I can imagine. I wonder if I'll recognize her when I get home? These thoughts make me quickly turn away from the child on the beach, taking refuge in Matsu's garden where the sweet, summer blooms of deutzia and crepe myrtle soothe my fears.

I was in the garden this afternoon when Matsu came back, mumbling about all the people in his way as he walked past me. "Half of them don't know if they're coming or going," he said. Then he stopped momentarily to hand me a blue envelope which was addressed to me from Pie.

Dear Big Brother,

Just a short letter to let you know how terrible I feel that we aren't coming to visit you in Tarumi. Mah-mee broke the news to me last night, and I admit I didn't take it very well. In fact, I threw a tantrum that makes me almost embarrassed to think about now. It was finally Ching who dragged me to my room, telling me Mah-mee didn't need that from me now. "What about me?" I asked. "You have more than you know," Ching answered. It was then that I almost wanted to tell her about my work at the Red Cross, but I thought better of Mah-mee finding out so I remained quiet. I do feel ashamed of myself for acting like a child, but first our Christmas holidays were cancelled, and now our summer vacation. I really wanted to see you. It doesn't seem like too much to ask. After all, it's almost a year since you left.

Sometimes I wonder if you look different? I bet you're still as handsome as ever. The girls at Lingnan must really miss you. Lots of them have come home from school for the summer. A few of them have been brave enough to come to the house asking about you, especially Sheila Wu, who has come by twice. Even if I'm not crazy about her, she has guts. Unfortunately, I still look the same, homely as ever with this short hair that Mah-mee feels is less trouble than long. It does stay out of my way when I'm rolling bandages, so I don't complain too much.

I hope everything is all right with you. I really wanted to see this village Yamaguchi that you've written about. I might have even been of some help. But now that I won't be seeing you this summer, I feel it's too long and hot. Even Anne and Henry refuse to come home. They would rather stay in Macao, so Mah-mee has hinted we might be going there.

I have to go now, Ching is waiting for me to go to the market with her. I'll write again soon. I miss you.

Love,
Penelope (Pie)

JULY 25, 1938

This afternoon the crowds were so noisy, I gave up trying to paint and walked toward the woods. It was significantly cooler under the shady pines. I wandered through the shadows thinking of how Sachi had hidden under a thick pile of leaves and pine needles, frightened and all alone until Matsu found her. As I stood there, lost in my own reverie, I heard the crackling sound of leaves and looked up to see Keiko in the near distance. She walked slowly, her head bowed in thought. My heart began beating as I waited for her to move toward me. I didn't want to frighten her so I waited quietly until the scent of her jasmine perfume reached me first.

"Keiko-*san*," I said, stepping forward.

Keiko looked up, startled. "Stephen-*san,* what are you doing here?"

"I wanted to get away from the crowds."

"So did I," she smiled.

We spent the next hour walking through the woods, speaking in low tones until we both fell into a comfortable silence. The air was warm and sweet. When I reached over and took her hand in mine, Keiko didn't resist. It wasn't until we reached the main road that she reluctantly let go of my hand and slowly slipped away from me.

AUGUST 8, 1938

The days have been hot and slow. I haven't seen Keiko again. I've tried to keep myself busy by painting or taking long walks to avoid the crowds. Then after dinner this evening, Matsu came into my room carrying two short-handled nets. "Come along," he said, "and wear something you don't mind getting wet."

By the time I had changed, I found Matsu waiting for me in the garden carrying an oil lamp, two unlit torches, a wooden bucket, and the nets. I took the torches and followed him out onto the road. It was dusk, just before night and our shadowy figures in the gray haze seemed unreal. We turned toward the road to Yamaguchi and walked in silence. The sound of crickets filled the warm night, interrupted only by my own voice asking, "Where are we going?"

"Not far," Matsu answered. He turned off the road and onto a narrow trail which led through the trees. He stopped a moment and lit the lamp, illuminating the dark path in front of us. The deeper we walked, the cooler it became, the smell of dank earth and eucalyptus growing stronger. After a while, we came to a cove surrounded by trees and rocks.

"Here we are," Matsu said. He lifted the lamp so I could get a better look.

The light set the dark green water aglow. I stepped back when I saw something leap from the water and fall back in again. "What's that?" I asked.

Matsu laughed. "Tomorrow's dinner," he said, as he set down the lamp. He slipped off his sandals, rolled up his pant legs, then proceeded to light a torch. He handed one to me and lit the other. Carrying his torch and one of the nets, Matsu began to walk into the water. As the glare of his torch illuminated the water, I could see silvery-white flashes leaping up all around him. He swung his net in midair, quickly collecting a number of shrimp as big as my fist.

I picked up the other net and stepped into the water, swinging my torch slowly from side to side, ignoring the sucking pull of the cool mud around my feet. It wasn't long before I felt the shrimp scratching against my legs, leaping up, and splashing all around me. I quickly raised my net, and let them catch themselves one after another as they jumped toward me. By the time I turned back toward Matsu, he was emptying his catch into the wooden bucket filled with water. I could hear the dull scratching of the shrimp on top still jumping, squirming wildly with their last breath.

174

AUGUST 16, 1938

I hadn't lied to my father after all. Matsu had plans for the *O-bon* Festival and asked if I would like to join him. I said yes, even before I found out that Fumiko, Matsu's older sister, was returning to Tarumi from Tokyo. Her imminent visit lifted our spirits considerably. Something almost boyish suddenly emerged in Matsu as the days grew closer to the celebration. Not only was it a day to honor the dead, it was a homecoming, a celebration of *"furusato,"* one's birthplace and spiritual home. People born and raised in Tarumi would return yearly for the *O-bon* Festival. After a trip to the Buddhist Temple to visit the graves of their ancestors, there would be food and dancing in the village to entertain the returned spirits.

On the day Fumiko was to arrive, I walked to Tarumi with Matsu and waited anxiously with him at the train station. It wasn't just that I was curious to see another member of his family; it somehow still surprised me that Matsu really was part of a family. He seemed to be on his own so much of the time, I'd forgotten that he was once someone's son and still someone's brother.

The train station was already crowded. The summer visitors were much different from those during the rest of the year. Many women dressed in Western-style clothing held an air of sophisticated boredom at the slow, lazy pace of Tarumi. After almost a year here, I'd grown used to the village life, and sometimes I wondered if I'd ever be able to return to the fast pace of Hong Kong.

We waited beside a group of locals who anticipated relatives home for the holidays. More people pushed their way onto the wooden platform as time went by, until you could hardly move and the hum of voices grew increasingly loud. But painfully obvious to me once again was how the women and children outnumbered the men. The sparse group of men who smoked and milled around the station were well past the fighting age. It still bothered me, as if I were supposed to be somewhere else but had somehow missed the train.

Matsu glanced at the clock, appearing more and more anxious. He wiped his forehead with a handkerchief. And though he was dressed in a worn, dark-blue kimono, I noticed he was cleanly shaven and his kimono freshly pressed. Suddenly, we heard a low

175

rumbling, and in the near distance we could see a flood of smoke as the train screeched, moving in slow motion as it approached the station. The crowd seemed to move in one breath, pushing forward even though there was no place to go.

When the train came to a full stop, Matsu told me to wait for him as he inched up toward the doors. It seemed to take forever for the first passenger to step down. I stood back, trying to follow Matsu above the sea of heads, but he had disappeared into the crowd.

Voices filled the air with greetings.

"Tadaima, I'm back," someone said.

"Okaeri naisai," another answered, welcoming him home.

I watched the homecomings, and wondered how it would feel to wait for my family to come off the train. There would be the usual nervousness in the pit of my stomach, the anxiousness of time moving too slowly. If things had gone as planned, I would be greeting them all now, but because of my father's indiscretion and the Japanese advancements in China, everything had vanished into the air. A sensation of homesickness swept through me as I watched strange faces and bodies disembark, looking for some familiarity among them. I was staring off in a different direction when I felt a hand on my shoulder and I turned around to see Matsu and his sister, Fumiko.

"He's daydreaming again," Matsu said, laughing.

Fumiko smiled and bowed. The top of her gray head bent toward me and I could faintly smell narcissus. I bowed back and when we both stood erect, she was shorter than I imagined. The thickness of age showed on her body, and like Matsu's, there was a certain strength in it. But it was Fumiko's face that captured my attention. It was one I would have loved to paint. She wasn't beautiful, not in the way that Tomoko must have been, nor did she have the roughness of Matsu. Her attraction wasn't in the form of perfect features, but from the deep wrinkles, age spots, and eyes that have seen much of what life has to offer. Fumiko had a face that had been enriched through time.

"I'm very happy to meet you," I bowed again.

"You are just as Matsu described you," she said, looking toward him.

"And how did he describe me?" I asked, speaking louder, above the noise of the crowd.

"That you looked just like your *ojī-san,*" she said, as she raised, then lowered her voice.

Fumiko insisted on making lunch when we returned to the house. I couldn't get over how easily she had stepped into our lives, settling in like another summer flower in the garden. We sat around the wooden table in the kitchen as Matsu directed her from his stool. As always, he felt uncomfortable when he had nothing to do.

"You must know by now, Stephen-*san,* that Matsu cannot sit still. Even as a young boy, he had to be doing something."

"You sure it isn't Tomoko you're talking about?" Matsu asked. He stood up and helped her place a pot of water on the stove.

"Both of you," Fumiko said.

I listened, thinking how it was the first time I had heard Matsu speak of Tomoko as if she were alive. And suddenly, it was as if the ghost of her filled the room with us. Matsu became young again with his older sister chiding him.

"It wasn't easy living with you two," he teased.

Fumiko dropped thick *udon* noodles into the pot, making sure they were separated and wouldn't stick together as they cooked. "I suppose so," she said, "but then, you didn't pay any attention to us anyway!"

Matsu sat back down and began to peel a peach, anything to keep his hands busy. "I couldn't understand either of you then," he said.

Fumiko stopped what she was doing and turned around. "I don't think I did either," she said. "If I had, I might have been more understanding."

For a moment, I thought I should get up and leave, that their conversation should belong just to the two of them, but it was Matsu who suddenly cleared his throat, placed both of his hands squarely on the table, and pushed himself up. He mumbled something about the garden, left the peeled peach on the wooden table, and was just as quickly gone from the kitchen.

"It's Matsu's way," Fumiko said softly, as she watched her brother leave. She turned back and stirred the noodles. "He always has had difficulties speaking of Tomoko, even after all these years."

"Were you still here when Tomoko . . ."

"Killed herself?" she asked, turning toward me.

I nodded.

"I was five years older than Tomoko, and had already been married. I had moved with my husband to Tokyo just six months before. I always thought she would join me there one day. Tomoko was always a dreamer, she never had her feet on the ground." Fumiko shook her head. "It was such a tragedy, because she was a beautiful girl, so full of life. I remember the day I received the telegram telling me of her death. I thought it was a big mistake. I told my husband, so he wired back only to receive another telegram confirming Tomoko's suicide. I sometimes dream of her as a grown woman, still beautiful and living happily. But then I wake up. And after so many years, I still return every year to honor her spirit, hoping that she has found some peace in the other world, which she couldn't find here."

"How was Matsu?" I asked.

Fumiko rinsed and drained the noodles. She then gently dropped the steaming bundle into another pot of boiling broth. "He was always quiet and hardworking. Did you know he was the one to find Tomoko?" she asked, not waiting for an answer. "During her last days," Fumiko continued, "my mother said Tomoko was closest to Matsu. It seemed so ironic, since before then, she would have little to do with him. I sometimes wonder if I could in some way have helped Tomoko through her despair."

Fumiko's voice trailed off, then stopped. The boiling noodles bubbled and sputtered. The steam rose and coiled itself around the small kitchen.

"After our parents died," Fumiko continued, "I asked Matsu to come to live in Tokyo, but he refused. 'I wouldn't know what to do there,' he said. He did come to visit once, but his heart has always been in Tarumi. Even though he won't say what, there has always been something or someone holding him here, something as deeply rooted as the pines covering these mountains."

I smiled to myself, and wondered how Matsu had managed to

keep Sachi a secret for so many years. It's true, Fumiko had moved to Tokyo early on, but she was the only family he had left now. How could he not shout Sachi's name out, and tell Fumiko that she was the reason he couldn't leave Tarumi? And how could he not make Sachi more real, more rooted in his life by acknowledging her presence? These thoughts turned around in my mind as I watched Fumiko divide the noodles into three bowls, place some fish cake on top, then set the bowls one by one on the table.

AUGUST 17, 1938

The low sounds of murmuring voices woke me. It took a few moments to realize that it wasn't a dream, but the soft hum of Matsu and Fumiko whispering in the kitchen. It was very early and still dark outside. I lay quietly as the warm, sweet smell of cooking drifted into my room, slowly drawing me out of a half-sleep. By the time I dressed and joined them in the kitchen, I could see that they must have been up for hours, preparing food to bring to the graves of Tomoko and their parents. On the table were bowls of pickled vegetables, deep-fried tofu, rice balls filled with red beans, and salted fish.

"I was just about to wake you," Matsu said, when he saw me standing in the doorway. "We have to leave the house very soon."

"I'm ready," I said. I wiped the sleep from my eyes.

"Here, Stephen-*san,* drink this," Fumiko said, handing me a cup of steaming tea.

I sipped it slowly, watching the two of them work side by side. I could see there was a warmth between them. It was the same way I felt with my brother or sisters, the kind of calm familiarity that comes from having grown up together. It felt good to see Matsu in this morning light, so unlike himself. Sometimes they spoke in whispers, or not at all, their hands slicing and wrapping, moving in perfect rhythm.

We left the house just as the sun rose a red-orange. My thoughts drifted to Sachi and what she might be doing for *O-bon* in

Yamaguchi. There were already many others making their way down the dirt road, carrying *furoshikis* filled with food for the graves of their family members. We joined the long procession which grew as we entered the village and lengthened down the road which led to the temple. The village itself seemed lighter, cleaner, as preparations for the festivities had begun. Long thin wooden poles about six feet tall or more stood every three feet down the length of the dirt road. Small hooks which protruded from the top of the poles awaited the lanterns to be hung on them. I looked around and felt relieved at not seeing Keiko and her family. Her father had made his feelings toward me clear the last time we were at the temple, and I didn't want either Keiko or myself to be embarrassed like that again.

By the time we reached the cemetery, there were already bowls of food and clay cups of tea and *sake* left at the graves. In Hong Kong, we also used to make the yearly pilgrimage to honor our ancestors during the Ghosts' Feast: first Ba-ba's side, then Mah-mee's. While the gravestones here in Tarumi were plain and simply engraved, many of those in Hong Kong were large and elaborate, most of them containing small photos of the deceased embedded in the stone. I had always enjoyed walking slowly down the crooked rows of gravestones, somehow moved by the faces staring back at me. They were images of youth and glamor, age and wisdom. It didn't matter. I walked away each year taking these faces with me, as if in that short time I had somehow come to know them.

So I felt let down by the time we came to Matsu and Fumiko's family plots. They were distinguished only by gray stone markers with names and dates written on them; there was no trace of personality surviving. I realized then I had never seen what Tomoko looked like. All I knew was that she had been beautiful as a girl. I wondered if Matsu had a photo of her tucked away somewhere.

Matsu and Fumiko unpacked the *furoshikis* and placed bowl after bowl of food on the three graves in front of them. Then came another surprise: Matsu stepped forward and began chanting something under his breath, almost in song. His voice was surprisingly soft and melodious. When he had finished, he and Fumiko bowed low toward the graves, and from where I stood a few feet

180

behind, I did the same. Afterward, Matsu suddenly excused himself and began to walk across the cemetery. He carried another *furoshiki* with him.

"Where is he going?" I asked Fumiko, who was busy washing the dirt off the gravestones with an old rag and a can of water.

Without looking up from her work, she answered, "To see Kenzo-*san*."

I wondered what Matsu had told her about Kenzo's death. Did she know he had hung himself? Could she have any idea of the cause? I watched Fumiko silently scrub the stone, then glance up just in time to see Matsu turn around the corner of the temple.

By the time we returned to the village, it had come alive with people and laughter. Large and small paper lanterns hung from the thin poles, lighting the way for the ghosts to arrive and depart. The lanterns came in all shapes, some resembling the figures of animals and houses, while others were simpler, painted colorfully in red, black, or white. Each dangled from its pole like an ornament. The smell of frying fish, *mochi* in soy sauce and sugar, and red bean cakes made my stomach growl. Music flowed through the air. It was time to entertain the spirits, to dance and rejoice at their return. The street was filled with people eating and drinking, people who had traveled hundreds of miles to be in Tarumi. There were so many new faces in the village, I felt as if I were somewhere else. Groups of women and children lingered in the street. Old men mingled, trying to remember names and faces from the past. The one thing all these people had in common were the dead they returned every year to honor.

I looked over at Kenzo's teahouse which stood dark and empty. I could almost imagine seeing him last year during *O-bon*, his trim figure rushing back and forth, carrying trays of drinks to thirsty customers. He might have slapped Matsu on the shoulder and invited him in for a beer. Only this year he was gone, leaving Matsu to honor him with food and drink. And what must Sachi be feeling this *O-bon*? I wondered if they were celebrating the dead in Yamaguchi?

It was hard to imagine what the future would bring to any of us.

All over Japan they were celebrating the dead, even as more and more Chinese were being slaughtered. There would be no one left to celebrate them. I looked around at all the smiling faces, at Matsu and Fumiko who moved slowly beside me, and wished that one of them could explain to me what was going to happen.

AUTUMN

September 5, 1938

*T*he first signs of fall have already made themselves noticed in the garden. The smells were first to change, the perfumes sweeter and heavier. Next will be the colors as they turn to the reliable shades of crimson, saffron, orange, and scarlet. There's something more serious about the fall than any other season. Maybe it's the light that gradually grows darker, making everything seem less trivial, forcing you to look harder to find your way.

Most of the summer crowds had departed by the last week in August, leaving Tarumi quiet again. When I walked outside this morning I was overcome by a feeling of nostalgia, a memory of being younger and knowing I would have to return to school soon. And though passing another autumn in Tarumi wasn't exactly like going back to school. It felt the same as returning to something I had lived before.

Of course, all these thoughts dissolved when Matsu called me over to the back of the garden to take a look at something.

"Look," he said, pointing down to a globe-shaped plant he called *"Kerria."*

I looked down to the yellow-orange flowers, their five-petalled blossoms resembling small chrysanthemums. "They're beautiful," I said, trying to share in his enthusiasm.

Matsu squatted down and fingered the small petals. "They're more than that," he said. "They usually only bloom one week in the spring. It is a sign of good luck to see blossoms this late in the year."

"Do you think we'll have any good luck?" I asked.

Matsu looked up at me, then back down at the blossoms. "As long as we don't have any bad luck," he answered.

I went down to the beach this morning. It was the first time in weeks that there haven't been crowds of people. Somehow it feels as if it belongs to me again, that I've stayed away all these weeks waiting for an empty stretch of sand. Just as I've been expecting Keiko to return again. I found out not long after the *O-bon* Festival that she and her family had gone to Osaka to visit her mother's family. Actually, it was Matsu who returned from the post office one afternoon and casually mentioned that they were away. First, he handed me a postcard from Pie, sent from Macao where she and Mah-mee finally went to visit Anne and Henry. Then he said, "That pretty friend of yours went to Osaka with her family. She's due back in a few weeks, according to Yoshida-*san.*" I nodded my head, then thanked him for the mail. Even when I turned to walk away and had begun to read my postcard, I could feel his eyes follow me.

Everywhere on the beach there are still remnants of people having been there. Carelessly dropped paper wrappers, a plastic shovel partly embedded in the sand, small mounds of what used to be castles and moats still stand. I felt lonely seeing these things, not for those who'd left them, but for all the things I've had to leave. The worst part of being sick was the fatigue, a weakness that set me apart from the rest, which left me nothing more than a spectator. At school I could only watch friends swim, play basketball and cricket. While convalescing at home, I was always a room away from the laughter. But after a year in Tarumi I finally felt stronger than I had in the past two years. Now I couldn't help but wonder how long it would be before I had to leave Tarumi behind also, and begin to participate in my other life again.

Lately, the news about the war in China had been sporadic, which simply meant no large Japanese victories, but the silence didn't fool me any longer. Sometimes I felt as if we were all just suspended in time, waiting.

I walked along the beach, until a flash of light caught my eye. It came from above the dune, and at first I thought it was just the sun playing tricks on me. But when I saw it flash again, I slowly began to distinguish someone walking through the waves of heat to the beach. I stood there and waited, until the slim figure disappeared again behind the dune. The soft crunching of the sand grew louder as Keiko finally rose up and over the dune.

"Keiko-*san!*" I waved to her.

Keiko saw me and waved back. She tried to move faster, but her wooden sandals made it difficult to run. She stopped for a moment to take them off, then carried them in her hands, freeing herself to run to me.

"I had hoped to see you," she bowed. Around her neck was a silver chain and pendant I hadn't noticed before. It must have been what had flashed in the sunlight.

"So was I." I bowed back. "I heard you were away with your family."

"Yes," she said, "we went to Osaka to visit my grandparents." She looked down toward her feet, then up and away from me toward the sea.

"Is everything all right?"

Keiko hesitated at first, then said quickly, "I won't be able to see you anymore, Stephen-*san.*"

"What do you mean?" I asked. It felt like she had just slapped me across the face.

"I'm sorry, but it must be this way," she said, looking me in the eyes. "I have to go now."

Keiko quickly turned around and began to walk back in the same direction from which she came. I wanted a better explanation, and instantly followed her back toward the dune. I reached out and grabbed her arm just as she was about to make her ascent. She still carried her wooden sandals in her hands, and as she swung around, they hit me in the chest.

"What's wrong with you?" I asked, squeezing her arm harder than I had intended to. "Has your father changed your mind about us?"

"There can never be any 'us,' " she answered.

Then Keiko pulled away from me, and for a moment I thought she was going to strike me with her sandals again. But she simply stepped away from me, as she fingered her silver chain with one hand and cradled her sandals in the other.

"Not without an explanation," I said.

"Don't you see, nothing could ever come of our friendship now." She looked behind her, checking again to see if anyone were watching us. "My brother was killed at Hsuchowfu. We just received word when we returned from Osaka."

At first I was stunned. Hsuchowfu! That meant that her brother had been killed back in May. I couldn't imagine what it must mean for her family to lose their only son. I pulled Keiko close to me and held on tight. I could feel her body choking back her tears, moving up and down in small hiccups. We stayed like this for a long time, until she pulled away just enough that I could see her face was wet. I assumed her tears were for her dead brother, but then she lifted her hand to touch my cheek, pressing her warmth there for a few moments. I thought about kissing her, but I was afraid she might pull away and leave me even faster. When at last I released her, Keiko looked into my eyes but said nothing. She simply turned quietly around and made her way back up the dune. This time I didn't follow her. I stood there and waited for something, the slightest nod of her head, the light of the sun on her necklace, any small sign for me to follow. But Keiko never once turned back. I watched her climb to the top, then little by little disappear beyond the sand dune.

I haven't been able to sleep. I got up to write this all down, hoping I could purge myself of Keiko and the ghost of her brother. I wondered how many Chinese he had killed before his own death? I suppose the question held no relevance to a Japanese family who had lost their only son. But what of all the Chinese civilians killed during the last year? Did Keiko and her family grieve for those sons and daughters, mothers and fathers? The madness of war destroyed much more than just the soldiers fighting in it. It picked apart everything in its way, so that no one escaped its clutches. Not even someone as decent and humane as Keiko would be left without scars.

SEPTEMBER 16, 1938

I dreamed of Keiko last night. She was running to me on the beach, but no matter how fast she ran, she could never get any closer to me. I'm not sure what I was doing in the dream, just standing there or running toward her. All I know is, when I woke up, I was sweating profusely, my futon and pillow damp, so I must have been running.

Matsu knows something has changed between Keiko and me, but he hasn't asked any questions and I haven't volunteered any information. I'm not sure what to tell him, since we had barely gotten started before our friendship ended. I've tried not to be too sullen, but like not having enough to eat, there's always that longing for more. Once or twice I thought I'd seen her at the beach, but it was only my "imagination playing tricks," as Mahmee would say.

The things you remember about a person when they're gone are funny. No two people will feel the same way, though usually it has to do with scent, or expression, the sound of a voice, an unusual gesture. For me, I can still see the colors of Keiko; the black of her hair against creamy pale skin, her dark blue kimono with white circles, the deep orange persimmons falling from the brown basket she carried. The ache in my heart grows larger every time I think of these colors, and how as each day passes they continue to fade from my eyes.

SEPTEMBER 23, 1938

It has rained for the past week. Then today, the first day of autumn, the rain stopped as if on cue, producing one of the most beautiful days. The sky this morning was a cloudless pale blue. The air was fresh with the damp salty smell of earth and the sea. It was a perfect day to celebrate *Shubun No-Hi,* the Autumn Equinox, with Sachi.

We left for Yamaguchi in the morning. I hadn't been there in a long time and was anxious to see Sachi again. It wasn't a very pleasant hike up the mountain with the earth saturated and muddy. I slipped on several occasions and by the time we arrived, both Matsu and I were splattered from head to toe, our shoes and the cuffs of our trousers caked with mud. Sachi simply looked at us, covered her mouth, and began to laugh when she saw us sloshing up to her doorstep.

We went around the back of the house to the garden, the

stones still dark and shiny, steamy from all the rain. We took off
our shoes and carefully rolled up the cuffs of our pants before
stepping up to the back door. Sachi was waiting with two *yakata*
robes for us to change into.

"Would you like to bathe?" Sachi asked, eyeing us up and
down.

Matsu looked at me, then shook his head. He gestured to the
side of the house. "We'll just rinse and take off these clothes."

Sachi bowed in agreement, handing him the two robes as she
quickly turned back into the house. Matsu led me to the other
side where there was a barrel of water. Nearby was a large wooden
tub in which to bathe.

"Take one of these," Matsu said. He handed me a robe, which
I could immediately tell was too large for me. Matsu removed his
clothes, rinsed them off, and slipped on the robe which fit him
perfectly. I did the same, no longer embarrassed by my nakedness. I had gained back some weight over the year, and with all the
swimming I'd been doing, I was in better shape than ever before.
But when I put on the robe, I could still easily have wrapped it
twice around me.

By the time we stepped into Sachi's house, she had hot tea waiting for us. The table was already set, with covered lacquer dishes
neatly arranged in the middle.

"*Dōmo arigatō,*" I said, as I accepted the tea. The robe hung
loosely from my body and almost fell open as I bowed.

Sachi smiled.

"How have you weathered all this rain?" I heard Matsu ask. He
stood by the back *shoji* door and stared out into the garden. There
was something different about his manner that I couldn't quite
pinpoint.

"It has been fine," Sachi answered.

Matsu walked around the house and looked up at the ceiling,
checking for any signs of leaking. When he found none, he smiled
to himself, went over to the table, and sat down with an ease that
comes from knowledge and assurance. At that moment I saw him
for what he was: the master of the house. I realized for the first
time that he'd never had a place of his own. Matsu had spent the
entirety of his adult life living and taking care of my grandfather's
beach house. Before then, he lived with his parents. But I could

see that this house, lovingly built with his own hands for Sachi, was just as much his. And suddenly, all the years of service fell away. He sat at the table with his dark robe on, looking happy and content as he motioned for us to join him.

I sat back and watched as Sachi served Matsu marinated eel, fried tofu, and rice. Then she stood quietly to one side, and watched him take his first mouthful, chew, then nod his head approvingly as her lips curved upward just slightly into a smile.

It was something I'd seen hundreds of times when I was young and my father was home. It became a nightly ritual. Though my father wore a mask of indifference on his face as Ching stood by his side, waiting for him to taste the food and give his approval, she appeared as anxious as a small child. Every evening she planned our dinner, mumbling to herself if something wasn't to my father's liking. I'd always felt uncomfortable being waited on, even by Ching, who has worked for my family ever since I can remember. But it was evident that after so many years Ching had a certain power over our family. My father trusted her with his food and his children. My mother told Ching secrets, then listened to her like a wise older sister, never daring to scream too loud at Ching when she was angry, for fear she might go to work for another family. It was easy to see that without Ching, my mother would be lost.

And with my mother and father so often away for business and pleasure, Ching stayed behind, raising all of us children as if we were her own. She brewed us bitter teas when we were sick, and scolded us when we were bad. And in many instances, it was Ching whom we all turned to instead of my mother with our skinned knees and broken hearts. She served us all the time, and in so many ways. I remember once asking her if she had any children of her own. "I have all of you," she said, "no one else."

After that I felt better, as if we also served some purpose, because without us, she might have simply drifted away with nothing to hold her down.

*   *   *

Matsu raised his bowl up and asked Sachi for some more rice. She rose before he even finished his sentence. At the same time he poured more tea into her cup and there seemed to be a perfect balance. I knew neither of them would ever drift away from the other.

"Would you also like more rice, Stephen-*san?*" Sachi asked me.

"Yes, please," I answered, lifting my bowl up toward her so she wouldn't have to reach.

SEPTEMBER 28, 1938

I woke up feeling anxious this morning. While Matsu was in the garden pruning and raking up leaves I went back into his room and turned on the radio. There was nothing new, the same old voice speaking of the Imperial Emperor and Japan's courageous struggle against foreign imperialism and communism. I clicked the radio off and went outside.

In Matsu's garden, and all over Tarumi, chrysanthemums were blooming in abundance. Matsu squatted by a black pine, pruning back its branches. When he heard me come up behind him, he sat back on his heels and said, "I could use some help."

"Just tell me what I should do," I said, grateful to have something to occupy myself.

"Hold this," he said, directing me to take hold of a branch so he could clip it.

"Like this?" I asked, but Matsu had already clipped what he had wanted.

"Sometimes it's easier to have two people doing it," he said. Then he lifted himself up off the ground and grabbed a bucket of soil. "You don't want to swim anymore?" he asked, turning around.

"I don't really feel like it," I answered. I thought it might be a good time to mention what had happened with Keiko. "I'm not seeing Keiko-*san* anymore," I blurted, wishing it had come out smoother than it did.

Matsu looked up at me, then simply pointed to another branch and asked, "Can you hold that one down?"

I did as he asked, while Matsu moved slowly, meticulously to cut back the branch in just the right place.

"Isn't it interesting, Stephen-*san,*" he said, "how sometimes you must cut away something in order to make it grow back stronger?"

I nodded.

"It may seem lonely and barren at first, only to flower again in the spring."

I thought it just like Matsu to relate human emotions to a tree. "Keiko isn't a pine tree," I said, annoyed at the comparison. "Her brother was killed at Hsuchowfu."

Matsu shook his head. "The stupidity of it," I heard him mumble. Then after a moment, he said, "We aren't so different, humans beings and plants. We are all a part of one nature and from each other we learn how to live."

"Even as one person destroys another?"

Matsu slowly got up from the ground. He stood back and looked approvingly at the black pine. "I won't say we human beings still don't have much to learn. Sometimes we love and hate without thought. We expect too much from one another, and often we are wrong. Take that flower," he said, pointing to the crepe myrtle. "It has a short life span, but you know just what to expect of it. The leaves are turning yellow-orange, so you know within a week they'll fall. Fortunately—or unfortunately—we human beings have much longer lives. And that makes for many more complications. But in the end, Stephen-*san,* you can only look back, hoping everything that happens in your life is for a purpose. Whether you see Keiko-*san* or not anymore won't take away from your having known her. If she is important, she will stay with you." He picked up the bucket of soil.

I offered to help him, but he shrugged his shoulders. "There will be others," he said, walking away from me, "many others. No reason for you to quit swimming."

SEPTEMBER 30, 1938

It's Pie's birthday early next month, so I spent a good part of the afternoon in the village looking for something to send her. The mail seems to move slower and slower. I haven't received anything from Hong Kong or Kobe for the longest time—no letters, not even a newspaper from my father.

The village was quiet. At first I'd stayed away, not wanting to run into Keiko. But then, like a page turning, I suddenly hoped I would see her again. Even if it was just a quick glimpse, at least I would know she still existed. But there were very few people in sight. It was as if the entire village had fallen asleep.

There was only one general store, near the post office, where I'd any hopes of finding a gift for Pie. Although she had everything she really needed in Hong Kong, I wanted to send her a keepsake, something she might look back on one day that would mark this year of separation. The store was very dark and cool inside. An old woman bowed and gestured for me to look around. I walked slowly down the crowded aisles hoping to find something, but there were only the essentials; canned goods, tea, ginger, fishing line, or knives. I was disappointed at not being able to find anything for Pie. Instead, I picked up several small cans of pickled vegetables, rice crackers, dried seaweed, and bought them from the grateful old woman.

Outside again, my eyes watered from the glare of bright sunlight. Two old men were sitting in front of the store engrossed in conversation, unaware of my presence. They spoke of the war, of Japanese honor, and how the Imperial Army must quickly capture the south before any more Japanese blood was shed. Neither of them mentioned Chinese losses, whose numbers were so large, so unreal, that it would take the shrill-voiced woman on the radio days to count them all.

OCTOBER 5, 1938

I woke up this morning wanting to go for a swim. Weeks had passed since I'd last seen Keiko at the beach, and I felt as if her shadow had finally been lifted. There was a chill in the air when I left the house. The warmth of summer had given way to a cool, breezy autumn. There was a kind of sadness in the air, the smell of saltwater mixed with the decaying flowers and fallen fruits. I tried not to think of anything morbid as I made my way down the path, over the dune to the water. The sea came in a flurry of small waves, rolling in white and furious.

I slipped out of my clothes and stepped slowly into the water. It was already much cooler than a few weeks before. I hesitated at first, then ran in, letting the cold water shock my body, awakening me. I swam until I was entirely numb from the cold, then just let my body roll back to shore on a wave like a lifeless piece of seaweed. It sometimes amazed me to think how powerless I was.

By the time I got back to the house, Matsu had left a note telling me he had gone into the village. I was still numb from head to toe after my swim so I decided to take a hot bath. The wooden tub in the back of the house stood empty and waiting. I filled the tub with water as I seen Matsu do time after time and lit the coals in the iron box underneath. Then I went to wash my body before the soak.

By the time Matsu returned, I was still soaking. It was one of the many customs I would miss when the time came for me to return to Hong Kong.

"You're going to have heatstroke," he said, coming out of the kitchen. He carried several newspapers and a few letters in his hand.

"It feels good," I answered.

"Looks like it all came at one time," he said. Matsu put one of the letters into his pocket. "From Fumiko," he added, balancing the rest of the stack on an uneven stone a few feet from the tub. Two more letters lay on top.

I quickly lifted myself out of the hot water, as the cool air embraced my body and sent goose bumps from my feet to the nape of my neck. I stepped out of the tub, towelled off, and slipped on my trousers and shirt. Matsu was already back at work picking up leaves, ignoring me. So I grabbed the mail and hurried into the house.

I didn't go to my room, but instead sat at the kitchen table as I'd seen Matsu do a hundred times before, his head buried in one of his magazines. One of the two letters was from King and the other from my father. I hadn't received anything from King in so long, and I was anxious to know if he was all right. I ripped open the envelope which had been mailed just over two months ago from Canton.

August 2, 1938

Dear Stephen,

I bet you think I've forgotten you. Well, no such luck! It's just that things have gotten quite difficult for us over here, and writing and studying between the blackouts has become an art. Don't I envy you there on the beach, without the incessant threat of bombs exploding in the distance. Don't laugh, but it has gotten so I dream with dull thuds in the background.

In all seriousness, things are awfully hot over here. We are rationed on everything from rice and tea to soap and toilet paper. I've finally found something to do with all my old exams! It doesn't matter anyway, the number of students here at Lingnan has dropped to just a handful. Most are trying to return to Macao or Hong Kong while they can. I wanted to write to let you know, Stephen, I'm finally leaving for Hong Kong next week too, if everything goes smoothly, so you can expect to see me there when you return. It seems kind of funny sending this letter to Japan, since they are the ones we curse every morning and every evening before we close our eyes. That is, if the distant bombing allows us to sleep.

But how are you? It has been much too long since I've heard any news. I'm not sure if you're having too good a time to remember your old friend, or if the mail isn't coming through. Whatever it is, when I see you next, we will certainly have grown older.

Oh yes, do you remember Vivian Hong? The pretty girl from primary school? She was killed last week when a bomb hit the apartment building she was in. It makes you realize just how fragile we all are.

I miss you, my friend. I look forward to the day we will meet again in Hong Kong.

Take care,
King

I tried to remember what Vivian Hong looked like. It disturbed me when I couldn't. The images of several girls came to my mind, but I wasn't sure Vivian was any of them. A feeling of guilt, then deep sadness, came over me to think she could already be forgotten.

I reread King's letter and imagined him already safely back in Hong Kong. He might be playing cricket, or eating noodles down in Wan Chai, or catching a movie in Central. Whatever, I suddenly ached to be doing the same thing. It had been over a year since I'd last seen my family and friends. I wanted to be like everyone else again, but I felt like a stranger, like I no longer belonged anywhere.

I looked down at the newspapers which all had headlines that said the same thing. The Imperial Japanese Army continued to thunder through China and were advancing every day. I threw the papers aside and then remembered the other letter from my father. I opened it carefully, as I imagined he would do. It began like all the others, inquiring about my health and hoping I continued to improve. I almost skipped the rest, thinking I knew just what he was going to say, how it might be just another obligatory letter. But something in the last paragraph caught my eye: He had to go on a short business trip to Tokyo. "I will be taking the train from Kobe up to Tokyo for a few days, and will have some time free for pleasure." My gaze ran over the next line several times before its meaning settled in. "Would you be interested in coming along?" he wrote.

OCTOBER 11, 1938

I wrote my father telling him I'd like to accompany him to Tokyo. This morning he sent back a telegram saying he was pleased.

I can't remember if I'd ever gone on a trip alone with him as a young boy. There's a faint memory of my being in a very large, open marketplace with high voices, pecking chickens, and bone-thin dogs sniffing at my legs. It smelled terribly of burning incense and salted fish. I held onto a man's hand, being dragged along through the crowd. I squeezed the hand so tight, my own felt numb and tight at the knuckles. I was afraid to let go, afraid of being lost among the throng of people, voices, and smells. But even now, I can't remember ever knowing for certain if it was my father's hand, or that of a servant's or uncle's I was holding, only that it was big and warm as it pulled me away from any harm.

OCTOBER 19, 1938

Yesterday we visited Sachi. I wanted to see her before I left. She was in village when we arrived, having just left Tanaka-*san*'s house. When she saw us walking toward her, I could see her lips part slightly, and pull upward into a smile. The faint scent of eucalyptus filled the air as we walked back to her house. When I told her about my trip to Tokyo, Sachi became quiet—a flicker of longing in her eyes. I realized she had been hidden away in Yamaguchi for so long she could only dream of the bright colors and fragrances that left her behind. I started to say something, but Matsu changed the subject and moved closer to Sachi, causing her soft kimono to brush against his arm.

Matsu saw me off on the train today. My father would be waiting for me at the Kobe station. Then we would leave almost immediately for Tokyo to stay for three days. I had only packed a small bag which Matsu insisted on carrying as we walked into Tarumi. Once there, Matsu shuffled his feet as we waited on the platform. He always seemed nervous when someone was coming or going.

When the slow-moving train finally arrived, Matsu handed me my bag and stepped quickly back as if crossing over an invisible line which separated us. Without saying a word, he slipped me a piece of paper with Fumiko's number and address on it, just in case of an emergency. I bowed and boarded the train, but by the time I found a seat and looked out the window, Matsu was no longer there.

As the train rumbled and ground its way to Kobe, I realized it was the first time I'd been away from Tarumi in over a year. The rocking motion suddenly made me tired. I hadn't slept much the night before, just thinking about what it would be like in Tokyo. I remember our entire family going there together once, when I was still too young to appreciate it. It seemed then just as crowded and congested as Hong Kong, filled with bright signs and people. My father and mother went dancing every night and we children were left at the hotel with Ching. Ching was always set in her ways. She would only eat Chinese food, so she brought her own white rice, long beans, lotus roots, and soy sauce chicken in jars and clay pots. Pretty soon the rich aroma filled our room so that if we closed our eyes, we couldn't tell if we were in Tokyo or at home.

I leaned my head back against the seat, knowing that within a few hours I would see my father. For a moment my heart raced as I tried to think of what we would talk about for three days. Still, if we had learned anything in the past year, it was how to dodge the more complicated subjects. My mother always topped that list.

By the time the train pulled into Kobe, I had napped and was looking forward to seeing my father. I grabbed my bag and followed the other passengers out of the train. The station was noisy and crowded. Train departures and arrivals were announced over a scratchy loudspeaker. I looked for my father, then finally saw him. He stood to one side, away from the crowd, his leather valise and briefcase by his side. He raised his hand straight up when he saw me, as if he were in a class and knew the answer to a question.

"Ba-ba." I put down my bag and bowed.

"You look very well," my father said, pleased. "We have a short time before our train departs. Let's get something to drink. Are you hungry?" he asked.

"Matsu packed some rice cakes," I answered, "but I wouldn't mind something to drink."

My father smiled, then leaned over to pick up his baggage, but I grabbed his valise first. He led me through a throng of people and I noticed many more soldiers lingering around the station than the year before. They eyed us up and down when we passed, gripped their rifles tighter, but said nothing.

We came to a small, standup bar to one side of the station which served drinks, beer, and small snacks. Both of us ordered coffee.

"How was your trip?" my father asked, as he sipped his coffee.

I finished spooning sugar into my coffee, then answered, "It was comfortable. It's hard to believe it's my first time out of Tarumi in over a year."

199

"You're certainly in much better health now than when you left here a year ago." My father added, "I see you've put on some weight."

"Let me show you," I said, taking off my jacket so he could feel my arm. I was proud of how solid I'd become.

My father squeezed my arm and laughed. "You're catching up with Henry," he said, referring to my large younger brother.

"I'm feeling well, Ba-ba. I sometimes wondered if I ever would again."

My father left his hand on my arm, giving it another squeeze. "Drink up," he said, "then we'd better catch that train."

OCTOBER 20, 1938

Tokyo seems enormous. Yesterday, after we arrived at our hotel I went out for a walk before dinner. My father had some business to attend to so it gave me a chance to look around. We stayed near the Ginza, a willow-tree-lined street more spectacular and flamboyant than anything I'd seen before. Even Hong Kong paled compared to the number of shops and restaurants that lined this large street, branching off to alleyways housing more shops. Long strips of cloth hung from doorways, characters announcing what each shop offered, from sushi and dumplings to souvenirs and tin windup toys. Women and men were dressed in both kimonos and Western clothing as they elbowed their way from one place to another. Compared to the slow-moving Tarumi villagers, they appeared sharp and humorless. And though the sounds of Tokyo felt flatter than Hong Kong, they were just as frantic. Large trolley cars rattled down the center lane as Western horn-honking cars and hand-pulled carts inched their way up the street. Noodle peddlers stood by their pushcarts playing their flutes in time to the *clock* of the wooden sandals against the pavement. And everywhere there were military vehicles and groups of Japanese soldiers who appeared young and excited, but who were none-the-less menacing with their rifles hanging loosely from their narrow shoulders.

I kept on walking. The Imperial Palace loomed up ahead, stately and imposing. It had stood majestically in the middle of Tokyo for centuries, housing the Imperial Emperor and his family. I walked around its outer walls, built mostly of wood and tile, surrounded by Japanese who came religiously to honor their Emperor. Groups of young boys and girls marvelled at its sheer size—not its modest height, but the vastness of its spread over so many acres, protected by moats and walls, housing hundreds of servants and workers in addition to the Imperial family. It felt strange being so close to the one person for whom an entire nation would go to war and die.

I walked by a group of young women dressed in kimonos who were sitting together on a bench by a fountain. They were talking quietly, sewing scraps of brightly colored cloth with dark threads. When I returned to the hotel later, I found out from my father that they were making *senninbari,* amulets made from embroidered material, which were then cut out and sewn together for the Japanese soldiers fighting overseas.

We ate dinner in a restaurant near the hotel where my father said they served the best marinated eel in all of Japan. We ordered steaming rice to eat with it. The small room was crowded and noisy with discussion. It wasn't long before I realized most of the conversations taking place were about the war in China. Even my father refrained from speaking Chinese there, and spoke only Japanese in his soft, measured tones. Toward the end of the meal he told me that perhaps I should return to Hong Kong before Christmas.

"Are things getting bad?" I asked in Chinese, keeping my voice low.

"You're well again, and your mother will be pleased to have you back with her," he answered in Japanese.

"Will Hong Kong be safe?" I continued to question him. I knew he heard things through his business connections, so he had a clearer picture of the situation than any of us.

"For now it is," he answered, this time in Chinese.

OCTOBER 22, 1938

Canton fell yesterday. The news came over the wireless and was announced from a loudspeaker at the hotel. For a moment it seemed as if everyone and everything froze, listening. After months of continual bombardment, the Japanese had simply executed a surprise landing in Bias Bay. I imagined the Cantonese, already anesthetized by constant bombing, dazed by the defeat.

My father and I were having lunch at the time, and the news felt like an unexpected blow to my stomach. All the Japanese in the restaurant cheered to hear news of the last major Chinese port to be captured, while I struggled for air and simply couldn't say anything. I watched my father look up from his plate sadly. Then shaking his head slowly, he simply said, "We'd better go."

With those few words, everything changed. I knew it was time to leave Tokyo. I no longer felt welcome. On the way to the train station, I sensed I was being watched. Even as the men and women passed me on the street and tried to keep their eyes lowered, I knew they couldn't help noticing that I somehow didn't belong.

Last night I stayed at my father's apartment in Kobe. We arrived on the evening train and I wasn't able to catch another train back to Tarumi until this afternoon. It felt good to spend even a short time with my father, to see him in the shadowy light as he sat in his leather chair uncertain of what he should do. He appeared older and tired, cradling a brandy in one hand. He stared out into the darkness for such a long time I thought he'd forgotten I sat across from him. Then in the end, having decided I should return to Hong Kong alone, he looked up at me. He would stay a little longer in Kobe to finish up some business while he waited to see what the Japanese would do next.

Matsu was waiting for me at the train station. He looked uncomfortable as always as he stood there alone, but once he saw me step off the train I could see his face relax.

"I received a message from your father saying when you were to return, so I thought I would meet your train," he said, taking my bag. "How was Tokyo?"

"Big and crowded," I answered. "It's really good to see you and be back in Tarumi," I said, admitting how much I had missed him.

"It was quiet here without you," he said, as he turned to leave.

"I'm sure you heard about Canton," I said, catching up to him. He grunted.

"I have to return to Hong Kong soon," I said.

I wondered if my father had also told him in the message that I was to sail back to Hong Kong in the next week or so. My father felt there was no need to wait any longer if he were able to book passage back.

Matsu simply looked at me and said, "I thought as much."

OCTOBER 24, 1938

There never seems to be enough time to do all the things you want to do. I hadn't expected it to be so difficult to leave Tarumi, but just the thought of it can make my eyes begin to water. This evening as Matsu prepared dinner and listened to his radio, we heard that Hankow had been captured by the Japanese. It was still hard to believe what was happening to China, and how swiftly it was occurring. Matsu quickly walked over to the radio and turned it off.

"Would you like to go to Yamaguchi tomorrow?" he asked.

I could barely answer, "Yes, I would."

"I think it would be better if you saw Sachi alone," he said.

OCTOBER 25, 1938

I found Sachi at work in her garden this afternoon. She looked up when I came through the sleeve gate, but she didn't seem at all surprised. I was carrying a gift I had bought for her in Kobe. It was a burnt-sienna-colored *yakishime* vase protected by old newspapers.

The night before, I had dreamt about Sachi. She was wrapped in bandages, sick, and all alone. And though she cried out for help, no one came. I wanted to know where Matsu was. But I could only feel afraid for her, without any voice that could be heard in a dream.

"Stephen-*san*." Sachi stood straight and bowed. She didn't ask where Matsu was.

"I wanted to bring you this gift," I said, returning her bow. "Matsu thought it better that I come to see you alone this afternoon," I quickly added.

Sachi smiled. "I am very honored," she bowed again as I handed her the vase. "What brings you all the way up here, and with such a serious face?"

"I've come to say *sayōnara,* Sachi-*san.* I'll be sailing back to Hong Kong in a few days."

I looked down at the stones as Sachi slowly began to rake through them, still cradling the vase in one arm. When she stopped a moment later, she stood silent. She looked so fragile I wanted to put my arms around her.

"Perhaps if the gods smile upon us, Stephen-*san,* we will have the chance to meet again," she said. Sachi put down the rake and bowed low to me. When she stood up again, the damaged side of her face seemed to glow in the sunlight.

I swallowed hard and touched the sleeve of her kimono. "I know we will," was all I could say.

Then Sachi bent down and, picking up the rake, handed it to me with a gesture. I began moving the rake through the stones, pulling it back and running it through again. The crackling sound it made was strangely soothing.

"There's something that has been bothering me," I said, as I stepped back and stood at the edge of her sea of stones.

"What is it?"

"Who will take care of you if something happens to Matsu?" I asked.

"What makes you think of that?" she asked.

"I dreamed you were all alone," I finally said.

"I am," she said, without hesitation.

"But Matsu was gone and you were sick . . ."

"Matsu will be gone one day, or perhaps I'll leave first. Either way, one of us will be alone. There are no guarantees of anything, Stephen-*san.*"

"But what will you do if Matsu should leave first?"

"I'll live the rest of my life the best I can," Sachi said. She gestured around the garden. "Look at all that I have to keep me busy," she smiled.

I nodded, then slowly began to rake through the stones again.

"You don't have to worry about me, Stephen-*san*. I've had a good life." Then Sachi held out her hand to stop the rake. "You have given us the one thing we've lacked."

"I don't understand."

Sachi's fingers closed tightly around the wooden rake. "You have been the *musuko* we lost so many years ago."

"There was a child?" I asked, astonished.

"It was a difficult birth, and in the end he was stillborn." Sachi's words hung heavy in the air.

"I'm sorry," I heard myself say.

I couldn't imagine how terrible it must have been for her. It seemed too unfair that Sachi should bear such a loss after all she'd been through. How could the gods take away the one person who might have made their lives easier? I grew angrier with each thought. And in my mind I saw Matsu lift his dead son in his hands, knowing that he would soon have to bury him in the cold earth, never to see him grow.

"Come with me," Sachi said, her voice startling me. She let the rake drop where we stood.

I followed Sachi back to her house, still feeling the shock of her words. I removed my shoes before I stepped in. The familiar room warmed me immediately, easing my anxiousness. Sachi walked to the low table where she pulled an arrangement of pine branches out of a dark vase. Then she unwrapped her new vase and carefully arranged the pine branches. Placing it on the table, Sachi stood back and smiled. "It adds new life to this room," she said.

"It's beautiful," I agreed.

Sachi turned and bowed to me again. "Thank you again, Stephen-*san*."

Then before I could say anything, she leaned over the table, and said, "Now I would like to give you a very small gift in return, to carry back on your journey home." She reached for my hand and held out her closed fist. In the palm of my hand Sachi placed Tomoko's two shiny black stones, collected so many years ago for their magic powers.

The only time I said good-bye to Sachi was when I first arrived in her garden today. Yet, the finality of the word seemed to echo through the air all afternoon. I sipped the green tea Sachi brought me and ate several red bean cakes, checking from moment to moment to be sure the two smooth stones were still in my pocket. I couldn't stop looking at Sachi's face every chance I had, even when she lowered her eyes in embarrassment. She was still very beautiful. Then when her face slowly faded in the darkening shadows of late afternoon, I began to grieve.

OCTOBER 26, 1938

I spent the entire day on the beach. I swam in the cold water and lay on the last strip of sun-warmed sand. In a matter of weeks it would be too cold to swim. I tried to imagine what my life would be like when I returned to the noise of Hong Kong, and how I'd thought I would never be able to adapt to the quiet here. But just thinking about going back was stifling.

All day I've wanted to see Sachi again. When I left her yesterday, it was as if part of me stayed behind. I felt like I needed to reclaim that part, ease the misery I was feeling. I daydreamed of what it would be like to stay in Tarumi and take care of Matsu and Sachi, make a quiet life for myself away from the noise and war. It would be so simple.

I opened my eyes and lifted my head when I thought I heard something in the distance. I almost dismissed it as just another phantom sound or vision that I had had a few times when I was alone on the beach. I once heard that if you really wanted something, your mind could create it. And I felt lonely for company. I sat up and looked at the dune and waited. I always expected to see Keiko come up and over it, half-running to meet me. But I knew deep inside it was just one of those waking dreams. It was like waiting for a letter that would never come. Only this time I wasn't wrong, someone slowly emerged over the top of the dune. In the next moment I could see Matsu walk toward me carrying a *furoshiki* filled with lunch.

OCTOBER 27, 1938

Today I began to pack. My father booked passage for me on a ship that departs in three days. The day after tomorrow I'll catch a train to Kobe and the following day I will sail for Hong Kong. It doesn't seem possible that I've been in Tarumi for over a year, but in packing up my belongings, I'm amazed that I've gathered so many possessions—my grandfather's paintbrushes, clay pots, shells from the beach. What I'd originally brought seems to have grown three times. Still, I hoped to get most of my packing finished, so Matsu and I could spend my last day in Tarumi without extra burdens.

My grandfather's house feels heavy with silence. Matsu brought me a few boxes this morning, then lingered in the doorway to watch. He hasn't said much since my father wired my departure date. Most of the time Matsu and I don't know what to say to each other. He wanders from one room to the next trying to keep himself busy, but I know we both feel lost. It's as if the house is slowly becoming a stranger to us. Matsu stares hard into each room as if he already sees it as it once was, silent and uncluttered.

Sachi came down from Yamaguchi to be with us this afternoon. It was like a wish come true. The gate creaked open and she walked into the garden unexpectedly, daring all in the bright light of day. Yet, somehow it didn't surprise either one of us as we watched her lower her veil and smile, reassuring Matsu that everything was well.

"I just wanted to see you and Stephen-*san*" was all she said.

Neither of us asked another question.

Later, as I lay in my bed, I tried to hold on to every moment of our evening together. Sachi had brought back a strange lightness to us. Matsu talked and laughed with ease. I couldn't stop watching them together as we sat down to eat around the old wooden table. I wanted Sachi to stay the night, but she insisted on returning to Yamaguchi. As always, Matsu accompanied her back. At the gate, Sachi bowed low to me, saying nothing more. It was only after I was alone in the house again that I realized that this time she had come down for Matsu.

OCTOBER 28, 1938

By the time I woke up this morning, Matsu had left breakfast for me on the table and was already gone. He didn't leave a note telling me where he went and I couldn't help but feel let down that he had disappeared on my last day in Tarumi. But this thought soon passed when I heard the gate open into the garden. I stepped into the *genken* just in time to see Matsu walk in carrying two parcels wrapped in brown paper.

"I thought it was better to take care of my business in the village early today," he said, walking over to me. He lifted up one of the packages. "I went to buy our dinner." The other package stayed safely tucked under his arm and remained a mystery. He appeared much happier after Sachi's visit.

"I thought you were trying to get rid of me a day early," I tried to joke.

Matsu suddenly stopped. "It never crossed my mind," he said.

Matsu prepared lunch while I cleaned up the last of my belongings in grandfather's study. The brushes and paints were neatly stored back in their cases, the empty white canvases left for Matsu to pack away until my next visit. I looked up at my only completed painting of the garden which had sat on the easel since the day it was finished, so many months ago. I decided then I would give the painting to Matsu.

After lunch when I had presented the painting to him, he stood stunned for a moment, then bowed so low I thought he would fall forward. "I am very honored," he said quickly, his eyes directed to the floor in formality.

I returned his bow. "It isn't half as good as having the real garden, but I thought you might enjoy it anyway." Then I took the chance to tell him, "I don't think anyone else could have done a better job taking care of me."

He never lifted his eyes from the floor, but his voice was firm and clear. "I sometimes think it has been the other way around," Matsu said.

We returned to the Tama Shrine in the afternoon. Matsu was surprised when I chose to go there. I was anxious about leaving and I wanted to walk somewhere. Somehow I felt going to the shrine might give me the sense of peace that I needed. This time after I entered the three *torii* gates, I went through the ritual of washing, removing my shoes, and bowing three times without taking any cues from Matsu. It wasn't that I had gone there with any special intention to pray at the shrine. I knew all the praying in the world wouldn't stop the war from continuing, or make my parents love each other again. I wanted to leave a message on the wall by the altar, tacked alongside all the other hopeful requests so that even if I never returned to Tarumi, something of me would remain.

OCTOBER 29, 1938

Last night Matsu prepared salmon and sliced cucumbers topped with miso paste. I watched him prepare the entire meal with the delicacy of hand which has always amazed me. All the while, he sipped from a glass of beer and acted as if it were just another evening in a series of many more. I tried to act normal, too, though the anxiousness gnawing in the pit of my stomach was a constant reminder I was leaving.

After dinner Matsu didn't remove the bowls as usual, but stayed at the table talking as we had done the evening before with Sachi. I told him I hoped to begin taking classes again once I was back in Hong Kong. He said he might eventually go to Tokyo to visit Fumiko for a few days. She'd been trying to get him to go for years, and it might be a good time. I agreed that it would be a perfect time for him to make a visit. After that he would spend time with Sachi, maybe eventually move to Yamaguchi. I saw him watch me closely as he told me this, but I simply agreed with a smile. Then when we had exhausted our conversation, Matsu stood up and took the *daruma* doll I had given him down from the kitchen shelf. He turned its face toward me so I could see he had plainly drawn in one eye. "When you return, I'll draw in the other," he said. "Now you should get some sleep, you have a long journey tomorrow."

I was up very early, moving quietly through the house and out into Matsu's garden. Fall had deadened some of the colors, but there still remained the quiet beauty I would always miss. Nothing had given me more solace those first few days I was in Tarumi than sitting in the garden. In it, life seemed to have stopped, and a separate life contained itself in its beauty. I sat by the pond for the last time, remembering. I had learned the difference between a Japanese flowering cherry tree and a weeping *Higan* cherry tree. I could almost see Sachi again when she came down from Yamaguchi after I'd been hurt, leaning over with Matsu as they planted a new tree. I felt Keiko's white blossoms that flowed over the fence and dusted my head. These images turned around and around in my mind as I listened to the wind crying through the bamboo fence.

I was about to go inside when I heard a small sound by the front gate. I had grown accustomed to checking on these ghostly occurrences with hopes that they might be real. I moved quietly toward the gate, so I wouldn't scare whoever or whatever it was. I couldn't see any shadows between the bamboo slats as I strained to listen for another sound. Except for the wind, there was nothing out of the ordinary. I grasped the handle of the gate and quickly swung it open. The road was empty, but this time Keiko had really been here. Attached to the gate was a single pressed white blossom.

Even if you walk the same road a hundred times, you'll find something different each time. It was dark and overcast when we started out for the train station. The air felt heavy with rain. For the first time, the road ahead of us looked dark and menacing. Gray waves pounded hard and loud. I strained to take one last glimpse of the garden before Matsu closed the gate behind us. Then he turned around and began to walk down the road at a quick pace. Even loaded down with my possessions, he didn't slow his pace.

By the time we reached the station, it had begun to rain lightly. Matsu and I put down my suitcase and boxes and waited in silence. My throat was so dry, it was all for the best that we didn't talk. I could barely swallow. Suddenly I wanted Matsu to leave at once. His waiting only made it more difficult.

"Why don't you go back before it really begins to rain? The train will be here any minute. There's no use our both being here," I said, swallowing hard.

210

Matsu looked uneasily around the station. "What about all the boxes?"

"I'll get the porter to help," I answered. "You'd better go," I strained, my voice breaking.

Matsu looked at me and understood. "I think you will be fine, Stephen-*san*," he bowed.

But instead of bowing back, I waited for Matsu to stand straight again before I put my arms around him in a hug. For a moment, he simply stood there frozen, but I didn't back away until I felt him lift his arms around me.

Only then did I let go. "So we'll write. And you'll take care of Sachi?" I asked, my voice sounding high, much younger as it searched for reassurance.

"As always," he answered.

I thought of what a fine father he would have been. "I hope the war . . ." I began, trying to say something about it, but not finding the words.

"It is another life. It will never have anything to do with us," he finished. "I wish you a safe journey, Stephen-*san*."

Matsu bowed low, then looked at me a moment longer before he left. At the edge of the station he paused. I was tempted to run after him, but my legs wouldn't move. I could only lean forward and watch him disappear from sight.

I sat back in the train, and wanted to cry. Outside, a splattering of rain ran across the window. Though it was only half-filled, the car felt hot and airless. I noticed the people settling in their seats, and it was only then that I saw a brown parcel tucked in among my belongings. I knew immediately it was from Matsu. I unwrapped the paper to find two black leather-bound books. There was no note. I let my hand run over the thick, soft leather covers before flipping through the empty white pages. Then as the train rattled toward Kobe, taking me away from Tarumi, I took out my fountain pen, opened one of the books, and began to write.

F 1 WEEK   Tsukiyama, Gail.
c.1
           The Samurai's
           garden.

$18.95

DATE